PLEDGE TO KILL

Printed in the United States of America

First Printing, 2015

ISBN-13: 978-1517545710
ISBN-10: 1517545714

PLEDGE TO KILL

by

Judy Goodspeed

Prologue

Ten minutes was all the time Debra Hayes had to get to the post office and then to the library to meet her sister Jane. She fairly flew up the post office steps, tripping on her long skirt a couple of times.

Her heart skipped a beat when she opened the mailbox and found a letter inside. Holding her breath, she tore open the envelope and unfolded the crisp white sheet of paper. "Dear Miss Hayes, The University of Texas is happy to inform you that your application for an academic scholarship has been accepted." Twirling around in delight, she placed the letter inside her history book. She could hardly wait to see Jane so they could read the details together.

It was a warm afternoon, this May 13, 1968, in Decker, Texas. A good day for a walk, Debra thought, as she hurried down Fifth Street and made a right on Pine. She stopped when a sharp pain in her head caused her to drop her books. The letter drifted away, but she didn't notice. Something was wrong. Jane! This was about Jane.

Debra began to run, not to the library, but to the park. Jane always cut through the park after music lessons. Panicked, Debra rushed down walking paths and through the picnic area. It didn't make sense that Jane would go into the woods, but Debra felt compelled to look there anyway. She took about three steps along a narrow path surrounded by dense foliage and found one of Jane's shoes. Following a trail of trampled grass, she came to a deep concrete drainage ditch. Jane lay in the bottom of the ditch. Debra slid down the steep incline, frantic to get to her sister.

Jane was unconscious. A large abrasion covered the left side of her head; her face was discolored with red whelps, and her legs scratched and bloody. Debra shook her head, trying to clear the pain, so she could comprehend what had happened. Why was Jane naked? Then it dawned on her. Someone did this to her sister. She began to scream. A man walking his dog in the park heard her and came to investigate. When he saw the situation, he tied the dog to a tree and ran to find a phone. Desperate to do something, Debra removed her own long cotton slip, covered her sister's torso, and held her hand.

By the time the man returned, Debra heard sirens, and in a short time, Police Chief Sam Hurley and Sheriff Tom Davis arrived.

"Which twin are you?" Chief Hurley asked.

"I'm Debra."

"Debra, this is Sheriff Davis."

"Do you have any idea what happened?" Sheriff Davis asked.

"No. I don't understand why someone would hurt Jane. Oh, please help her," Debra pleaded.

Before the chief or sheriff could ask any more questions, the ambulance driver slid down the concrete side asking, "What happened?"

Debra replied, "I don't know."

He checked Jane's pulse. "She's alive," he said.

Two volunteer firemen rappelled down, bringing a backboard and a blanket. One of the men took charge and gave orders, "Stabilize her neck and head, but be careful of the contusion on the left temple. Her right arm appears to be broken, but just immobilize it for now. There isn't severe bleeding, but there are bruises on the neck, face, arms and legs. Keep her warm."

Chief Hurley asked, "Do we need some kind of equipment to get her out of here?"

"No. Give us a hand with the ropes."

They soon had Jane strapped on the board, ropes tied to the handles.

Hurley said, “I’ll guide the board. You two climb up and haul her out. Try not to bump the wall.”

Debra stood out of the way, not knowing what to do. In a flash Jane was out of the ditch and being carried down the narrow trail to the ambulance. As they were leaving, one of the firemen pitched the sheriff a rope, saying, “Help get Jane or Debra out of there, I can’t tell them apart, and bring her to the hospital.”

Sheriff Davis pulled Debra up and escorted her to his police car. When he turned to walk away, she asked, “Where are you going? I need to get to the hospital.”

“I’ll just be a minute.”

He walked over to Chief Hurley. “What do you make of this?” he asked.

“I don’t know what to think. Just from what I’ve seen, it looks like she was running from someone and didn’t see the ditch.”

Not knowing the girls, the sheriff suggested, “Maybe she came out here with her boyfriend. They got to necking, things got out of hand. She changed her mind, and he got rough.”

“Don’t think so. Not this girl. From what I’ve heard, they aren’t allowed to date. Their father is very strict and very religious. I think she was attacked and ran for her life. I’ll look around and see if I can find where this started. Her clothes should be close, unless he had her in a car and she jumped out.”

Sheriff Davis paused for a minute, “Both tall blondes, with sparkling green eyes and beautiful olive skin. How could anyone hurt one of them? I’ll be back after I take the sister to the hospital,” he told Hurley.

On the ride to the hospital, Debra sat in stunned silence, trying to wrap her mind around what was happening. Sheriff Davis didn’t try to make conversation.

Once there, Debra rushed to the desk, “My sister was just brought in. I need to be with her.”

“You must be talking about the Hayes girl.”

“Yes. Jane is my twin.”

"I'm sorry, but the doctor is with her now. When he's finished examining her, he'll come out and talk to you. Just make yourself comfortable in the waiting area."

"Comfortable? Who could be comfortable anywhere in a situation like this?" Debra asked the sheriff.

"I totally agree," he said, then added, "Has anyone contacted your parents?"

"Oh my gosh, I'd better call Mrs. Simpson and see if she'll go tell Mother."

"You don't have a phone at home?"

"No. Dad won't allow one."

Mrs. Smith agreed to go tell Mrs. Hayes about the accident, and she arrived at the hospital in about twenty minutes.

Mrs. Hayes told the sheriff her husband drove a truck and had left early that morning on a long haul. Sheriff Davis promised to get in contact with the company he drove for and find out his route. If they couldn't contact him, the highway patrol would be called and asked to locate him. It was a couple of hours before Mr. Hayes called the hospital. He had already turned around and headed home, but estimated the drive would take about seven hours. He gave strict instructions that no medical procedures were to be performed until he got there, and his wife was to call church members and get a prayer chain started for Jane.

Doctor Adams came to Mrs. Hayes. "We need to remove part of Jane's skull to relieve the pressure on her brain. I can't even risk moving her to Dallas, so a neurosurgeon has agreed to come here. This is very serious and I need your permission to operate."

Mrs. Hayes refused to make a decision without her husband.

"Mrs. Hayes, if we don't do this surgery immediately, your daughter will suffer brain damage and perhaps even death. We don't have time to wait for your husband," the doctor explained.

Debra begged her mother to allow the surgery, even offering to take the blame herself, but Mrs. Hayes ignored her. By the time Mr. Hayes arrived, the damage was irreversible.

His first words to Debra were, “This is your fault. You were supposed to be with her.”

According to her father, she was the oldest and therefore responsible for her sister--even though she was only seven minutes older.

Later that evening, Sheriff Davis came to the hospital to see if Jane had regained consciousness. He told the family, “We haven’t found any witnesses, but it’s a small town. Surely someone knows something.” Turning to Debra, he asked, “Miss Hayes, can I talk with you for a minute?”

She followed him to an empty conference room. “How can I help you?” she asked.

“I’m sorry about your sister,” Davis said.

Debra simply nodded her head.

“How did you find her?”

“We always meet at the library after Jane’s music lesson. I was on my way there when I experienced a strange feeling that something had happened.”

“What kind of feeling?”

“First a sharp pain in my head. Then I couldn’t get my breath. I knew Jane was in trouble.”

“What did you do?”

“I ran to the park because she takes a shortcut through the park to the library. When I saw her shoe, I kept looking until I found her.”

“That’s odd that you knew all of those things.”

“Not really. We’re identical twins and very much in tune with each other.”

“Do you know who might have done this?”

“No.”

“What about a boyfriend?”

“We aren’t allowed to date. Tom Morrison pestered Jane to go out with him. She explained why she couldn’t, but he kept bugging her anyway.”

“Isn’t his dad the banker?”

“Yes.”

“I’ll have a talk with him. Thank you, Miss Hayes. Call me if you think of anything that might help. Again, I’m sorry about your sister.”

Debra walked back to the waiting room, wondering how she could explain what it was like to be a twin. One gets hurt, the other cries out. That’s always how it had been for Debra and Jane.

Davis came back to the waiting room. “I hate to bother you again, but can you tell me what your sister was wearing?”

“She had on a blue cotton skirt, white long-sleeved blouse. No jewelry except a gold locket just like the one I’m wearing.”

Giving her hand a squeeze, he said, “Thanks, you’ve been a big help.”

When she returned to the waiting room, it was full of people from their church. Some were on their knees in front of chairs and sofas, others stood, but all were praying, some quite loudly. The only person that Debra was glad to see was Mrs. Scott, Jane’s music teacher. It was seeing this kind wonderful woman that opened the horrible grief and fear that Debra held inside. She walked into Mrs. Scott’s open arms and the tears began to flow.

Together they walked to the ICU ward, sank to the floor by the door and sat with arms linked, not talking, just waiting.

Some hours later Mrs. Scott left, but Debra remained sitting, a thousand thoughts running through her mind. Why had this happened? Would Tom Morrison stoop this low? Probably. He’d been pestering Jane for months to go out with him and Tom didn’t hear the word no.

When her father insisted she go home, Debra refused.

“She needs to know I’m here, and this is where I’m staying,” Debra said.

She was surprised when he turned and walked away without saying another word.

Debra didn’t know what lay in store, but she did know she would take care of Jane. She would find out who did this, and one way or another, justice would be served.

Chapter One

June 10, 1978. Debra watches from her hiding place as a nurse guides Jane past the live oak tree laden with Spanish moss, and seats her in the gazebo near the fishpond. It's Nurse Wilson, the only one who leaves her unattended while she sneaks in a visit with Jim Matthews, the guard at the front gate. This is dangerous because, even though the gate isn't far away, it is out of sight of the gazebo.

Jane stares into space, unaware of the pink hibiscus and white clematis vines surrounding the gazebo. A white butterfly flits around her and finally lights on her golden hair, but she doesn't acknowledge its presence. She remains alone, which is usually the case when Nurse Wilson is on duty.

Patients walk the grounds while nurses visit, but they all remain in designated areas. Doctors come and go from buildings, busy with their regimented schedules.

After months of diligent observation and planning, Debra is sure she can drive in the back entrance and take her sister while Nurse Wilson is flirting with Matthews. Once she has Jane in the car, she'll drive to the park across the street. There, Debra will leave one of Jane's shoes at the edge of the water and throw the other one farther out. That will be the only clue as to where she has gone.

Debra will never be suspected because she's a regular visitor. She knows Jane's schedule, and over the years, has gotten her medications through contacts at the hospital where she works.

According to the schedule, Ms. Wilson and Jim Matthews would be on duty for the next two days. Debra can put her plan into action.

Early the next morning, Debra spotted Dr. Naomi Richards' black BMW in its usual place and breathed a sigh of relief. The BMW was the perfect car for her kidnapping plan.

If Doc followed her routine, her lab coat with her identification tag hung in her office and an extra set of car keys were in the top right hand drawer.

On her way to the parking garage elevator she checked to see if Dr. Craig Morton's Jag was where he always parked. Yes! Hopefully, the Jag would be gone in the morning, but Dr. Richards' BMW would remain. The affair between Morton and Richards had been going on for months.

Debra stepped from the parking garage elevator, walked down a long corridor just like she did every evening when she went to work as an assistant to the doctor who was on night duty. She entered the double doors marked MORGUE. Getting the key to Dr. Richards' office might be risky because Dr. Nichols, who was chief examiner of the morgue, kept the spare key tucked away in a vase on the top shelf of his bookcase. One day when Dr. Richards left her keys at home, Debra learned of its location.

When she walked into the exam room, Dr. Adams looked up from performing an autopsy.

"What are you doing here?" he asked, pushing his glasses back on his face with a forearm.

"I think I left my checkbook in my locker."

"Want to help out?" he pleaded. "Susan didn't show up again."

"Sorry Doc, I have some business to take care of."

Debra continued on her way, but instead of going into the locker room, she slipped into Dr. Nichols' office. Thank heavens he never locked the door. In a flash, her fingers closed on the sharp edges of the key. Going back through the exam room, she waved her checkbook at Dr. Adams.

Dr. Richards' office was near the double doors. If anyone walked in and glanced to their right, they could see through the window in the door. Taking a deep breath, Debra inserted the key and gave it a turn. Didn't work. She removed the key and tried again, this time jiggling it a little as she turned. Bingo. It worked.

Once inside, she locked the door and went to the desk. Grabbing a tissue from the box sitting on the bookcase, she used it to open the desk drawer and pick up the keys. Dropping them into her pocket, she turned and took the lab coat from the peg on the wall. After unpinning the badge, she slipped the I.D. into her pocket with the keys.

Debra left the office, locked the door, and wiped the doorknob clean. If tomorrow went as smoothly as today, next week would find her and her sister in route to Texas.

June 12, 1978. Debra drove into the University Hospital visitor's parking lot. Taking her bag, she entered the main entrance to the hospital, walked into the first restroom she came to, and locked the door. She twisted her long golden hair into a bun and placed a red wig on her head. Leaning close to the mirror, she put brown contacts over her lime green eyes. Her reflection revealed a few loose strands of hair, which she tucked under the wig. She removed the I.D. badge from her bag and pinned it onto her lab coat. One final check in the mirror revealed a lady that could easily pass for Dr. Richards.

She walked down the corridor to the parking garage elevator. Just as she started to push the button, she heard footsteps. Oh no, it was Dr. Loftis. Fortunately he wasn't looking her way. She left as if going to her car and waited until she heard the elevator doors close. The close call made her decide that the stairs might be safer.

The BMW sat in the usual spot. She unlocked the door, took a plastic sheet from her bag and arranged it over the front seat, and then placed more plastic on the back sheet. Last came the gray blanket. Next she removed Dr. Richards' license plate and replaced it with one she had stolen from a car on the upper level of the parking garage the night before.

"I'm ready now," she said to herself as she pulled out of the garage and began her drive to Deer Creek Mental Hospital. God help her if there was road construction. She was on a tight schedule.

Twenty minutes later she drove past the main entrance to Deer Creek. The familiar sight of Matthews on duty at the front gate relaxed her. Things looked fine, but when she stopped at the service entrance, an unfamiliar face peered through the guard shack window--her heart stopped. Where was Al? He never checked a thing. A schedule change? Al kept busy either eating junk food or sat with his boots on the counter, his nose buried in some paperback. What if this new guy stopped her and asked a lot of questions? She'd come up with something. Today had to be the day.

When the attendant opened the window, she pointed to the I.D. and then to her watch. The guard nodded and she drove through without a hitch. Debra parked near the corner of the female residence building where a hedge blocked her from the guard's view. She left the car unlocked and walked toward the building. Most of the patients were still eating lunch, and those on the grounds were involved in feeding the ducks or attempting to play croquet.

Alone in the gazebo, the woman sat head down, hands folded in her lap. Debra stepped into the structure and took her hand saying, "Jane, come with me. I'm taking you home."

Like a little child Jane allowed herself to be led from the gazebo to the car. Debra gently situated her in the backseat and told her to lie down. Debra covered her with the blanket and drove past the guard with a wave and a smile. He looked over his glasses long enough to give a salute back.

A block down the street from the hospital, Debra drove to a small park. Dense vegetation and trees surrounded walking paths. At the end of the road, a short rail fence blocked an inlet of a large swamp. Alligators sometimes wandered near the fence and occasionally moved inland. This was a part of the Everglades, but Debra had noticed that few people came to this area.

She parked in a secluded spot that couldn't be seen from the street, removed her lab coat, then took Jane's loafers from her feet and put them on. Carrying her own shoes, she stepped over the fence and walked into the edge of the water. Being careful not to lose both shoes, she left one in the mud and threw the other one as far out into the water as she could. Once back on solid ground, she put on her shoes, ruffled the grass where she had stepped and wiped the mud from her hands on an old towel she brought for that purpose.

Debra checked the time and saw that she had only a few minutes to get out of the park and down the road before Nurse Wilson returned to her patient. Ten years of watching and waiting were finally over. At last she could look after her sister and take care of some unfinished business in Texas.

She returned to her personal car in the hospital parking lot. She hated to leave Jane in the car until she returned the BMW, but she couldn't come up with a better plan. She also had to replace Dr. Richard's tag.

Once back at the car, she put Jane into the back seat of her Chevy Nova.

"You stay put until I get back. I'm going to crack the windows so you won't get too hot. I'll be back in a few minutes."

There weren't many cars in the parking lot. Debra found a space she could back into and replace the tag. She was crouched behind the car when a man asked, "Do you need help?"

Debra tore the skin from her knuckle as she jerked up and answered, "No thanks, I just dropped my keys."

The soft-spoken gentleman smiled and went on his way. With shaky hand, she secured the last nut. She had fifteen minutes to get the car back.

Safely parked in Dr. Richard's parking place, she removed the plastic from the seats and stuffed it into a bag. She wiped the interior of the car clean, then the door handles, and lastly the trunk and tag. Grabbing her bag, she headed for the elevator, then changed her mind and took the stairs. Better to be safe even though she was in a hurry.

She was winded by the time she reached her car. After checking on Jane, she sat for a minute to catch her breath and remove the wig. Once back in control, she drove home, pulled into the garage and closed the door. With shaking fingers, she unlocked the back door and guided Jane into the house.

"Well, here we are. What do you think of my little abode? Come let me show you your room, and we'd probably better make a stop at the bathroom. Then it's medication time," Debra said as she led Jane down the hall.

Jane refused to take her medication. At her wits end, Debra at last remembered Jane's love for chocolate milk. "Please take your medicine. I'll give you chocolate milk."

No response. Debra went to the refrigerator and poured a little milk into a glass. Jane took the medicine. "That's my girl. Now, time for a nap. I'm expecting a phone call any minute, so I'll have to leave you alone for a little while."

The phone rang as Debra was putting Jane to bed. "I'll bet that's the hospital telling me you're missing. You stay put. Take a nice nap, and when I get back I'll fix your dinner."

Captain Jack Stone responded to the call reporting a missing patient from Deer Creek Mental Hospital. He was puzzled because Deer Creek was very secure. He couldn't remember this happening before. Bill Jenkins, the hospital administrator, met Stone as he was getting out of the car.

"Thank goodness you're here. The hospital's reputation will be ruined if we don't find Ms. Hayes."

"I'm concerned about the patient, not the hospital's reputation. Fill me in on the details."

"Nurse Nancy Wilson was in charge of Jane Hayes this afternoon. She took her on an outing to the gazebo. Ms. Wilson had to leave for a moment. When she returned to the gazebo, Jane Hayes was gone. As soon as Nancy reported her patient missing, the hospital security guards began a search of the grounds and surrounding area. One of her shoes was found at the edge of a swamp, but there was no sign of a body.

"What's this girl's story?" the captain asked.

"She's been a patient here for ten years," Jenkins said. "Jane was gang raped when she was seventeen. As she was trying to get away from the park where it happened, she fell into a drainage ditch. Unfortunately, the fall caused severe brain damage."

"How disabled is she?" Stone asked.

"She's mute, but responds when given simple verbal instructions. Her motor skills are limited and she never moves without assistance. That's why this is so bizarre. I can't believe she walked away."

"Excuse me," Stone said as he punched the talk button on his radio. "Any news?"

"Negative."

"Where's Nurse Wilson?"

"She's in my office. I thought you'd want to question her."

"What did she tell you?"

"She said she was called away for a minute for a personal emergency. Jane was gone when she returned."

"What kind of personal emergency?"

"I think it had to do with her monthly. I didn't ask point blank, but that's what I gathered."

"Oh, I see. I'll question Ms. Wilson and the other staff members who care for Miss Hayes. I'd also like to talk to the guard on the front gate. And it would probably be a good idea to see if any strange vehicles came through the service entrance. You do have a surveillance camera, don't you?"

"Yes, but we had a substitute guard today, and he forgot to turn it on."

"That's great."

"The guard didn't notice anything unusual. The other staff members will be on duty. You can talk to them whenever you like."

"Has the family been notified?"

"Yes. Her parents live nearby, and her twin sister is on her way here now. Debra found Jane the day she was attacked. Seems she sensed something was wrong, and sure enough, she was right. Mrs. Hayes visits Jane often and is steadfast in her belief Jane will be well someday. They'll be here soon."

"What was Jane like before the rape?"

"According to her family, she was a straight-A student, sang like an angel, and was asked to enter a beauty contest. You'll see an exact replica of her when you see Debra. She should be here any minute," Jenkins said, glancing at his watch. "We'd better get back to my office."

They were rounding the corner of the administration building when Stone observed the blonde's approach. Late twenties, five-eight, thin, she walked with her shoulders back. She wore tan slacks and a lime-green blouse. Darn attractive, but aloof. Her green eyes flashed like gems when their gazes locked for an instant.

"This is her sister," Jenkins said. "Miss Hayes, Captain Stone."

"Have you found Jane?" she asked.

Stone shook his head. "Only one shoe."

His radio crackled and a policeman reported that a search of a deserted building revealed nothing. They were moving on to a vacant lot near the building.

"Do you have any ideas or suggestions?" Stone asked Debra.

"No, I can't imagine her leaving on her own. Take me to the place where you found the shoe. Maybe I can sense something."

Once at the site, Debra walked about for a few minutes looking at the ground, and then she gazed out over the swamp. "I can't believe she could have walked this far. I'm sorry. This is upsetting me more than I thought it would. Could you please take me back?"

Debra was silent on the drive back to the hospital. When they arrived, Jenkins came out to meet them.

When she got out of the car, she asked Jenkins, "Where was Jane when the nurse last saw her?"

Jenkins led the way to the gazebo where her sister was last seen.

"I don't sense anything at all. I just feel numb and short of breath," She turned and headed back toward the building.

"Your parents should be here soon." Jenkins said, hurrying to catch up with her.

Debra dabbed her eyes with a tissue saying, "I'm afraid I'll break down when I see Mother, and she doesn't need that. Will you tell them I'll call later?"

"Of course," Jenkins said, "I just can't understand how this could have happened. We have an excellent staff, and I'm sure someone will remember something. I'm confident Jane will be found."

She nodded and, head down, walked to the car.

When Mr. and Mrs. Hayes arrived five minutes later, Stone and Jenkins filled them in on the events of the past few hours.

"We're doing all we can," Stone said, "but there aren't many leads to go on."

"Don't stop looking!" Mrs. Hayes begged Stone, "Please don't give up."

"We're not close to giving up," Stone assured her.

Jenkins spoke up, "Debra was here. She'll call you later."

"She should be with us," Mr. Hayes stated. "Her mother needs her."

Stone's radio sounded. Everyone listened while he discussed the next plan of operation.

"We're going to start dragging the swamp. Jenkins, can Mr. and Mrs. Hayes stay in your office so they can be by the phone?"

"Certainly."

Stone said goodbye and walked to his car. In his gut he felt sympathy for them, but he doubted their daughter would be found alive. He still couldn't understand how she could have left the grounds without being seen. There were guards on duty at both entrances. What prompted Jane to walk away--or was she lured away? Could be an inside job, but for what reason? The Hayes family didn't appear to be wealthy. He'd do some research when he got back to the office.

Debra smiled as she drove away from the hospital. Planning every detail had made it easy. Captain Stone would have to search a long time if he found Jane. Checking her watch she stepped on the gas pedal. It was almost time for Jane's supper and very necessary to keep her on schedule. If she got upset, she wouldn't eat at all. Then the only option would be tube feeding. That thought made Debra push the pedal harder.

Jane was exactly as she had left her. Debra managed to coax her to the kitchen table. Dinner was chicken soup, milk, and chocolate pudding.

Spoon-feeding Jane was a slow process. Debra reminded Jane of the time Jane had fed her soup when she had the mumps. Jane had laughed and teased her because of her fat jaws, all the time waiting on her hand and foot. Jane's nursing service only lasted two days, however, before she joined Debra in bed.

Debra continued talking about childhood incidents while she cleaned up the kitchen. Occasionally she would look at Jane and ask her a question. The blank expression on her sister's face never changed.

Once the kitchen was clean, she called her parents. Her mother answered the phone.

"Hello Mother. Have you heard anything about Jane?"

"No, they're still searching. Captain Stone said he would call if they find anything. How are you?"

"I'm okay, just worried. I'm going to work, but will call you in the morning."

"I can't believe you're going to work. Are you sure you're up to it?

"I don't want to go, but the other assistant is sick."

"Please be careful. I couldn't stand it if something happened to you."

"I'll call you tomorrow. Try not to worry. Goodbye."

"Come on, Sis. Doesn't a shower sound nice? I'll shampoo your hair and fix it for you.

"Raise your arms so I can get your shirt off. Here you go, put both arms up. That a girl. Now put them down. Raise your foot so I can get your jeans off."

That method didn't work so she unfastened Jane's jeans, slipped them down, and then sat Jane in a chair.

"Pick up your feet so I can slip your jeans off."

"Okay, I'll pick them up for you. There we go. Stay put and I'll get the shower going."

"Shoot, I'll get in with you."

She turned the water off and then wrapped a towel around herself before drying Jane. Dressing her was the same process as the undressing. It was slow going.

"Let's dry your hair. Do you like your new hair cut? Last week my stylist cut yours just like mine."

"It's bedtime. I'll tuck you in and read you a story after you take your medication. Tomorrow night you can read me a story. We'll take turns just like we did when we were kids."

Story time over, she smoothed Jane's hair back, kissed her on the forehead and gently touched her cheek. "You have no clue who I am, do you?" Wiping away a tear, she finished dressing for work.

The sound of rain on the garage door sent her back into the house for her umbrella and raincoat. A final check on Jane and then she was out the door and on her way to work

She pulled into an underground parking garage and backed into a parking space. The morgue was located on the ground floor, just above her. This was not a popular place, which was one reason Debra transferred there after Cole's death. Her job was interesting and isolated.

She stepped through the double doors at eleven o'clock. Good, Dr. Nichols was on duty tonight. He did his job well and didn't ask questions about her personal life. "Good evening, Ms. Hayes," Dr. Nichols greeted. "Are you ready for a busy night?"

"Why? What's on the schedule?"

"We have a cancer victim, a suicide, and a homicide. Oh, and we can get John Doe ready for shipment to the crematorium; a family member finally showed up today to identify him."

"It's about time someone showed up, poor man," she said as she hung up her shoulder bag and then placed her raincoat over it.

Dr. Nichols was already uncovering the body of what appeared to be a middle-aged white male. All data was tape-recorded, as the autopsy was performed.

When the first procedure was completed, Debra asked, "Do you want me to prepare John Doe for shipment while you get the homicide ready?"

"Do you think you can handle him by yourself?"

"Yes, but if I have any trouble, I'll come and get you."

"Okay, go ahead. That will save us a lot of time."

She went to the storage room to get one of the cardboard coffins used for those who were to be cremated. After placing the coffin on a gurney, she got the shoulder bag that contained Jane's hospital clothes and two pieces of plastic. On her way by Dr. Nichols' desk, she picked up the instruction sheet concerning the body.

According to the instructions, Mr. Amos Mayfield was to be picked up at seven a.m. and taken straight to the crematorium. Well, that was simple enough. She pulled open the door to drawer fifteen and slid Mr. Mayfield out, then lowered the gurney and placed it beside the body.

"Hang on, Mr. Mayfield, while I pad the bottom of your coffin." She removed the lid of the coffin and placed Jane's clothes and the plastic sheets inside.

"Okay, here we go. I'm going to slide you into this box. First, your shoulders and then the rest of you. Now, I'll tuck everything under you and cover you with a sheet. Everything looks good so I'm going to put on the lid and secure it with tape."

Pushing the gurney in front of her, Debra went back to the autopsy room.

"Dr. Nichols, Mr. Mayfield is ready if you want to sign the release."

"Did you have any trouble?"

"Not at all."

"I'm at a good stopping point. Let's go ahead and take a break. I'll sign the release when we start back to work."

"Okay. Do you want something to eat or drink?"

"Grab me a cup of coffee, if you're going to get something."

"I'll be back in a minute."

"Take your time. I need to return a couple of calls."

Debra made sure Dr. Nichols was in his office before she left. This was the perfect opportunity to return Dr. Richards' keys and I.D. She was approaching Dr. Richards' office door when the double doors opened and Dr. Richards walked out. Debra stopped dead in her tracks, not sure what to do.

Dr. Richards approached her, back straight, eyes blazing.

Oh no, she's found out that someone moved the car. Should I run?

Instead of running, she said, "Hi Doc, how are you?"

"Furious. Is Michael working?"

"He's in his office returning calls. Can I help you?"

"Only if you can get rid of Hudson."

"Are you talking about our administrator?"

"I certainly am. He's talking about changing to twenty-four hour shifts."

"That doesn't sound good. I'm going for coffee. Would you like some?"

"Love some. I'll be in Michael's office."

Once Dr. Richards was out of sight, Debra hurried to unlock her office door and return the items she had borrowed. Now she had to return the key to Dr. Nichols' vase.

She probably could have put the key in the vase when she delivered the coffee. The two doctors were busy studying their new schedules and discussing the chief of staff. They barely managed a thank you when Debra set the coffee on the desk.

Dr. Richards left after about fifteen minutes of ranting and raving. She stormed out of the room, headed for her office.

Debra's hands were shaking as she handed the forms to Dr. Nichols for him to sign. If he noticed, he didn't say anything.

When the release was completed, she wheeled Mr. Mayfield to the loading area, locked the wheels on the gurney and made sure the tape was still secure. Satisfied, she returned to assist Dr. Nichols.

When quitting time rolled around, Debra was recording what Dr. Nichols recited about the homicide. He spoke while he examined the brain. "Victim's death is the result of a large caliber bullet which entered the left frontal lobe and exited the lower right quadrant of the back of the skull. The exit wound is large and caused extensive damage. I would guess the projectile came from a high-powered rifle, such as a .308. My only other finding is that the victim appears to be at the end of the first trimester of pregnancy." He looked up at her. "I wrote down the detective's name on a yellow pad in my office. Would you mind getting it for me so I can jot down a few notes before I call him?"

"Not at all."

She picked up the yellow pad and then reached up and dropped the key into the vase. Mission complete. If Rest Haven did their part, she would be out of here in a few minutes.

The Rest Haven hearse pulled up to the loading ramp at seven fifteen. The driver signed the necessary forms and loaded the coffin. Debra took the papers back to the file cabinet and sighed with relief.

Dr. Nichols was pulling on his jacket when she passed his office.

"Have a good day, Dr. Nichols."

"Thank you, Debra. Same to you. I'll see you tonight."

But she knew he wouldn't see her that night. She had a promise to keep. Now she must hurry home and check on Jane.

Arriving home, Debra found Jane just as she had left her the night before. "Time to go to the bathroom. I'm sorry I was late, but a shower will fix everything."

When Jane was clean and dressed, Debra fed her breakfast and then sat her in a chair in the bedroom.

She talked as she changed the bed. “I won’t leave you any more except to go back to Deer Creek this afternoon. I’m sorry I was late getting home this morning, but you won’t have to lie on wet sheets again.”

After the sheets were in the washing machine, she took Jane to the kitchen with her. She poured two cups of coffee and set one in front of her sister. Taking the other cup, she sat at the table.

“It’s been a long time since we chatted over a cup of coffee together. Would you like me to catch you up on the last ten years of my life?” She looked into blank eyes, knowing she needed to tell her story aloud whether Jane could understand her words or not.

“After I graduated from high school, Mom and Dad decided we should move and find a good hospital for you. Mother wanted to live in a warm climate so Florida became the first choice. I didn’t care where we went, just so we got out of Texas. We more or less lucked out finding a hospital. I think Mother called several doctors and then checked out the private hospitals they recommended. She chose Deer Creek, a beautiful hospital, located across the road from Everglades National Park. Mom and Dad moved to Paolita, Florida, so they could be close to you. Once you were situated, I found a job in Miami and bought this house. Of course Dad had a fit when I moved out, but I was determined to get away from him.”

She got up and poured herself another cup of coffee. “Need a refill?” Jane had not touched the first cup, so she emptied it and refilled it with fresh coffee.

“I found a job at University Hospital working in the lab. At first I was just a delivery girl, but quickly became a lab assistant. An opening came up for the third shift, so I switched to get a pay increase, and that’s when I met Cole.”

Debra looked at the schedule mounted on the refrigerator and said. “Bathroom time, Sis.” She led Jane to the bathroom and sat her on the commode. “While you take care of business, I’m going to change clothes. I’ll fill you in on Cole while I fix lunch. You would have liked Cole. He was a gentle, sweet man.”

Back in the kitchen she warmed leftover roast beef, opened a can of green beans and prepared instant potatoes. When the food was ready, she put servings of each in the blender for Jane. The result was a brown gruel that looked far from appetizing. Surprisingly, it smelled like roast beef and green beans.

"Lunch time." She tied a bib around Jane's neck and began feeding her. Lunch was a slow process, but she was patient. By the time she had finished feeding Jane, her own food was cold and she didn't have much of an appetite, but she fixed a plate and warmed it in the microwave. After the kitchen was cleaned, she took Jane to the living room and sat her in the recliner.

"You stay put while I get the clothes out of the dryer." She returned to the living room with a basket of clothes to fold. While she folded, she told Jane about Cole Roberts.

"My first evening on third shift I was assigned to be Cole's assistant. I shuddered when I read I would be working with a man. I was chastising myself for not requesting a woman when this tall handsome man said, "I'm Cole Roberts. You must be Debra. May I help you get situated?

"Jane, he had the most beautiful brown eyes I've ever seen. When I looked into his eyes, I knew I had nothing to fear. Here was this guy who was six feet four, built well, but a little on the thin side. He had thick auburn hair, and a voice that could soothe demons. In five minutes he had me laughing and completely at ease.

"We had worked together a month when Cole became very ill. I visited him in the hospital and continued to visit him when he went home. He had been in a gay relationship and became infected with Hepatitis C.

"Promiscuity was common in the gay community and Cole's partner was an active participant. By the time he found out about Hal's infidelity, it was too late. His days were numbered and he had no one to whom he could turn. You see, his family didn't know he was gay and would never accept him if he told them.

"During Cole's illness we became close friends, and I opened up a little to him. When he learned I wanted to go to college, he offered to help me. We found that we could help each other. His family had been pressuring him for years to get married and he wanted to die knowing they were happy.

"When Cole was well enough, we were married. Of course, it was for appearance only. I could take care of him, and in return, he would leave me well fixed financially.

He called his parents and told them he was bringing his new bride home to meet them. They were not thrilled and I was not looking forward to meeting them. Oh, they were nice enough, but it was obvious they had expected Cole to marry a rich Southern belle and oversee their massive orange groves. We stayed two days, but it seemed like a month.

"I took care of Cole for over a year. His many friends helped me care for him and made it possible for me to go to school. His health deteriorated rapidly and there wasn't much that could be done to help him. I came to love Cole much like I love you. He was kind, gentle, and very intelligent. He appreciated every act of kindness, no matter how large or small. I was showered with gifts, and he told me I brought much happiness to him.

"While we were together I learned, mostly from his male friends, how to dress fashionably, style my hair, and apply makeup.

"I called Cole's parents when Cole was dying, and they came immediately. They chose to stay in a hotel rather than with me, which was a relief. With the doctor's help we managed to convince them Cole died of pneumonia, complicated by a bad case of the flu. They left after Cole's memorial service, taking his ashes with them. I was not invited to the service held at their home. They did send me a check for fifty thousand dollars, contingent on me signing a release from any rights to the orange plantation. I signed the release.

"Cole left me his house, car, and ninety thousand dollars. I could finish college without worrying about money. I worked part time just for the experience and to learn some things I would need in the next few years.

"Oh, look at the time. I must go to Deer Creek, so I'll help you to the bedroom for a nap. When I get back, we'll have supper and watch television."

She put Jane down for a nap, changed clothes, and left. She wondered if Captain Stone would be there. He didn't appear to be suspicious of her, but who knows what goes through the mind of a cop?

Upon arriving at the hospital, Debra talked with Mr. Jenkins for a few minutes before joining her mother.

Mrs. Hayes looked up as Debra entered Jane's room. "Hi, sweetheart, how are you?"

"I'm okay, Mom. How are you?"

"Tired. Very tired and afraid your sister won't be found."

"I know, Mom. I'm afraid, too."

"Captain Stone doesn't think they can continue the search much longer. He seems convinced she waded into the swamp and was dragged away by an alligator. The nurse admitted she left Jane alone for a few minutes while she talked to the guard. They have both been dismissed, but that doesn't help matters now. You'd think one of the other attendants would have noticed her walking away, but no one did. Two of her regular nurses admitted that she walked away a couple of times before. Once they found her in the laundry room, the other time in a hall closet. They didn't think it was significant enough to put in her chart. I think she came to herself and was looking for a way to get home."

"Mom, if she'd known what she was doing, she wouldn't have walked into the swamp. You know Jane didn't like water."

"I thought you were the one who didn't like water.'

"Well, I'm not too crazy about it, but she was terrified of water."

"There isn't anything we can do here. Let's go find your father."

Mr. Hayes and Captain Stone had returned from the swamp and were sitting on the bench near the front gate. Both men stood when Debra and her mother walked up.

"Still no luck?" Debra asked Captain Stone.

"Not a clue, but we're still looking. I'm not sure how long the chief is going to let us continue. But we'll keep digging until he says to stop."

"Have you looked in nearby cities?"

"We've alerted police departments within a fifty mile radius."

"Good." She looked at her watch and said. "I have to go. Let me know if you find out anything, or if there is anything I can do to help."

She hugged her mother and said good-bye to her father and Captain Stone. Waving, she pulled away from the curb and then directed her attention to the heavy traffic.

Sleepy and tired, she let down the car window. The fresh air revived her enough for her to get home without falling asleep at the wheel.

Home at last, she unlocked the back door, and called "Jane, I'm home."

She listened for footsteps as she placed her purse and keys on the kitchen counter. Of course there weren't any footsteps. Jane was just as she had left her. Sitting on the edge of the bed, she gently smoothed the hair out of Jane's eyes, hoping to see some spark of recognition. There was nothing but a blank lifeless stare. Taking a tissue from the box on the nightstand, she wiped the drool from her sister's chin and dabbed the corner of her own eye.

Taking Jane's hand, she said, "Get up, sleepy head. Time to go potty."

After the bathroom duties were cared for, she took Jane to the kitchen and sat her at the table. "Did you know I'm a dentist now? I'll tell you about dental school while you eat supper." Once the leftovers were warmed and blended, Debra took up her story.

"I enrolled in dental school the fall after Cole died. I kept my job and still managed to stay on the honor roll. Suffering from lack of sleep was my biggest problem, but sometimes I could sneak in a nap at the hospital.

"I dreamed about us going to college, maybe even dental school together. We could have had a great future. Open up. Now swallow. Good girl."

Debra finished feeding Jane and fixed herself a steak sandwich. Carrying her sandwich and a glass of milk, she said, "Come on to the den and watch the news with me."

She set her sandwich and milk on the coffee table, then clicked on the television and returned to the kitchen to get Jane. "Sit in the recliner. Here, let me put your feet up. Now, are you comfortable?"

Debra knelt beside the chair and put her arms around her sister. "Why do I ask you questions when I know you can't answer?"

She remembered she needed to call the hospital and tell them she wouldn't be in for work. Debra dialed the number while she ate. Suddenly very tired, she stretched out on the sofa to watch television. She woke up to the music of the late show and rushed to the recliner to check on Jane. Her sister hadn't moved and seemed to be asleep. Debra didn't try to move her but covered her with a light throw from the sofa.

Checking Jane one last time and satisfied that she would sleep through the night, Debra slipped between the sheets and let her thoughts drift back over the last few years. Although she had graduated from dental school, in order to keep her identity a secret, she continued to work as Debra Hayes at the morgue. In a short time, however, if all went as planned, she would be far from here and known as Rae Lyn Roberts, D.D.S.

Chapter Two

Friday afternoon Captain Stone ended the search. The only hope left was the possibility that Jane walked to the swamp and then changed direction.

Debra and her mother packed Jane's things into cardboard boxes. Mrs. Hayes seemed numb with shock and disbelief. "I just can't imagine not seeing her again. They haven't looked long enough."

"Mom, you know she wouldn't wander far, and she couldn't do without her medication for this long. The thought of not seeing her is killing me."

"Does that mean you have given up hope?"

"No, I guess I'm preparing for the worst but still hoping some miracle will happen. Like a telephone call from someone who has found her and is taking care of her."

When the last item was packed, they closed the door and carried the boxes to the car.

Debra felt a sharp pang of guilt as she said good-bye to her mother. It didn't bother her that she wasn't saying good-bye to her father. They had never gotten along. Samuel seemed to go out of his way to make life miserable for her.

For years Debra had tried to please her father but gave up when he wouldn't allow Jane to have surgery. The person she loved most in the world was robbed of a future because of his fanatical religious belief.

She drove away realizing that in order to accomplish her objective, she would never see them again. They would not understand the pledge she had made to her sister and the things she would have to do to keep that pledge.

Debra checked on Jane as soon as she got home. She hadn't been there ten minutes when Jane suffered a seizure. That didn't happen often but it was hard to watch. The look of fear and panic in Jane's eyes, like some animal caught in a corner with no escape, broke Debra's heart. She had to get something done for her sister soon.

What to feed Jane was becoming a problem. Remembering that she was out of chocolate milk, Debra walked to the corner supermarket to buy some. Before entering the market, she went to a pay phone and called her realtor.

The couple that bought the house belonging to Mrs. Cole Roberts would be ready to close on Monday. They wanted the house with the furnishings. Debra would only keep her personal things, which she would pick up Monday. They agreed to meet at 9:30 a.m. to take care of the paper work.

Jane hadn't moved while Debra was gone. She lay with her eyes open, arms at her sides, and legs straight as boards. Getting her to the bathroom was quite a chore. Debra glanced toward the mirror. The only difference in their looks was the emptiness in Jane's eyes and the tiny drool from her mouth. They were beautiful women; even brain damage couldn't change that.

After supper Debra called her parents. Her mother answered the phone.

"Hi, Mom. How are you?"

"I'm here, but that's about all. How are you?

"Pretty much the same. I called to tell you I'm going to be out of town for a few days."

"Has someone called about Jane? Have you found her?"

"No, Mom. I just need to get away so I can get some sleep."

"Come home and I'll take care of you."

"Thanks, but I can take care of myself."

"When will you be back? Are you going alone? Where can I call if I need you?"

"I don't know when I'll be back, probably in three or four days. A friend is going with me."

"I guess I can't stop you, but I wish you wouldn't go."

"Sorry Mom, but I need to get away. I'll call you when I get home."

Next, she called the hospital and asked for a week off, which was not a problem. She had many vacation days accumulated and could probably take off a month.

She hated to think of the pain she was going to cause her mother, but there was no other way if she carried out her pledge. Feeling like a caged animal, she began walking through the house. Perhaps the feeling would pass if she didn't dwell on the next three days. Still she paced as she went through a mental checklist of what she had left to do.

In the night she got up and went to check on Jane, who was sleeping peacefully. Lying down beside her sister, she took her hand. Memories of their childhood filled her mind. Tears trickled down her face when she thought of the love they once shared.

At home, Jane was the one who could always deal best with their Dad. She could reason with him and often saved Debra from unjust punishment. Jane was kind and loving to everyone, even those at school who delighted in teasing her. Debra wanted to punch them or call them names, but Jane always stopped her.

"Now you see what happens to nice people."

Debra met the morning with mixed emotions. Even the simple task of preparing breakfast almost overwhelmed her, but she got through it and fed her sister. She showered Jane and made her comfortable in the recliner.

Looking at Jane she said, "You are so beautiful, inside and out. How could God let this happen to you?" She left the room, intent on cleaning up the kitchen. Suddenly, giving way to hysteria, she sobbed, picked up a cup and flung it against the wall. "Where were you when five rapists went unpunished?" Flinging another cup she said, "I'll take care of them myself." Debra stumbled to the bathroom and threw up until her body ached from heaving. She sank to the floor and rested her head on the cool tile for a few minutes. Weak and trembling, she pulled herself up to the washbasin, turned on the cold water, and splashed her face.

Still weak, Debra walked to the kitchen and fixed a piece of toast. After she ate the toast, she cleaned up the broken glass.

Now that she was in control again, Debra returned to business. The rest of the day she spent cleaning house and taking care of Jane. That evening they watched television until midnight. Then, Debra put her sister to bed and took a sleeping pill.

Sunday, she kept her twin near her all day as she worked in the house. As the day passed, she worried. Was she forgetting anything? Dismissing her fears, she fed Jane a light supper and cleaned up the kitchen.

"I'm going to the store and get a few things for our trip. I'll be right back. Just think, tomorrow we'll be on our way to Texas, and I'll find a place in Dallas where you'll be safe and happy. Best of all, we'll get rid of the horrible headaches."

Needing to relieve stress, Debra walked to the supermarket. She was in the checkout line when a sharp pain shot through her temple. As she placed her items on the conveyor, the pain became more intense. Her head was throbbing by the time she gathered up the two bags and rushed out the door saying, "I'm coming, Jane."

She left the bags on the step, unlocked the backdoor and rushed to Jane's bedroom. When she stepped into the room, a sour, sweet smell caused her to gag. As she approached the bed, the odor became stronger. Jane lay still, eyes open, and body relaxed. Vomit covered her face and the pillow. She grabbed Jane, rolled her onto her side, ran her index finger in her mouth to make sure there wasn't an obstruction. The corner of the sheet was clean so she used it to wipe away the vomit, then pulled Jane onto the floor. She pinched Jane's nostrils together, tilted her head back and blew two quick breaths into her mouth. Five chest compressions, one breath, five compressions, one breath. "Breathe, please breathe." Continuing until she was exhausted, Debra sank to the floor beside her sister.

Sobbing, she gathered Jane into her arms. "What am I going to do?" How can I live without you?"

Debra sat with Jane's body all night. There was no one she could call. She must decide what to do with a body that shouldn't be in her house. She picked up the phone to call her mother, but put it back in the cradle saying, "If I turn myself in, those five bastards will get away with it. Think! I've got to find a way to see that they get what's coming to them."

She walked to the bedroom and removed the soiled bedding. Jane looked so peaceful, so beautiful. "That could be me," Debra said. And then it hit her. "Everyone will think it's me. A note, some spilled pills, and the gold locket from around my neck will convince my parents that I killed myself. Dad will never allow an autopsy. By the time they discover that I'm not coming back from my trip, Jane's body will be decomposing."

The sun was shining by the time she finished cleaning the bedroom, washing Jane's hair and changing her pajamas. Jane looked beautiful and at peace lying on Debra's bed. "Good-bye, Sis. I love you and I'll keep my pledge," Debra said as she removed the gold locket from around her neck and put it on Jane. On the nightstand she set a bottle of sleeping pills, and a note explaining that she couldn't live without her sister.

She went to the refrigerator and took a small package out of the freezer. The package and a wad of cash were placed in her fanny pack. Then she closed the front door and used a duplicate key to lock the dead bolt. Oblivious to the rain, she walked down the street to the nearest pay phone and called a cab.

Debra paced the sidewalk while she waited for the cab. She wanted to be away from here, far away. It seemed like hours before the cab got there.

"Where to?" asked the driver.

"Downtown Holiday Inn."

The cabby tried to converse with her, but Debra only answered his questions. He finally gave up talking and drove to her destination. He glanced at the rear view mirror often as though he was studying her. Wondering what he was so curious about, she moved to sneak a look in the mirror. The image was not pretty. Her wig looked like a wet dog, and her mascara was smudged under her eyes. The slapping of the windshield wipers brought her attention to the fact that it was raining. He probably thinks I'm some crazy woman out to kill a cab driver.

"Tonight wasn't a good night to have a fight with my husband," she said. "He kicked me out of the house, but at least I have enough money for a room."

"Are you hurt?"

"Oh no. He isn't physically abusive, just verbally. He'll be okay in a couple of days."

"Does this happen often?"

"About every three or four months."

"Here we are. Do you need help?"

"No, I'm fine. Thank you."

Debra paid the cabby and walked through the glass doors. She had reserved a room yesterday so all she needed was a key. The desk clerk eyed her suspiciously until she pulled out a roll of bills. Then he didn't seem to notice her disheveled appearance.

Once in her room, she began to relax. Breathing a sigh of relief, she drew a hot bath and called room service to order a hamburger, fries, and a Coke. When the food arrived she ate every morsel. Thoughts of Jane brought a stream of tears. The hamburger and fries were suddenly in her throat and she rushed to the bathroom. Once her stomach was empty, she looked in the mirror and said, "You have to get control. Your life as Debra Hayes is gone. Now keep your pledge."

She crawled into bed but couldn't sleep. She had been bad and should suffer so she went into the bathroom and lay on the floor. Memories of her childhood flooded her mind as she lay on the cold tile. This was her father's favorite punishment. All night she shivered, tossed and turned, but refused to seek the comfort of the bed in the next room. She kept reminding herself that Debra had died with Jane. Their suffering was over. Now it was time for Rae to deal misery to the bastards who killed her sister.

Morning came. She showered, dressed, and went to the buffet breakfast. Finding a secluded table, she ate some dry toast and picked up the morning paper. A familiar voice startled her, causing her to look around the paper in the direction the voice had come from. Captain Stone was sitting two tables away. She raised the paper, finished her coffee, and left. Her heart was racing by the time she got back to her room. The toast and coffee gushed up, and she barely made it to the bathroom.

Debra left her room and went to a pay phone. She took a piece of paper and some change from her pocket and dialed the number from the paper. In a few minutes she had arranged to be in Myrtle Beach in two days for a bit of plastic surgery.

Next she called Stewart Collins, a friend of Cole's, to ask if he would like an all-expenses paid vacation. She explained that she wanted to get away but needed an escort so she could enjoy the beach without being hassled. Stewart was happy to accept her offer, and since he didn't work, he had no scheduling problem. He spent most of his time on the beach playing volleyball or in the gym lifting weights. Stu was thirty years old with blond hair, blue eyes, and a build like Arnold Schwarzenegger. Stewart was a kept man. His lover was a business tycoon who very much wanted their relationship to be a secret, especially from his wife and three children.

Stewart was thrilled that Rae had thought of him, and anxious to go. She would pick him up at his house at 4:00 p.m. tomorrow.

Debra went to the lobby and called a cab. Noticing a discarded paper, she glanced through it to see if there was any mention of Jane. She didn't find anything. When the cab arrived, she gave the driver the address of the house Cole left her in his will.

Debra loved the house she and Cole shared the short time they were married. It was a large colonial style, with four bedrooms and a lovely landscaped yard. There was no practical reason to keep the house. She would never be back here again.

Who would have thought she would wind up owning two houses? Perhaps her mother would keep the house she left her, or maybe she would sell it and enjoy a few pleasures in life.

While waiting for the realtor, Debra packed the clothes she'd left in the house after Cole died. These few things would do until she got to Myrtle Beach. She went to the utility room and opened the cabinet where the hot water heater was stored. Reaching behind the heater, she fished around and found the wire attached to one of the pipes. She unfastened the wire and pulled out a black leather purse. Inside the purse was a wallet that contained a driver's license and a social security card in the name of Rae Lyn Roberts. Lastly she put one thousand dollars into the wallet and another five thousand in the zipper compartment of the purse.

A knock at the front door interrupted Debra's packing. She placed the purse on the bed and went to the door where she greeted two young women and a young man. The woman in the neat tan suit spoke first. "Mrs. Roberts, I am Leslie Dobbs. We spoke on the phone. This is Mr. and Mrs. Dillon Casper."

"Please come in. It's nice to meet you."

In thirty minutes the deal was closed, and Debra was richer by one hundred fifty thousand dollars. While the Caspers walked through their new home, Debra placed her luggage in the trunk of the white El Dorado Cadillac parked in the garage. When everything was loaded, Debra returned to the house, wished the Caspers well, and then said a final good-bye to the Cole Roberts segment of her life.

At ten thirty a.m. Rae Lyn Roberts pulled out of the garage and drove to the bank. The bank president met with her and suggested how she might invest her money to make the best profit. She thanked him and said she would think about it

After a nice dinner Rae checked into the Hampton Inn. She soaked in a hot bath and went to bed. Visions of Jane flashed through her mind even though she kept reminding herself that Jane and Debra were dead. Unable to sleep, Rae clicked on the television and found a movie to watch. Exhaustion finally took over and she slept.

Before picking up Stewart, Rae bought a large ice chest, filled it with fruit, bottled water, sodas and a bottle of bacterium she had been carrying in a small ice chest.

It was four fifteen p.m. when Rae pulled up in front of Stewart's house. He was out the door with his bag hollering, "Hello!" before she could come to a complete stop.

"I take it you're ready to go." Rae said.

"You bet. I've been ready ever since you called. There's nothing like a change of scenery to brighten your life. How are you?"

"Oh, I'm fine, and I quite agree a change of scenery will be great."

"Do you want me to drive?"

"Yes. I need a nap."

"Have you mapped out our course?"

"Yes, Highway 95 to Jacksonville, and then Highway 17 all the way to Myrtle Beach. Just a nice little drive along the coast.

"Stewart, I have a confession. I'm going to have a bit of plastic surgery while we're there. I may need you to fetch and carry for me until I recover a bit."

"I'm a wonderful nurse, but why in the world are you having plastic surgery? You're beautiful. Don't tell me it's on an unseen area."

Rae laughed. "I'm having the end of my nose straightened and the mole taken off my lip. The doctor promised me it wouldn't leave a scar."

"I love that mole. It's so sexy."

"Thanks but I don't agree. It's always bugged me."

Once Rae was comfortable with Stewart's driving she leaned her head back, closed her eyes and slept. When Stewart swerved to miss a dog she jerked awake.

"Sorry, I almost hit a dog."

"That's okay."

They drove until hunger overcame their thrill of adventure. Spotting a restaurant ahead, they agreed to give it a try. Rae reached into her purse and counted out five hundred dollars. "This should be enough for a while," she said, handing Stewart the money. "You get to pay all the bills."

Stewart said, "I can handle that."

In a flash, he was out of the car opening the door for her. Stewart was very much a gentleman. Taking Rae's hand, he said, "Food! I need food!"

The good meal made Rae and Stewart lazy so they decided to find a motel. Stewart rented single rooms next to each other and carried in their luggage. Rae checked the ice chest and found there would be plenty of ice until morning. Stewart went for a swim in the motel pool while Rae showered. They watched the news together; then Stewart went to his room.

Rae was up early the next morning putting on her wig when she realized she and Stewart would be sharing a room in Myrtle Beach. She doubted she could sleep in the wig without having a headache or maybe even losing it, so she would have her hair dyed when they reached Myrtle Beach.

Stewart knocked on her door just as she was closing her bags. They ate some fruit, had a cup of coffee, loaded up, and left. Stewart drove so Rae could enjoy the scenery. They arrived in Myrtle Beach about lunchtime and by one o'clock had found a hotel on the beach.

When Stewart went to check the beach, Rae called the hotel beauty salon and made an appointment. By four-thirty the wig was gone. Her auburn hair looked natural and felt wonderful. Rae met Stewart at the hotel bar at five o'clock. Over a drink they decided to go shopping before going out to dinner.

Stewart escorted Rae to the doctor's office the next morning and fussed over her as though she were having major surgery. The procedures took only a couple of hours, and the doctor assured her that she would be out of the bandages in a few days. He said it would be fine for her to go to the beach as long as she didn't get wet or get sand on her face. Rae didn't think she would be heading for the beach anytime soon.

Stewart took her to their room and made sure she was comfortable, then left to have her prescriptions filled. When he returned, Rae was asleep so he slipped out for a bit of exercise.

Rae was amazed that she felt so well the next day. She suffered only slight discomfort when she ate or brushed her teeth. Her nose was sore but not excruciatingly so. They headed for the beach that afternoon with Rae wearing a large hat and sunglasses.

After three days, she returned to the doctor to have the bandages removed. The rest of their time was spent shopping and enjoying the local entertainment. Stewart was a wonderful escort and fun to be with. He was by her side constantly, fussing over her like a loving husband. Rae found she rather enjoyed the attention.

They left Monday and arrived back at Stewart's on Tuesday. Rae thanked him and they chatted for a few minutes. She promised to call him if she decided to take another vacation. Driving away, she realized she would miss him.

Rae thought a dentist just starting a new practice wouldn't own a Cadillac. She hated to give up her wonderful car but it would be best, so she started looking for a used car lot. She found a nice Ford Torino station wagon. The salesman tried to convince her she would have to pay some besides the trade in, but she held firm. He wound up putting on a trailer hitch and servicing the car. She watched while they changed the oil, checked the air conditioner, battery, transmission, and brake fluid. Rae drove out of the garage with a set of belts, clamps, and hoses secure in the back seat. The salesman was shaking his head as he wished her good luck.

After a call to the insurance agent and a trip to the tag agent, she was legal and ready to go. Now all she had to do was rent a U-Haul and head for Texas.

Rae pulled up to the storage shed just before dark. It took about thirty minutes to load the boxes and a few pieces of furniture. She was tired, but thought driving might help her relax. She preferred to drive at night but didn't feel as safe as in the daylight, especially since she was carrying a large amount of cash. A .357 lying beside her made her feel more secure, but she still thought she would stop before midnight.

She headed out of Miami, and then as if pulled by a strong arm, took the exit to her former home. It wasn't wise to go by, but curiosity got the best of her. She drove slowly down the familiar street. When the house came into view she saw her parent's car parked in the driveway. Jane was in good hands. Without looking back, she turned the corner and drove away.

Rae took U.S. 95 to U.S. 75. She should reach South Bay, or perhaps Moore Haven, before midnight. There was no need to hurry. According to her calculations, it would take about thirty hours to get to Decker.

Pulling the trailer slowed her down some. When she reached South Bay at ten p.m., she stopped. A hot bath and a good night's sleep beckoned. The motel she chose wasn't fancy, but it looked clean.

By seven o'clock the next morning Rae had eaten breakfast, filled up the car, and was on her way. A light rain made visibility poor and the highway slick. She reminisced; it had been just this kind of day when she began her college career. It hadn't been too difficult to convince the dean that even though she was schooled by a religious order, she could pass the college entrance exam. He agreed to let her take the test. She passed with no problem. Rae Roberts was a college freshman with no record of high school on her college transcript and no social security number. Dean Nabors insisted that she apply for one.

It took her months to find a lonely male who worked at a social security office. She stalked him long enough to find he ate lunch every day at a little coffee shop near the office. He ignored her the first couple of times she spoke to him. When she asked to join him for lunch, he was befuddled, but said yes. They ate together for two weeks before he asked her out to dinner. In another two weeks, he was quite smitten and fell for her sob story about being born at home to a very young girl who didn't want her. She was given away and her birth never recorded. Could he help her get a social security number? One trip to bed and she had her card, and Bob soon had a broken heart.

For the next six years while remaining Debra Hayes at work and home, she was Rae Roberts at school and Cole's house. Cole was the only person who knew her as both Debra and Rae. Occasionally someone had asked if she were wearing a wig. She explained she suffered from a scalp disorder that made her natural hair thin and scraggly.

Cole never questioned her until just before he died. When he asked why she maintained the two identities, she told him she didn't want her family to be able to find her when she moved and started her practice. She explained that her father was an abusive drunk, her mother just a drunk, and they were constantly begging her for money. Since Cole had never met her parents, he believed her, and promised her secret was safe. It was easy and she had enjoyed her two identities. Too bad Debra had to die. She was a nice person, just a little dull. Rae, however, was full of life and loved adventure with only one care in the world.

Debra checked the gas gauge. She stopped at the next station and filled up. Then she drove across the street to the Dixie Quick. A foot-long and fries would probably give her indigestion, but she was going to have them anyway. While eating, she noticed a couple of guys in a tan pick-up next to her. They watched her every move. When she got out to throw away her trash, one of them whistled. Returning to the car she looked at the road map thinking they might leave, but they didn't. A couple of idiots didn't scare her. With that thought in mind, she left the Dixie Quick and drove back to the interstate.

Twenty miles down the road, she noticed the pickup. It was hanging back behind a Chevy sedan. The .357 was within easy reach and she knew how to use it. Cole insisted that she learn how to shoot a pistol, rifle and shotgun. In fact, she had brought Cole's twelve-gauge shotgun and her twenty-gauge with her. At first she resisted shooting lessons, but after a few practice sessions, she began to enjoy it and became quite good.

The sedan took an exit, but the pickup wasn't in sight. Maybe they decided to find another adventure. No such luck. They appeared again about ten minutes later. Surely they wouldn't try anything stupid on the interstate, but one never knew. They were right behind her flashing their lights, an old trick used to get drivers to pull over. She kept driving. They bumped the trailer causing the car to weave. The second bump was a little harder.

"Okay boys. You asked for it," she said aloud as she began to pull over to the shoulder. She stopped the car and opened the door. The pickup pulled up behind her. As the guys got out of the cab, Rae shot a hole in their radiator. She was pulling away before they could react. It would be a while before they could catch her even if they elected to try. Just for safety's sake, she would choose an alternate route. If they persisted, the next bullet would be aimed at one of them.

She stayed on the interstate until she found State Highway 27 and stopped at a motel earlier than she would have otherwise.

"I want a single, away from the street, if possible. I had a problem with two men down the road and I'd rather not have to deal with them again," Rae told the motel manager.

He asked, "Would you like me to call the police and report them?"

"No. I don't think they'll show up, at least not for a while. They'll probably do something to my car or trailer if they do find me."

"Tell you what. Let's take your car and trailer to the county barn and park it inside for the night. That way you won't have to worry about any trouble. I'll put you in a room near the office, and you can get a good night's sleep."

Rae was surprised that someone would be concerned, and though a little reluctant, agreed to the arrangement.

She unloaded her suitcase and the ice chest, and then followed the manager to the barn and parked her car. He took her back to her room and asked her out for dinner. She declined the invitation, although she was tempted. Cheese and crackers with fruit for dessert would suffice tonight.

After filling the ice chest from the ice machine, she enjoyed a long hot soak in the tub and was asleep before the news went off. Rae slept late, dressed and asked for a ride to get her car. After a good breakfast, she was on her way without seeing any sign of a tan pickup. She arrived in Decker, Texas, Saturday morning.

Chapter Three

The sign read, "Welcome to Decker, Home of 6,502 Friendly People." Rae added aloud, "And five rapists."

"Why did I manage to get here on a weekend?" She asked herself. "Oh well, I might as well buy a paper and see if I can find a place to live." The Decker Daily was on Main Street so she drove there and bought a paper out of the stand in front; it was Friday's, but that was okay. There were three furnished apartments listed with phone numbers but no addresses. Rae drove to a fast food place and used a pay phone to call. On her third try, she reached a lady who gave her the address and directions.

She turned into the driveway and admired the neat white frame house with a wrap-around porch, complete with swing. As instructed, she drove past the house to find the garage apartment. It was just as neat and well-kept as the house. Approaching the backdoor, she was met by a small woman with gray hair and a wonderful smile.

"You must be the one who called about the apartment."

"Yes, I just arrived in town and need a place to hang my hat."

"Are you from around here?"

"No, I'm from Alabama, but I attended dental school in Florida. I hope to start a dental practice here."

"You're a dentist? You look awfully young. Do you have family here?"

"No. I'm alone. Oh, sorry, I didn't introduce myself. I'm Rae Roberts."

"Well, Rae Roberts, as pretty as you are, you won't be alone long. My name is Doris Price. Come on, I'll show you the apartment. You don't party, do you?"

"No, I'm very quiet. Some people would call me boring."

"How did you happen to choose Decker if you don't know anyone here?"

"I wanted to live in a small town in the Midwest, so I did some research and found that Decker has only one dentist. Further research indicated that he is elderly and will probably be retiring soon."

"Well, you're right about the elderly part, and I hope you're right about the retiring too. Here we are. Look all you like."

The apartment was small, with only one bedroom, but it was immaculate. Hooray, it wouldn't need cleaning. The only drawback was Mrs. Price. She was nice and friendly, but Rae sensed she was a busybody.

"I like it. Would it be possible for me to move in today?"

"Don't see why not, everything but the phone is in working order. You can have the utilities transferred to your name Monday."

Mrs. Price insisted on helping unload the trailer. She helped with the television and a few pieces of furniture, and talked incessantly. Rae didn't know if she was tired from unloading or from listening to Mrs. Price.

Once everything was in the apartment, Mrs. Price said, "I'll leave you to put your things away."

"Thank you for your help. I can make it fine now," Rae said as she ushered her landlady out the door.

After Mrs. Price left, Rae took the bottle of botulism culture from the ice chest and placed it in the freezer compartment of the refrigerator. Tired from the days of traveling she only unpacked the necessities. She was debating about going out for dinner when there was a knock on her door. She opened the door and Mrs. Price handed her a plate covered with foil.

"I thought you might like a home cooked meal," she said.

Rae's irritation toward her talkative neighbor faded. "Thank you, I was dreading cheese and crackers again, but you shouldn't have gone to so much trouble."

"No trouble, I love to cook. If you need to use my phone, feel welcome to do so."

"You're very kind, but I have no one to call."

The fried chicken, salad, mashed potatoes and gravy was delicious. Rae ate every morsel. Full and content, she locked the door for the night and took the newspaper to the bedroom. "Same old news, same old names as ten years ago. This is like stepping back in time," she said aloud as she refolded the paper.

They had moved to Decker when her father's trucking company relocated in Dallas. The move from Houston was welcome, but instead of living in Dallas, her parents chose Decker. They wanted their daughters to attend high school in a small town. Mr. Hayes' sister lived in Decker and loved it there. So with encouragement from Aunt Emily, the girls enrolled as freshmen at Decker High after having attended their first eight years at a church operated school in Houston.

Jane and Debra were excellent students, but because of their religious beliefs, they weren't allowed to take part in extracurricular activities. The only exception had been for Jane to take vocal music. Her father allowed her to enter the contest at a college in Dallas, and she won a superior rating all four years.

Most of the students were great with the girls and understood that their religious beliefs required the old-fashioned dress and hairstyle.

Some, however, were cruel. One of the cruelest was Thomas Juan Snodgrass, the local banker's son. Tom was handsome, cocky, and mean. He was a good athlete, but had a lousy attitude. He pretty much did as he pleased. He went out of his way to make fun of Jane and Debra.

Tom had three friends who followed him everywhere. They were also from wealthy families.

Stephen Paul Morrison's father was an oil tycoon. Steve was an athlete and very handsome. He was a nice guy when he wasn't around Tom.

Jackson Blake Cooper was the only child of doctors. Tall, skinny, with acne, he was tolerated by Tom and Steve. He hung with them and was their errand boy.

Dale Allen Smith was from a rich southern family who had made their fortune in real estate. He was nice looking, but not very bright. He, like Jackson, hung on to Tom and Steve's coat tails.

Even though they picked on Jane and Debra, Tom asked Jane out several times. She turned him down just as she turned down all other invitations. The other boys accepted her refusal, but Tom, who always got what he wanted, persisted.

Jim Garrett was the fifth boy included in the attack. He enrolled in school the second semester of their senior year. Jim didn't seem like a bad guy and no one really understood why he hung out with Tom and the others. He left Decker soon after graduation.

"Well, guys, we're going to meet again," Rae said as she turned out the light.

Awakened by singing birds and bright sunlight Rae was confused for a minute but then smiled and enjoyed a long stretch. She was eager to get dressed and start her new life. First, she must make a trip to the grocery store. After breakfast she would take a walk in the park and get rid of a few demons from the past.

Rae was stepping out of the shower when she heard a knock on the door. Mrs. Price was already becoming a problem. She opened the door and sure enough there was the pert little woman holding a plate, "Here's your breakfast, dear. Maybe next Sunday you will go to church with me."

"Thank you, Mrs. Price. You must quit doing this. You're very sweet, but before long, I'll weigh two hundred pounds."

"Honey, you look awfully thin to me. Won't hurt you to gain a pound or two."

Lord, the woman could cook, but she must put a stop to this. A house in the country was what she needed. She would start looking as soon as possible, but right now she had to get moving before Mrs. Price showed up with lunch.

She returned the U-Haul trailer and went to the grocery store. Mrs. Price was returning from church as she pulled into the drive. A handsome young man parked at the curb and walked toward the house. Jon Price had graduated two years before her. Afraid that he would recognize her, she grabbed a bag of groceries and went upstairs.

Dropping into a chair, Rae caught her breath, "I don't think he has any idea who I am. Better get control or I'll have a nervous breakdown."

Nerves under control, Rae began putting her groceries away. When that task was finished, she washed Mrs. Price's plates and was drying them when there was a knock on the door.

Rae went to the door.

"Would you like to join my son Jon and me for lunch?" Mrs. Price asked.

"No, thank you, I've already made plans. I was on my way to return your plates and tell you that I'll be gone this afternoon."

"Will you stop by and meet Jon before you leave?"

"Okay, I'll be down in just a minute."

The meeting was quick. Jon was nice and good-looking as ever, but Rae had other things on her mind. She excused herself and went to the park.

Several changes had been made. The wooded area along the creek where she found Jane was cleared of underbrush. There were also walking paths lined with Texas wildflowers, and a guardrail stood in front of the drainage ditch. Families were gathered at picnic tables for lunch, and a group of young men were playing softball.

She took a stroll around the park and then returned to her apartment. Rae looked through the classified ads hoping to find an office building space for her dental practice. The Chamber of Commerce might be able to help. She would check tomorrow.

Out of professional courtesy Rae visited Dr. Tooley's office. He was excited that she was opening a practice because he wanted to cut down on hours. They discussed possible building sites and the general atmosphere of the area. Dr. Tooley asked her to come back the next day, which she agreed to do.

Dr. Tooley made her an offer she couldn't refuse. He wanted to sell her his clinic. His plan was for her to work with him a couple of weeks so that his patients could meet her and she could check out his equipment. If all went well, they would begin the legal work.

After two weeks Dr. Tooley announced his retirement and introduced Rae as his replacement. The only bad part was his assistant was also leaving. Rae ran an ad in the paper. After many interviews, she hired a former classmate, Lori Farmer. Lori was a nice person, married and the mother of a five-year-old. A woman with a family shouldn't be too concerned with her boss's life, and Lori seemed to have no clue that Rae was actually Debra Hayes.

The newspaper ran an article on her, so Decker was now aware of the new dentist. After a slow first month, her practice was improving.

The Kiwanis Club invited her to lunch. She accepted the invitation and agreed to give a speech on modern dental techniques; however, she was disappointed that Tom Snodgrass, the president, was not at the meeting. If asked, she would join the club because she wanted to get acquainted with Snodgrass.

She did meet Sheriff Harley Davis who gave a short speech on the condition of the jail. Sheriff Davis had investigated Jane's case and did a very poor job. It was obvious he was influenced by money since he purchased a new Ford pickup right after the case closed. Rae could hardly stand to look at him, much less shake hands. Perhaps she should add him to her list.

Three months went by, and Rae didn't feel she had made much progress. Her practice was going well, but she hadn't found a place to buy, nor had she located all of the men she sought.

The holiday season was near and the town was swept up in the Christmas spirit. Lori decorated the office window and gave Rae a gift. Rae was surprised. She hadn't even thought of buying gifts. As children, she and Jane received one gift, always something they needed, such as underwear. All of their holiday seasons were spent at church activities.

Caught up in the holiday spirit, Rae allowed Mrs. Price to talk her into going to the Christmas program at church. Rae was having a good time until some girl sang "O

Holy Night." Jane sang the song every year at the school Christmas program. Rae was overcome with sadness and rushed out of the church, her eyes filled with tears, and she ran smack into Tom Snodgrass.

"Are you ill?" He asked.

"No, I just need some fresh air."

"You must be the new dentist."

"Yes. Who are you?"

"Why, my dear, I am the president of your local bank, Tom Snodgrass."

"Oh, so you are real. I've been to two Kiwanis meetings and you haven't attended one yet. I was beginning to think you were imaginary."

"Are you a member?"

"I'm planning to join."

"Well, I'll bet I don't miss any more meetings. Matter of fact, I may call for an emergency meeting or two."

Rae searched for a retort. Unable to come up with one, she went to find Mrs. Price.

Mrs. Price was concerned when Rae left and was sure she was coming down with something.

"You look pale and kind of green around the gills."

"I'm fine, Mrs. Price. You worry too much."

"Well I'm going to fix you some hot soup when we get home. You probably haven't eaten since breakfast."

This was true, so Rae didn't argue with her.

While they ate their soup, Mrs. Price chattered about the program. Rae asked, "Who was the girl singing "O Holy Night?"

"Oh that's Margie Tucker. Doesn't she have a beautiful voice?"

"Yes she does. Does she attend your church?"

"No, her parents belong to a very strict religious group, but they allow Margie to sing at special functions."

"Who are her parents?"

"Luke and Emily Tucker. They live outside of town on a farm. I think they have two other children."

So that was little Margie, her first cousin. Emily Tucker was Samuel Hayes' sister.

"Is something wrong, dear?"

"Oh no, I was thinking about Margie. She has a beautiful voice. Thanks for the soup. I feel much better."

"You really must take better care of yourself."

"I'll try. Goodnight, Mrs. Price."

Alone at last, Rae sat with a glass of wine thinking about Tom Snodgrass. He hadn't changed much. Age had improved his looks. He inherited his dark complexion and black hair from his Latin American mother. His blue eyes and height came from his father. Too bad his personality came from the devil. She was looking forward to the next Kiwanis meeting. She felt Tom would suggest a private get together. She'd rather be alone with a pit viper.

The talk around town was Tom spent his time at the Country Club playing golf, drinking, and chasing women while his dad ran the bank. His wife was a socialite and known for her affairs. Their two children spent most of their time with a nanny. In time she would find out more about Snodgrass.

This weekend she must buy something for Lori and Mrs. Price, and she had no idea what. Simple. She would phone Lori and ask what she thought Mrs. Price would like, and phone Mrs. Price and ask her what to get Lori. She needed to get the gifts Saturday morning because she planned to fly to Las Vegas Christmas Day. She didn't want to spend Christmas alone in her little apartment. She and Cole had gone to Vegas to get married and she enjoyed the city very much.

Her plan worked. Lori suggested a pretty robe for Mrs. Price. Mrs. Price suggested for Lori, a day of beauty package that included a massage, manicure, and haircut. They were thrilled with their gifts and Rae felt good about giving them.

She declined a dinner invitation with Mrs. Price and her family so she could pack. It would be good to get away from here. She would play the slots, catch some shows, and make plans for dealing with a certain local banker. Rae already had some thoughts as to how to rid the world of Tom Snodgrass, given the opportunity. There was no need to hurry.

Las Vegas fulfilled Rae's need to be active. She couldn't believe the town never slept, and once again she became a night person. The slots were fun for a while, but Black Jack became her game of choice. Cards weren't allowed in the house when she was growing up, so she learned the game by watching. There was always a gentleman eager to give her a few pointers, and of course, they also wanted a dinner date. When she felt she understood the game, she bought some chips and found a table. Even though the odds were with the house, she managed to break even. After a couple of hours, she began to win. She boarded the plane to Dallas, carrying more money than she came with.

She spent two days in Dallas shopping and getting her hair dyed. Relaxed and eager to deal with Tom Snodgrass, she drove to Decker. Too bad he would die quickly instead of suffering for years. How she wished she could arrange for him to be reduced to a drooling idiot.

Mrs. Price welcomed Rae back with a warm hug. Without an invitation, she followed her to her apartment, talking all the way. Rae was only half listening until Dale Smith's name was mentioned. Jerking to attention, she asked, "What did you say about Dale Smith?"

"He had a heart attack yesterday. It is hard to believe someone so young could have a heart attack. I think he was born with some kind of problem and was cautioned to be careful about diet and drinking. They think he will live but will be limited in his activities. But then his activities have always been limited to chasing women, spending money, and drinking."

"Mrs. Price, I can't believe you said that."

"Well, it's the truth. A day's work would kill him, for sure."

"I take it Mr. Smith is wealthy?"

"His parents are wealthy. His father made a mint in real estate. He's been spoiled all his life. Thinks he's better than everybody else."

"Shall I assume you don't care much for Dale Smith?"

"I don't like him one little bit. He's just a pretty face with a horrible attitude, but I don't wish him dead."

"What hospital is he in?"

"Oh, they flew him right to Dallas. No doubt, he will have the very best care money can buy."

"Well, I hope he makes it. Maybe this will scare him into changing."

Rae didn't add that she had plans for Mr. Smith.

Mrs. Price rattled on while Rae put up groceries and unpacked her suitcases. When she finally left, Rae felt like she needed another vacation.

It was still daylight so she decided to walk to the clinic and make sure everything was ready for tomorrow. She found the clinic in tiptop shape. Lori had been there before her. Picking up the appointment book, she looked over the list of patients for January 2nd.

Back at the apartment, she fixed a light supper and read the paper. Later when she was sure Mrs. Price wasn't going to pop in again, she checked the botulism culture hidden in the freezer. Rae smiled as she recalled how she came by the bottle of bacterium.

She had rushed to the lab one evening to leave a blood sample to be analyzed. Todd, one of the lab techs, was so absorbed in his work, he didn't notice her.

"You're working awfully hard. Must be something important."

"If this works, it will be your ticket to staying beautiful, beautiful."

"What are you talking about?"

"I can't tell you the details right now because it's still in the research stage."

"Interesting. Keep me posted on your progress."

"Will do. Something I can do for you?"

"Yes, I need a drug screening on this blood."

"I'm on it. I'll buzz you when I finish."

"I'm headed for the hazardous waste dump. Need me to take anything?"

"Hey, that would save me some time." Todd replied, "Sure you don't mind?"

"Not at all."

"What is this?" Rae asked as she looked at the bottle.

"It's a bacterium that can be fatal if ingested. Best known as botulism. Here's you a pair of gloves and a mask. Best not handle it without protection."

"Why are you destroying this? Weren't you working with it when I came in? Or can it even be used again?"

"This culture can be kept cool or frozen for a long time. Warm it up and the bacteria go full speed. I don't have approval for this particular research so I'd best not keep it around."

"Good plan. Holler when you finish the blood work-up."

"You got it. Don't drop that bottle."

Not only had she not destroyed the culture, she had packed it in ice and brought it with her. Thank goodness Todd enlightened her as to its great value.

January was a busy month at the clinic, so busy the day of the Kiwanis meeting caught her by surprise. Lori reminded her or she would have missed the meeting entirely.

Tom Snodgrass met her at the door. "You look lovely, Dr. Roberts," he said as he escorted her to a chair. He touched her arm as he seated her. Rae wanted to rush to the bathroom and wash the spot. When the meeting adjourned, Tom beat a path to Rae's side.

"I'll walk you back to your office," he said.

"That isn't necessary. I feel very safe." Rae replied as she started out the door.

"You never know what will happen these days, so I'll protect you."

He talked continually all the way to the clinic. When they arrived, he asked, "How about meeting me tonight for a drink?"

"Aren't you married?" Rae asked.

"Yes. Is that a problem?"

"You bet it's a problem. I don't go out with married men."

Tom laughed and said, "I love a challenge. See you, Doc."

Rae almost panicked just thinking about him touching her and the possibility of being alone with him. She snapped back to reality when Lori said, "Mrs. Taylor is here, Doctor Roberts."

"Send her in, Lori."

Rae's afternoon was booked so Tom Snodgrass was forgotten. She was walking the last patient out when a delivery from the flower shop arrived. Lori accepted the roses and then handed them to Rae. She set them on her desk and removed the card. It read, "Beautiful women should be appreciated."

"Gosh, Doc, I didn't know you have an admirer."

"Well, I'm more inclined to think of him as a dirty young man. I'm not interested in married men. Keep this under your hat, okay?"

"Sure."

"I'll have a talk with Mr. Snodgrass. He seems to have forgotten I have a responsible position to uphold. I doubt my patients would understand his sending me roses. Toss them in the trash."

"Throw these beautiful flowers away?"

"Take them home with you if you want to. Just get them out of my sight."

Lori took the flowers. Rae didn't even look to see what she did with them. She didn't know why she was surprised and upset. This was what she expected. Still fuming, she looked over tomorrow's list of patients, locked the clinic and walked home.

She debated about calling Tom but decided to let it ride. If he sent more flowers or started calling, they'd have a talk.

January had been extremely cold, which was unusual for Texas. The first week of February brought a winter storm that was even more unusual. The storm hit on a Tuesday afternoon and by four o'clock, the ground was covered with sleet and the temperature was below freezing. When the storm hit, Rae sent Lori home and prepared to go home herself. She was walking in the bitter cold when a car pulled up to the curb beside her. Tom Snodgrass let down the window and asked, "Would you like a ride?"

"No, thank you. I'm almost home."

"You'll freeze. And that would be such a waste."

"I'm quite comfortable," she lied.

"Okay, but don't say I didn't try."

Rae thought she might very well freeze before she made it up the icy stairs. Her feet were so cold she could barely feel them. She went to the bathroom to run a hot bath only to find the water pipes were frozen. She was wondering what to do about the water when the phone rang. Mrs. Price was calling to ask if everything was okay.

The storm blew itself out the next day, but it was three days before the temperature rose above freezing and the pipes began to thaw. Rae was Mrs. Price's guest during that time. She thought she would go crazy but instead she had a good time playing gin rummy and baking cookies.

Jon came over to check on them the second day. He drove Rae to the clinic so she could check the water situation. All was well there. On the drive back he asked her out for dinner Saturday night, weather permitting. Rae accepted the invitation and then wondered later if she had done the right thing. Jon was a kind, considerate man, but she didn't have time for a man in her life. More to the point, she didn't want a man in her life. Oh well, one dinner wouldn't hurt.

Dinner turned out to be pleasant but not exciting. When Jon asked her out again, she told him no. She could tell she had hurt his feelings, but he would get over it. Mrs. Price was a bit distant for a few days but soon was chattering again. Rae rather enjoyed the days of silence.

Tom asked Rae out again at the February Kiwanis meeting. She smiled and said, "I don't go out with married men."

"I'll get a divorce if that's what it takes."

"I'm not sure I'd go out with you anyway, so don't bother with a divorce."

"You don't know what you're missing."

"I'll live."

"I've got to be more exciting than Jon Price."

"I doubt exciting is the correct term. Jon Price is a very nice man."

"Boring, boring."

She left before she became angry and said something she shouldn't. The anger returned that afternoon when two-dozen roses were delivered to the clinic. The card read, "Let me excite you."

Rae was furious. Lori took one look at her face, grabbed the flowers, and took them to the trash.

That evening Tom called. "Ready for some excitement?" he asked.

Struggling to maintain her cool, she said, "I don't need your kind of excitement. Please don't call here again." Before he could respond, she hung up. The phone rang again but she didn't answer.

She fumed around the apartment for an hour or two and then decided she needed some fresh air. Walking at night was not something she usually did, but she felt as if the walls were closing in on her. It was still cold outside so she dressed warmly and, at the last minute, slipped the .357 into her coat pocket.

Once outside and away from the apartment she began to feel better. The air was so cool it almost hurt to breathe. She walked to the edge of town and found a clearing away from the city lights. The moon gave enough light for her to find her way. So many stars filled the clear sky that there wasn't room for one more. The cold began to creep through her clothing. Her toes, fingertips, and nose were beginning to tingle. Still she stood and marveled at the beautiful sky. How could God make such a beautiful world and then put horrible people in it? Sighing, she turned and started back to the apartment. Walking up the driveway, she noticed a car parked across the street. It was Tom Snodgrass. He waved and drove down the street.

So, Mr. Snodgrass was spying on her. Well, let him spy. He didn't scare her. She knew he was harmless unless he had his buddies with him.

She bathed and dressed for bed. The phone rang. Thinking it was Mrs. Price, she answered.

"Did you have a nice walk?"

"Yes, I did. You should try it sometime."

"I'd love to walk with you. Just name the time and place."

"Forget it. And quit spying on me."

"I'm not spying, just admiring."

Rae hung up and went to bed. She couldn't sleep so she read for an hour or two. The next morning the alarm went off much too soon. She got up feeling as if she hadn't slept at all.

Flowers arrived at the clinic that afternoon, and the card just had two eyes drawn on it. Lori sighed and took them to the trash saying, "He's beginning to get on my nerves now."

Rae laughed. "Think I could ask him to send money instead of flowers?"

"Can I carry it to the trash?"

They were both laughing as they left to go home.

Chapter Four

March came, bringing the hope of spring. The days started getting longer and warmer. People were cheerful and talked of planting gardens and crops. Rae wanted a place in the country where she could have a small garden and a flowerbed. She would call the realtor again.

She couldn't believe her practice was doing so well. There was seldom a day that wasn't filled, and some held interesting experiences. She would never forget Mrs. Cherry getting stuck in the dental chair, or Mr. Stevens swallowing his gold cap. Thank goodness they were both good-natured.

Snodgrass stopped bothering her, or at least he stopped sending flowers. The phone still rang at odd hours, but she didn't answer. When the Kiwanis meeting rolled around, Lori reminded her to attend. She almost didn't go, but since Lori hadn't scheduled a one p.m. appointment, she changed her mind at the last minute.

Tom met her at the door with a big smile and escorted her to the chair next to his. During the meal, he said, "I'm headed for Mexico as soon as this meeting is over. Got a private plane waiting at the airport. I'm going to spend five days fishing and partying with the natives."

"Where in Mexico?" Rae asked.

"A place so remote no one even knows about it."

"How did you find it?"

"A friend of mine has been there. Matter of fact, he's flying down tomorrow. Yep, me and old Steve are going to have a ball."

"Steve?"

"Yes. He's an old high school buddy. He owns a casino in Las Vegas."

"Must be nice. I hope that cap doesn't fall off while you're playing in the jungle."

"What are you talking about?"

"The cap on your upper right incisor looks loose and needs to be glued back on. If you'll meet me at the clinic, I'll fix it for you. As soon as this meeting is over, come to the back door of the clinic. Don't tell anyone I'm doing this, or I'll never have another lunch hour."

"Okay Doc, your secret is safe. See you in thirty minutes."

Rae slipped out of the meeting and rushed to the apartment. She pulled on a pair of gloves, took the bottle of bacterium from the freezer and placed it in a pan of warm water. It took more time than she wanted to get it to a liquid state, but heating it fast might kill the bacteria. She poured the liquid into a plastic container and rushed to the clinic. Tom knocked on the back door a couple minutes later.

"Come on in, and I'll have you fixed up in no time."

She sat him in the chair and examined the tooth. "Do I need to deaden this before I go to work, or are you brave?"

"Better deaden it. I don't handle pain very well."

Rae prepared the syringe of Novocain and gave it in the upper gum, both on top and underneath. She had to hurry. Lori would be back in a few minutes.

"I'll let that work a minute while I get the glue. You okay?"

"I'm fine. Just thankful you noticed the cap. Why the mask and gloves?"

"I've had a little bit of a sore throat. Would hate to give you a bug and ruin your trip."

Rae filled a paper cup with the botulism bacterium. She mixed some mint mouthwash with it to cover the taste. Returning to Tom she began on the tooth. She really didn't do anything except work at the gum line and then push the cap up. Finishing, she handed him the cup. "Drink this so you won't have an upset stomach. Sometimes dental work and flying don't mix. You may feel a little queasy, but you'll get over it in a little while." He drank the liquid and then said, "That stuff tastes awful. You sure it won't kill me? How much do I owe you?"

"No charge."

"I'll take you to dinner when I get back."

"Sorry. No dinners, no drinks, no walks. Go catch your plane."

"Thanks. Come go with me, and we'll have fun in the sun."

Rae pushed him out the door. He had just driven away when Lori came in the front door. Rae went in the bathroom and flushed the cup down the toilet. The plastic container would be taken care of later.

There wasn't time to think about what she'd done. Patients came in a steady stream all afternoon. Lori noticed no flowers came that day. "Maybe he's given up," she commented.

"I hope so. He was all in a whirl at the meeting, getting ready to fly to Mexico for a vacation."

Rae sent Lori home at five but she stayed for a while longer. She washed the container out with soap and boiling water and then dropped it into the disposal. If any questions were asked about his being there, she would just say he came by and asked her to go to Mexico. She doubted anyone would suspect any foul play when he got sick and died of food poisoning. She just hoped he got to Mexico before he started getting ill. He might even survive, but she doubted it. And she forgot to thank him for telling her where Stephen Paul Morrison lived.

Mrs. Price was waiting for her when she pulled in the driveway. She'd baked cookies and wanted to share with Rae. How could anyone refuse homemade cookies? Rae thanked her and climbed the stairs to her apartment.

She was nervous and couldn't sit still. She finally changed clothes and went for a walk. What if Tom told the pilot about going to her office, or lived until Stephen got there and told him? What if he didn't die and realized that he'd been poisoned? She really didn't think he would give a second thought about his visit to the clinic. Even if he did live, it would be hard to trace the poison to her. "Time will tell and worrying won't help, so get a grip," she told herself as she turned toward home.

Rae awoke before the alarm buzzed. She'd spent a restless night listening for the police. Instead of rolling over and going back to sleep, she got up and looked out the window. A beautiful sunrise greeted her. She had time for a short run before breakfast. Maybe a jog would take the edge off her nerves.

The air was crisp but not uncomfortable. Rae stretched, warmed up her muscles, and then jogged to the outskirts of town. It was going to be a beautiful day. Too bad she must work.

Lori was already at the clinic when Rae bounced in. Rae poured herself a cup of coffee and asked Lori, "How are you this morning?"

"I'm fine. Just having a little morning sickness."

"Does that mean what I think it does?"

"Yes, I think I'm pregnant. This is a surprise, but we're happy about the baby. Will you want to replace me?"

"No. You can work as long as you feel up to it. You're my right hand. I can't imagine not having you here."

"Thanks, Rae, for being so understanding."

"You just take care of yourself."

The morning passed with fillings, cleanings, and even an extraction. Just before noon Rae found a minute to call her realtor. The lady hadn't forgotten about Rae, she just hadn't found the right property. Rae thanked her and hung up.

A couple of days passed with no news about Snodgrass. She went to work thinking that he had survived the poison.

Twelve o'clock rolled around. Noticing the time, Rae said, "Let's go out for lunch, Lori. I'm going to make sure you eat well, but if you order pickles and ice cream, I'm leaving."

Lori laughed and said, "So far I haven't had any weird cravings."

They walked down the street to Sally's Café, hoping today's special was chicken fried steak. Lori's husband David joined them. Rae liked David and didn't mind him being around. They were eating when Richard White walked in and sat down with a group of men at the next table. Richard was the dispatcher at the police station.

Rae heard one of the men say, "You've got to be kidding. Tom Snodgrass dead? No way."

Richard said, "I'm telling you that's what came over the radio. Someone from the family is going to have to go to Mexico to claim the body."

"What happened to him?"

"They didn't say, but evidently there wasn't foul play because they are going to release the body."

"Who's going to get Tom?"

"His dad. Marlene is off on a ski trip in Colorado."

"What was he doing in Mexico?'

"Who knows?"

The café was soon buzzing with the news of Tom's death. Rae ate a hearty lunch and returned to work feeling great. She just hoped he was in horrible pain before he died.

After work, Rae cleaned her apartment. Cleaning was not her favorite task, but once she made up her mind she went to work. She was in the middle of scrubbing the kitchen floor when Mrs. Price knocked on the door. Rae hollered, "Come in."

Mrs. Price bounded in, stopping just short of the kitchen. "Have you heard the news?"

"What news?"

"Tom Snodgrass is dead."

"Yes, I heard about him at lunch."

"Probably drank himself to death or had a heart attack chasing some woman."

"Mrs. Price, you shouldn't speak ill of the dead."

"Maybe not, but he was a spoiled brat who got away with things others wouldn't have."

"Now what makes you say that?"

"His name usually came up if there was some kind of scandal. He was accused of rape in high school and was probably guilty. Ruined a young girl's life and got off scot-free. He had to get married right after graduation because the girl was pregnant. I could go on for a week."

Rae continued to scrub the floor while she talked to Mrs. Price. "Who was the girl?"

"Jane Hayes. She was beautiful and a lovely person. Her whole life was ruined. Some said she lost her mind. The family moved and put her in a private hospital."

"Was Tom the only suspect?"

"Oh, no. There were five involved, but all of them were little rich boys, so they went free."

"Don't you feel sorry for his wife and kids?"

"For the kids. They've really never had much of a life. I'll bet Marlene is married again in three months."

"I wonder what happened to him."

"No one seems to know. The old man will probably demand an autopsy."

"I would if it were my son."

"Yes, I suppose so. Well, I'll go and let you finish."

So the rape hadn't been forgotten, and it seems the citizens knew who the guilty parties were. Most people weren't sad that Snodgrass was dead. She wondered when the body would be back and where the autopsy would be performed, and if anyone noticed him going to her office.

The town was still buzzing the next day, but Rae was too busy to pay much attention. Lori wasn't upset about Tom, just sad for the kids.

She told Rae. "I went through school with Tom and even dated him. He thought he could do whatever he pleased and usually did. I was lucky I broke up with him. He wasn't above date rape or most anything else. Several of the girls he dated came into wealth all of a sudden. He and some other boys were suspects in a gang rape when we were seniors. The girl they attacked was one of the nicest people I ever knew. They destroyed her life. I've often wondered what happened to her and her twin sister."

"Mrs. Price was telling me about the rape. I couldn't believe no one was ever charged."

"That's what money will do for you."

Out of respect for her fellow Kiwanis member, Rae went to the service at the cemetery. The widow was dressed in black, complete with a veil. She was beautiful. Rae never once saw her speak or show any sign of emotion. "I wonder what she will do now," Rae thought. "Hopefully, she will find a man who will be decent to her."

She wanted to get a look at Stephen Morrison. She stayed back at the edge of the crowd so she wouldn't be noticed but could watch what was going on. Steve was a pallbearer and it didn't take Rae long to pick him out. He was still handsome even if he was a little thin on top. When he glanced her way, she turned her head.

The clinic was closed so Rae went to her apartment. She changed clothes and was considering a walk when someone knocked on the door. Mrs. Price entered all in a flurry about the funeral. She went on and on about the flowers, the beautiful music, and the wonderful service. Rae was relieved when she left.

As she munched on an apple, she glanced at the paper. She couldn't believe her eyes when she read an ad in the classifieds. This just might be her dream come true. The place was a two-bedroom log cabin on five acres. There was a pond, a stream, and a barn. Rae was so excited she could hardly punch in the phone numbers.

An elderly couple owned the place, but because of bad health felt they should move to town. The property was twelve miles southeast of Decker; five of those miles were gravel. She wasn't familiar with the area, but thought she could find it without much trouble. Grabbing her keys, she went down the stairs. There was a chill in the air. Glancing up she saw large white thunderheads in the north. They created a beautiful scene in the ice blue sky. In her excitement she dismissed the weather.

She headed south on Highway 52. 'The Lonesome No More' bar sat on the southeast corner. This was where she was to turn right onto a gravel road. The bar looked like a hole in the wall, but there were several vehicles parked in front. As she drove, she noticed the absence of houses, the neat fences, and the flat open country. This was what she was looking for.

The cabin sat on a little rise and was surrounded by maple and pecan trees. The drive from the main road was lined with a rail fence.

As she approached, she saw the couple sitting on the front porch. When she got out of the car, a small gray dog met her. She realized that the greatest danger from this animal was a good licking. The little dog raced ahead as she walked toward the porch.

The elderly gentleman said, "You're a brave woman. That dog is a natural killer. Welcome. My name is Bill Chitwood, and this is my wife Nancy. The noisy fur ball is J. B., short for James Bond."

"Hello, Mr. and Mrs. Chitwood, I'm Rae Roberts from Decker. Your place sounds like what I'm looking for."

"Can I get you a cup of tea?"

"No, thank you."

"I reckon you'd like to see the house?" stated Mr. Chitwood.

"I'd love to."

"Go in and look around."

"Aren't you going with me?"

"Why no. I see it all the time. Unless you figure on having a bunch of questions I can't answer from this chair."

Rae walked through the front door into a large living room. Facing the door was a beautiful fireplace made of native rock. To the right of the living room was a neat kitchen and dining area; to the left was a bedroom and bathroom. The upstairs loft contained another bedroom and bath, plus a snug study. A door opened from the loft onto a balcony over the back porch. This would be perfect for sunbathing or watching the sunset. From the balcony, Rae could see the pond, a small barn and a corral.

She bounced back down the stairs and out to the porch. Mr. and Mrs. Chitwood were gathering up their teacups and coming inside. "Looks like it's going to storm."

The cold north wind hit Rae and she realized Mr. Chitwood was right. It was going to storm, and soon. It was also getting dark outside. Rae asked a few questions and told the Chitwoods she would call or come back out the next day.

She was leaving when Mrs. Chitwood said, "You realize J. B. goes with the place?"

"Are you serious?"

"Oh, yes. He'd never make it in town. He's lived here all his life."

"But won't you miss him?"

"Maybe a little, but not as much as he'd miss roaming the wide open spaces."

"I've never owned a dog. I wouldn't know how to take care of him."

"Nothing to it. Just put his food out and give him a pat once in a while. J.B. pretty much takes care of himself."

By the time Rae left, the sun had set, the north wind was howling, and it was beginning to sleet.

In her excitement about the cabin, Rae hadn't thought much about the storm, but now she realized it was going to be a dilly.

Spring storms could be terrible, but they usually didn't last long. That thought comforted her a little as she pulled onto the highway. Sleet pelted the windshield and began to cover the pavement. She hadn't gone far when the car began pulling to the right. "Oh no!" She said aloud. "A flat tire and I don't have a coat!" Rae pulled onto the shoulder. The tires crunched on the ice-covered grass. When she opened the door, cold wind and stinging sleet greeted her. The right front tire was indeed flat. Back in the car she warmed her hands and thought about how she was going to change the flat without freezing to death. Thank goodness, the sleet seemed to be letting up some.

She was thinking about her situation when a pickup pulled out of the bar parking lot and headed her way. Good, maybe someone would help her. The driver passed by, stopped, and backed up. Three men got out of the truck and walked toward her car. Something about the way they approached and the silly grins on their faces made her think they weren't going to be much help. To be safe, she locked the doors and barely cracked her window.

The driver of the pickup walked up to the window and said, "Looks like you're in trouble, little lady."

"No, my friend will be here in a little while. He'll change the tire."

"Oh, and just how does your friend know where you are?"

"I told him where I was going and what time I expected to be back. He'll be along any minute."

"Come on boys, she has a boyfriend coming. He'll help her."

The three climbed back into the pickup and left, only to return in a few minutes. They blew her a kiss as they drove by and then turned into the bar parking lot.

Rae knew they would continue to check on her, and when no one showed up, they would be back. She was angry with herself for foolishly running off without a coat or her pistol. Well, she might freeze, but she was going to start working on the flat tire and hope the three jerks would drink a beer or two before they looked out again. Thank heavens it had stopped sleeting, but boy, was it cold.

She pushed on the emergency brake, took the keys, and after a struggle got the spare off its mount. God, she was cold. She rolled the spare to the front of the car, and then set the jack under the bumper. She had the jack in place and the hubcap off when she saw the trio coming. "Don't panic, she said, just get back into the car and warm up. Better take the lug wrench for a weapon, since you don't have your gun."

They pulled up behind her this time and just sat and looked at her. She ignored them. Maybe she could brain one of them with the lug wrench if they tried anything.

Evidently they didn't notice the spare or the jack because they drove by, turned around, and went back to the bar. She breathed a sigh of relief when they got out of the truck and went back into the bar. As soon as they were inside, she got out and started working on the lug nuts. As usual they were too tight, and she jumped on the lug wrench handle to break them loose. All but one was loose when she saw them coming again. She took the lug wrench, got back into the car, and started the motor. If necessary, she would drive on the flat.

The pickup pulled over in front of her car and the three helpful gentlemen got out. The driver walked up to her window and asked, "Give up on your boyfriend?"

`"No, I just thought I'd have everything ready so he won't freeze."

"Now ain't that sweet, boys. She's just gettin' things ready for him."

They all laughed and gathered at the back of the pickup. Sharing a bottle, they talked and watched her. She could tell they were discussing what they were going to do and she didn't think it was going to be good. If they intended to help, the tire would be changed by now.

When the bottle was empty, the driver threw it into the ditch and walked toward her side of the car. One of the other two picked up a tool out of the back of the truck. He walked to the passenger side of the car. As he drew back a wrench to hit the window, a truck pulling a horse trailer stopped behind Rae's car. She jumped out and ran to the truck. "I told them you'd be here. I knew you'd be worried," she babbled to a man she'd never seen before.

"I've been worried sick. Get into the truck before you freeze!" he said, sizing up the situation.

Rae climbed into the truck, taking a chance against one rather than three.

The three drunks made a hasty exit.

"Thanks," she said. "They've been harassing me for a while. I have a flat tire, but I can have it changed in no time if you'll just stay and keep watch."

"You stay in the truck and keep warm. I'll take care of the flat. I'll need that lug wrench if you can part with it."

Rae laughed and handed him the wrench.

He soon had the spare on, but it was low and shouldn't be driven on.

"Come on with me to the ranch, and I'll get a compressor and air it up. Oh, by the way, my name is Link Wood. I live a couple of miles from here."

Rae held out her hand, "Rae Roberts. I live in Decker. I hate to put you out, but I appreciate your help."

"No problem. Have you got your keys?"

"Yes."

"Okay, I'll lock your car and we'll get rolling."

Rae was surprised when he drove to an intersection, turned around, and went back in the direction of the Chitwood place. Link's ranch was only a few miles from what she hoped would be her future home.

Chapter Five

They arrived at Link's ranch in ten minutes or so. The entire place was surrounded with white board fences, and there were barns and sheds everywhere. The brick house in the middle of everything was neat, if not beautiful. Link pulled up to the house and said, "Go on in and warm up. I need to put up my horse and feed."

"If you have an extra jacket, I'd like to go with you."

"No problem. I have all sorts of gear in the tack room."

Link drove on to a big barn. "I'll unload Zipper. Then we'll go inside and get you a coat."

Rae waited until Link led the horse to the cab of the truck. Then she got out and walked with him to the barn. Link handed her the lead rope and said, "Hold him while I get you a jacket."

"Will he get wild and crazy or anything?"

"No. He's gentle as a lamb, besides being dead tired."

"What's he been doing?"

"Cutting calves at a quarter horse show."

"You'll have to explain, I don't know what you're talking about."

Link laughed and handed her a jacket. "I'll let Zipper show you if you'll come back out one of these days."

"I just might do that," Rae said as she gently rubbed the beautiful black horse.

They chatted comfortably while they dished out grain and hay to a dozen horses. When they reached the last stall, Link said, "Now, you get to meet a special lady—Maggie."

Rae stepped in the open door, and there stood the most beautiful animal she had ever seen. Maggie was a dark bay mare with a black mane and tail and four black stockings. She was small and perfect, even delicate. Maggie turned her head and looked at her with her big brown eyes. Rae said, "She is beautiful. Is she gentle?"

"She's a doll. Only problem is, I'm too heavy to ride her so she doesn't get much exercise. Pet her if you want to. She has no bad habits."

Rae forgot about drunks, flats, the cold, or the fact she was far from home with a stranger. She fell in love with Maggie at first sight. While Link finished his chores, she stayed with Maggie. When he came back, she was reluctant to leave.

"You'll have to come back and see her, maybe even ride her."

"I've never ridden in my life. Well, maybe once when I was small, and I don't think I liked it very much."

"You just need a few lessons."

"Maybe. Bye, Maggie. You're beautiful."

Link found the compressor, and after unhitching the horse trailer, drove her back to her car. He aired up the tire, and insisted on following her home.

When they arrived, Rae thanked him for his help and for sharing his horses. He told her to visit anytime. It was after he pulled away that she remembered his jacket.

"What an interesting day this has been," she voiced as she hung the blue plaid fleece lined jacket on the back of a chair.

Later, lying in the bathtub, she thought about Link. He seemed familiar, but she didn't remember ever having seen him before. He wasn't someone who stood out in a crowd, just kind of ordinary. Not especially handsome, but certainly not ugly. He was about five ten or eleven, just slightly taller than she herself, had hazel eyes, and dark hair that was showing a little gray at the temples. He had a stocky build, but didn't have an ounce of fat anywhere. His most striking feature was his beautiful white even teeth. She supposed being a dentist made her aware of a person's teeth. Well, he probably saved her from some horrible fate. He seemed like a nice guy, and he had some nice horses.

While soaking in the tub, she realized that she hadn't eaten and that she had failed to ask the Chitwoods how soon they wanted to move. Well, she could always drive back out, return Link's jacket and visit Maggie.

She ate a sandwich and went to bed thinking about log cabins, bay mares, and fuzzy dogs. Sometime in the night, a cowboy rode in on a black horse. Her dreams were interrupted by a phone call.

Lori's husband David was calling from the hospital. Lori was having pains and bleeding. He was beside himself. Rae told him she would be there as soon as possible.

When she arrived at the hospital, Lori was better. The doctor said the baby and Lori were going to be fine. David and Rae stayed with her until she went to sleep. David thanked Rae for coming and asked, "Can you work tomorrow by yourself?" Without hesitating she said, "I'll ask Mrs. Price to watch the front for me. She'll love it. You just worry about Lori. Everything will be okay."

Rae hit some slick spots driving to and from the hospital so there would probably be some cancellations today. When she turned into the driveway, Mrs. Price was picking up the morning paper. "No time like the present," Rae said as she let down the window and stopped the car.

Before she could speak Mrs. Price asked, "Is something wrong?"

"Sort of. Lori's in the hospital and I was hoping you could help out in the clinic today."

"I don't know how much help I'll be, but I'll try," Mrs. Price answered. "What time do I need to be there?"

"You can ride with me if you'd like. I'll leave in an hour."

"I'll be ready."

Mrs. Price was so excited Rae was a little concerned about how she would handle patients. Oh well, let the little lady have her day. She wouldn't be giving drugs or putting in fillings.

Mrs. Price worked like a trooper all day and the patients loved her. Rae was impressed.

When the last two patients canceled, Rae drove Mrs. Price home and went to check on Lori. She was doing fine and hoped to be back at work in two or three days. Rae talked to Lori about hiring Mrs. Price full time. Lori agreed that a receptionist was a good idea.

Maybe if I put Mrs. Price to work full time, she won't be so upset when I move, Rae thought as she left the hospital parking lot and drove to the gas station to pick up the tire she had left that morning.

The storm was over, but there was still a chill in the air and a few patches of ice here and there. The highways were clear so Rae saw no harm in driving back to visit the Chitwoods. She changed into jeans and a warm sweater. After finding a carrot for Maggie, she puzzled over what to take J. B. and decided on a couple of cookies. She had no intentions of a repeat of last night, so she picked up her pistol and Link's jacket as she walked out the door.

J. B. was Johnny-on-the-spot when she pulled in the driveway. He barked and ran around in circles. Rae laughed and gave him the cookies. Mrs. Chitwood met her at the door and asked her in. The fireplace was beautiful and gave welcomed warmth. Rae was soon seated on the hearth with a mug of hot spiced tea. She loved this place already and she didn't even know if she would be able to buy it. After chatting awhile, she asked the Chitwoods questions about water, wiring, the septic tank, and all other possible problem areas. Satisfied with their answers, she asked the selling price. Sixty-five thousand was a drop in the bucket, and Rae agreed without a second thought. On a whim she walked to the barn with J. B. keeping her company. It wasn't very big, but then why would she need a barn at all? Barns made her think of Maggie so she returned to the house and said good-bye to the Chitwoods.

When she started down the driveway at Link's she saw several horses out in a small pasture. She looked for Maggie, and sure enough, the little mare was one of them. Rae stopped, got out with a carrot in hand and walked to the fence. She called Maggie. The little mare came to greet her with all of her friends tagging along. She hadn't planned on feeding a herd of horses. She wasn't sure Maggie got a bite of the carrot, especially since she dropped it on the ground. After the carrot was gone, so were the horses, except Maggie.

The rattle of a feed bucket drew Maggie's attention. A sharp whistle put her on the run. Rae got into her car and drove to the barn. Link was in the granary, filling buckets. "Need some help?" she asked.

"Sure. How are you?"

"I'm fine. Thought I'd better return your jacket."

"I think you came back to see Maggie. Want to feed her?"

"You bet. What do I need to do?"

Link showed her how to mix sweet feed, minerals, and oats. Together they walked down the hall to Maggie's stall. Maggie was waiting at the back door. Link entered the stall and opened the outside door for her. Rae noticed the stall was clean and had fresh straw on the floor and fresh water in the bucket. Link poured the feed into a trough and then handed Rae a brush.

While Maggie ate, Rae brushed her. At first she just brushed her neck and one side because she was afraid to walk behind her. Then she saw mud on her belly so she cautiously brushed it away. Maggie kept right on eating. Rae took a deep breath and walked way around Maggie's rear. Link came along about then and said, "When you walk behind her, stay in close and lay a hand on her rump. Here, I'll show you."

Rae practiced a couple of times, and Maggie kept on eating. By the time Link came back, Maggie had been brushed all over, even her legs.

"The brush doesn't work too well on her mane and tail, but I tried."

"Follow me, I have just what you need."

Link went to the tack room and came back with a large wide-toothed comb. "Here you go."

"Does she like this?"

"She loves attention."

Rae combed Maggie's mane and tail, then stepped back and admired her work. Maggie was busy eating hay.

She took the brush and comb back to the tack room and went to find Link. He was brushing Zipper.

"How do you get him so shiny?"

"Brushing, brushing, and more brushing. Of course a good diet, clean stall, and fresh water help."

Link picked up a front foot and cleaned out the dirt.

"Should I have cleaned Maggie's feet?'

Link laughed, "Hooves. Yes, you should clean your horse's hooves every day."

"Will you show me how the next time I come out?"

"Sure. Want a bite to eat? I'm about to starve."

"Thanks, but I'd better get back to town. I want to check on my assistant. She's in the hospital."

"Sorry to hear that. What does she assist you with?'

Rae laughed. "I'm a dentist."

"Holy cow, dentists scare me to death!"

"Well, I'm harmless unless you're in my chair."

Link laughed and said, "I'll remember that. Be careful going back, and come out anytime you want."

"Thanks. I don't want to be a pest, but I really like Maggie."

The Chitwoods found a house after a week of hard searching, but it was two more weeks before all the paper work was completed. Finally, the day came when the cabin was empty and Rae could move in. Everyone was happy except Mrs. Price. She acted upset, but Rae knew she was really glad for her.

During the weeks she was preparing to move, Rae visited Maggie often. She allowed Rae to clean her hooves, brush her, and trim her ears and bridle path without blinking an eye. Link was a patient instructor and seemed unaffected by Rae's visits. He was friendly and polite, but never pushy.

Rae readily agreed when he offered to go furniture shopping with her. They left early on a Saturday morning for Dallas, pulling a freshly washed four-horse trailer, to haul the furniture home in. Link was a perfect gentleman and fun to be with. He never once acted like he was interested in her except as a friend. She was beginning to trust him, and that frightened her.

Sunday, David and Link unloaded the furniture while Rae, Lori, and Jake, Lori's son, did the arranging. By Sunday evening the cabin was looking like a home. Rae was happier than she had been in years.

Early June brought long hot days. Rae worked in the yard or spent time with Maggie almost every evening. She went to see the little mare even when Link was gone to a horse show.

Then one day she announced she wanted to try riding. Link showed her how to saddle Maggie and put on the hackamore. He saddled Zipper, and they led the horses to the arena. Rae had fun once she relaxed. Maggie was steady as a rock and seemed to enjoy the outing almost as much as Rae did.

Although she was sore, Rae was eager to get off work and ride again. She was going over the patient list for the next day when she came to the name, Dale Smith. “Well, well,” she said to herself, “At last I’m going to meet Mr. Smith. I wonder what he needs.”

She was preoccupied with thoughts of Dale Smith when she stopped by to groom Maggie. “I’ll do a better job tomorrow,” Rae told her as she latched the stall door.

Link gave her a puzzled look and asked, “Did you have a bad day?”

“No. Just a long day. I seem more tired than usual.”

“Zipper and I have a cutting show coming up Saturday. Would you like to go?”

“I’ll let you know later in the week.”

Link didn’t push the issue.

At home she was short with J. B. He tucked his tail and went to the barn. She unlocked the front door and dropped her purse and keys in a chair. Dale Smith was all she could think of. The scum was going to be in her clinic tomorrow. What should she do? She couldn’t just walk in and shoot him, which was what she would like to do.

Nervous and in an inner rage, she went for a walk along the creek. J. B. joined her, and she petted and talked to him. “You aren’t guilty of any crime, are you, little guy? I’m sorry I was short with you earlier.”

J. B. was happy again and bounded ahead to scare away any dangerous animals. Rae had to laugh when the brave dog ran from a bullfrog. The walk helped, but she was still agitated when she got back to the cabin.

She couldn't possibly decide what to do with Mr. Smith until after she saw him. It might even be necessary for him to make a second visit.

Sleep was almost impossible that night, and she felt sluggish as she dressed for work. Smith's appointment wasn't until afternoon. This was going to be a long morning.

Mrs. Price was her usual cheerful self when she entered the clinic. She met Rae with a cup of coffee and a hearty, "Good morning, how are you?"

Rae assured her she was fine, took the coffee and went to the back to find Lori. She found her taking equipment out of the sterilizer. "Hi, how are you feeling?" Rae asked.

"Bigger than a homecoming float but not nearly as pretty."

Rae laughed and glanced at the name of the first patient. Rosemary Howard was coming in with a toothache. "Well, I guess it's time to get rolling," she said as she traded her coffee cup for safety glasses and latex gloves. The glasses bothered her but, as well as being a safety measure, they disguised her somewhat.

The morning passed without any surprises. The ladies called in an order for lunch rather than going out in the heat. At ten after one, Mrs. Price brought Dale Smith back.

"Good afternoon, Mr. Smith. What can I do for you?"

"I have a terrible toothache, and my regular dentist is on vacation. My physician called in a prescription for an antibiotic, but he can't give me anything that will stop the pain because I have a heart condition."

"Let's have a look. Which tooth is it?"

"Lower right side, in the back."

She examined the tooth and then took x-rays. Looking at the film she said, "This tooth will have to be pulled. You've lost half of it so a filling would never stay. A root canal and cap is an option but would take too long and require more sedative than an extraction."

"Can you pull the tooth without killing me?"

"I won't touch it unless you agree to go to the hospital where you can be monitored. I'd also like for your physician to assist."

"Sounds sane to me. My doctor's name is Tom Mackey. Can you call him or do I need to?"

"I'll talk with Dr. Mackey and then give you a call at home. In the meantime, stay on your antibiotic. So we're talking about the first of next week. Until then, I'll pack the tooth with a medicated filling. That should stop the pain until we can get it pulled. Is that agreeable with you?"

"Yes. Anything to get rid of the pain."

"You shouldn't have any pain once it's filled. You know, of course, there is always a risk with a heart condition. We'll take every precaution, but that's all I can tell you."

"Will you knock me out for surgery?"

"I'll discuss that with Dr. Mackey, but the usual procedure is to give you enough anesthetic to put you in a dreamlike state. You won't actually be asleep."

"Let's go for it. I'll take a risk with a beautiful woman any day."

"Okay. I'm going to give you a little gas and fill your tooth with medication. This is only a temporary job, so be careful and don't chew on it."

In less than fifteen minutes the tooth was filled and Mr. Smith was ready to leave.

"Set it up, Doc, and give me a call, or better yet, have dinner with me and give me the details."

"I'll call you and let you know when to check into the hospital. If you have any problems with the tooth, come to the clinic and we'll work you in."

Rae asked Mrs. Price to call Dr. Mackey. He called back just before closing time and agreed to assist with the extraction. They set it up for Tuesday morning of the following week. This would give them both time to clear their regular schedules. Rae expressed her concern about Dale Smith's heart condition. Dr. Mackey was also concerned but knew the procedure was necessary. He was going to arrange for an anesthesiologist.

By the time she got home, Rae was making plans for Mr. Smith. She was in a good mood so she changed clothes and went to see Maggie.

The nature of animals amazed her. No matter what her mood or behavior, Maggie and J. B. still loved her. They greeted her with warmth and happiness every day.

True to her nature, Maggie greeted Rae with a nicker and ran to get her carrot. Rae petted and talked with her before leading her to her stall. She was brushing Maggie when Link walked up leading Zipper.

"Hi, how are you?" he asked.

"I'm fine. How are you?"

"Doing good. I'm going to check the heifers in the north pasture."

"May I tag along?"

"Sure, but it's a pretty long trip. We won't be back until dark."

"That's okay. Will you watch me while I saddle Maggie and make sure I do everything right?"

"Want me to saddle her for you?"

"No, I need to practice."

Link watched while Rae put on the blankets and then tossed the saddle up on the little mare.

"Looks like a professional job to me. Let's go for a ride."

They rode across the pasture, along the creek, and over a couple of hills to get to the north pasture. She felt no fear, only freedom, as they trotted along side by side, not talking, just riding. Reaching their destination, Link counted the heifers and looked them over to see if they were near calving time. "I need to move them next week," Link said as he opened the gate for Rae to ride through.

"Can I help?"

"Sure, an extra hand is always welcome. What day is good for you?"

"I think Tuesday will be a good day."

"Tuesday it is. Have you decided about the horse show Saturday?"

She hadn't thought about it but suddenly decided to go. "Yes, I'd love to go. What do I wear?"

"Jeans and boots will be fine. I'll pick you up about eight Saturday morning."

"Great, I'll be ready, except I don't have any cowboy boots."

"Loafers will do."

It rained all day Thursday and most of Friday so Rae didn't ride Maggie. She did go by and groom her both days.

Rae was up and dressed by seven o'clock Saturday morning. She had hardly thought about Dale Smith. He would sometimes just pop into her head at unusual times like when she was brushing her teeth, or now as she sat waiting for Link. Just a few more days and he would not be thought of anymore. A honking horn jerked her into action. She quickly grabbed her purse and was out the door. J. B. got a pat and orders to guard the place as she climbed into the pickup.

"Good morning. You look nice." Link said.

"Thank you. How are you this morning?"

"Nervous, but otherwise raring to go."

"How's Zipper?'

"He's fine. He ate a good breakfast and is probably taking a nap by now."

They had been driving about thirty minutes when Link spotted a donut shop. "Want a donut and cup of coffee?"

"Sounds great, but I'd prefer a chocolate long john please."

"Do you want to go in or eat on the road?"

"On the road's fine."

Over pastries and coffee, they chatted during the last miles of the trip. When they pulled into the fairgrounds, Link asked, "Do I have crumbs all over my face?"

Before she realized what she was doing, Rae wiped his mouth with a napkin. Link laughed and said, "I must have been a mess."

There were trailers everywhere. Rae was excited to see so many beautiful horses. She was firing questions right and left. Link answered as he unloaded Zipper and tied him to the trailer.

"Come with me, and I'll get you seated."

"Wait. Aren't you afraid someone will steal Zipper?"

"No. He'll be fine."

"Okay. Do I cheer, or is this a quiet affair?"

"You'll catch on after the first contestant. Zipper and I are number ten."

They walked up the alley to the arena and Link spoke to almost everyone they met.

"Do you know all of these people?"

"Most of them. We've been competing against each other for years."

Once Rae was seated, Link left to exercise Zipper. He looked very handsome in his white shirt, starched Wranglers, chaps, black boots, and straw hat. She had never seen him wear spurs, but later found they were just for appearance.

She didn't move throughout the cutting contest. Watching the way the rider and animal worked together was awesome. When the first woman competed, Rae made up her mind she would ride a cutting horse someday. Everything and everyone was forgotten as she enjoyed this new world.

Link and Zipper were a pleasure to watch. Link rode with grace and confidence, never moving the reins, just cueing Zipper with his legs. The beautiful horse worked with his ears back and his eyes focused on the calf he was to keep away from the herd.

Rae cheered and clapped with the rest of the audience when the winners were announced. Link and Zipper won second and earned enough points to enter the National Quarter Horse Show that would be held in Oklahoma City in the fall.

Link chuckled when Rae said she wanted to ride a cutting horse. He said she could, just as soon as she rode Maggie a little faster than a trot. They talked horses an competition over dinner. The day was over much too soo

Sunday morning Rae cleaned house and did instead of going to see Maggie.

When she stopped to eat lunch, she found the cupboards were bare. Grumbling to herself, she made a list and drove to the grocery store.

Rae planned to go by the hospital Monday after work but decided since she was in town, she would go now to look over the operating room.

There weren't any doctors at the hospital when Rae arrived, but the head nurse was glad to show her around. She checked the equipment and made a list of things she would need to bring from her clinic. From surgery, they went to the ICU, and then to a hospital room. Everything looked okay so she thanked the nurse and left to go to the store.

Back home, Rae put away the groceries and fixed a light lunch. When she finished, she went to see Maggie.

Link was gone so she didn't ride. She wasn't comfortable enough to ride alone and besides, it was too hot. It would be wonderful to be confident enough to saddle up and ride across the countryside. Maybe she would get there someday. She was content to just be with Maggie today. Her grooming was beginning to show. Maggie's coat was sleek and beautiful, her mane and tail neat and without tangles. Rae laughed and said, "You look like a model, not a hair out of place."

Link drove in just as she was leaving, and Rae was surprised to see a woman with him. He waved and she waved back.

She drove home thinking about Link and how different he was from most men she knew. He had never expressed any interest in her other than friendship, yet she could feel an underlying current. She didn't feel threatened and Link was easy to like. She was surprised that she was a little jealous of the blonde with him.

She couldn't shake the feeling she had met him before. Perhaps she should get brave and ask him about his past, but then he would question her. Best leave well enough alone.

J. B. greeted her with open paws and eagerly joined er when she said, "Let's go for a walk." The little dog was in constant motion. Rae laughed at him and even welcomed a warm lick when she sat down to watch the sunset. "Thanks boy, that's just what I needed," she said as she wiped her cheek.

The sky was brilliant with reds and golds as the sun sank to the edge of the horizon. Dusk slowly surrounded the peaceful countryside. The stillness soothed her troubled soul. She picked up a stick and wrote "Jane" in the damp earth at the edge of the pond. As a tear slowly slid down her cheek, she rubbed out the name with her shoe and then walked to the house.

Later that evening she sat on the porch and listened to the night sounds. Frogs called to each other in the pond and insects buzzed from every direction. Whippoorwills sang their lonely song from the distant woods. Occasionally a coyote howled. It was late and she should get some sleep, but she didn't want to move. Finally she made herself go inside.

Sleep eluded her, so she picked up a book, but couldn't concentrate. Restless and not the least bit sleepy, Rae walked onto the balcony.

It was a little cooler now but still uncomfortably warm. Lightning bugs were everywhere. She smiled as she remembered childhood days when she and Jane caught the little bugs and put them into a fruit jar. It was great fun to catch them and let them go at evening's end. Reluctantly she went back into the house. It was going to be one of those nights. Rather than fight it, she took a sleeping pill and went to bed.

Monday morning was hot and hectic. Patients were out of sorts, and Rae felt about the same. Somehow she made it through the day without losing her temper. She only wanted to choke Mrs. Price a couple of times. The little lady remained cheerful despite the heat and ill nature of others. Lori, cleaning up at the end of the day, was obviously exhausted. Rae, taking a deep breath, asked, "Lori, what do you think about finding someone to fill in for you until the baby's born?"

"Probably would be a good idea, especially if you want me to help train her."

"Do you know of anyone?"

"Not right off hand, but Mrs. Price might know someone that needs a job."

Mrs. Price entered the room about that time and Rae said, "Lori needs to stay home and rest more. Do you know of a possible replacement for her?"

"I'll do some asking around," Mrs. Price replied. "I bet I can find someone."

Rae reminded them she would be at the hospital the next morning. They didn't need to come in until after lunch. Lori helped Rae gather up the tools she would need for the extraction and wished her good luck.

Mrs. Price asked, "Do you need me to go with you in the morning?"

Rae replied, "Thanks, but that won't be necessary."

She didn't stop to see Maggie. Her entire focus was on Dale Smith. With luck, he would join his friend in hell.

Chapter Six

Rae couldn't contain herself once she got home. She paced the floor until she was at the point of exploding. A drive might help. Before she realized it, she had driven thirty miles. By the time she drove back home, her plan was perfected.

The hospital was a beehive of activity Tuesday morning. Rae went to surgery at eight a.m. to scrub in. Dr. Mackey greeted her as she walked into the scrub room. He was much younger than Rae expected. They discussed Dale Smith as they scrubbed, agreeing that the procedure was dangerous but no more so than a chronic infection.

At nine a.m. they met with Dale and the anesthesiologist. When everyone was ready, an injection instantly put Smith into a dreamland state. Rae pulled the tooth with ease. She then packed the cavity with gauze.

Dale asked, "When are you going to pull it?"

Dr. Mackey replied, "It's gone. Dr. Roberts is very efficient."

Certain that he was stable, they moved him to a private room and remained with him for about thirty minutes. After a short discussion, they agreed the IV should be left in to keep his fluid levels up and to be available if he should need medication.

Dale complained of pain and a horrible taste in his mouth. Dr. Mackey ordered something for his pain and Rae told him she would wash his mouth out as soon as the bleeding stopped. She also told him that he needed to keep an icepack on his jaw.

He howled like a wounded animal when the nurse handed him the icepack. Rae wanted to slap him, but instead she assured him it would only be for a little while. Once he settled down, Rae and Dr. Mackey walked out into the corridor.

"I think he'll be fine, but I'll hang around for a little while and see if the bleeding stops," Rae said.

"He should be okay. I'll be in the hospital checking on my other patients. You go on and do what you need to. I'll check on him in a few minutes."

Everything was going as planned. Rae drove to the clinic to return her equipment. Mrs. Price was busily cleaning and answering the phone.

"What are you doing?" Rae asked.

"I thought this would be a good time for cleaning. Besides I was bored at home."

Rae laughed and said, "Well, I'm sure the cleaning is needed. I'll help in just a minute."

"Oh, no, you won't. You go eat breakfast and relax while you have the chance. How did the extraction go?"

"Without a hitch. I'm going back to check on him after I go home and change clothes."

"I think I found a girl to fill in for Lori."

"Who?"

"Margie Tucker."

"Do I know her?"

"She sang at the Christmas program, remember?"

"Yes. She's a lovely girl. How old is she?"

"This is her first year out of high school so I assume she's eighteen."

"Good, hopefully she can work full time. When's she coming by?"

"I told her to come by tomorrow about five fifteen. Is that okay?"

"Sure. I'll be happy to visit with her. I'd better run so I can get back to the hospital. See you later, and don't work too hard."

Rae drove home and fixed a bowl of cereal. As she ate, she thought about Margie Tucker. It would be strange to be near a family member, but she liked what she knew of the girl so she would give her a try. Before leaving, she removed the syringe that was taped to the calf of her left leg. She carefully placed it on the vanity. After she changed clothes, she slipped the syringe containing five cc of undiluted potassium into her smock pocket.

She heard Dale Smith long before she neared his room. He was complaining about the icepack and how much pain he was in. Nurses scurried in and out like ants. Rae couldn't believe he was carrying on so.

"What's the problem?" she asked.

"I'm in terrible pain. This icepack makes my jaw hurt, and when do I get rid of the I.V.?"

"Soon, if you behave. I need to check and see if the bleeding's stopped."

"Can you take the gauze out? It makes me have an awful taste in my mouth."

"The gauze stays for a few hours unless you would rather bleed to death or have a dry socket. Now open up so I can see what's happening."

Rae examined him, turned to the only remaining nurse and said, "I need to change the gauze so I might as well rinse his mouth while I'm at it. Would you get me a saline-filled syringe and some gauze please?"

While the nurse was gone, Rae removed the gauze and threw it away. When the nurse returned, Rae had Dale cover his eyes with a towel so there was no danger of getting saline in them. She rinsed his mouth, and then he spat into the emesis basin.

"I think I'm going to need another saline syringe please."

When the nurse left, Rae quickly removed the syringe from her pocket and injected the potassium into the I.V. She then placed the syringe in her pants pocket. All this time, the towel remained over Dale's eyes and Rae assured him he would be fine.

"I don't think I'll need that after all," Rae said as she packed fresh gauze into the cavity. "Bite down and keep pressure on that so it won't start bleeding again. I'll be back to check on you this afternoon."

Just as she reached the front desk, a "Code Blue" and Smith's room number were announced over the intercom. Rae raced back to the room.

Dr. Mackey and a nurse were working on Dale. Nothing seemed to be helping.

"What happened? He was fine a minute ago."

The nurse answered, "He threw the icepack at me and tried to spit out the gauze. He started ranting and raving. Then wham! He had a heart attack. I'm sorry, I couldn't do anything for him."

"It wasn't your fault. He refused to help himself." Rae turned to the doctor. "I'm sorry, Dr. Mackey. I wouldn't have left him if I'd thought he was going to do something like this."

"It certainly isn't your fault. You did an excellent job. If he'd done what he was told, this wouldn't have happened."

"Do you want me to call his family?"

"No. I'll take care of it. I know them well. They were advised this was a risky procedure."

Rae walked into the clinic reminding herself to act upset. There was no one there so she rinsed the syringe with water, filled it with Novocain, and emptied it. Just as she threw it into the disposal the front door opened. Mrs. Price and Lori were coming back from lunch. Mrs. Price rushed to Rae and wrapped her in a hug. "I'm so sorry about Dale Smith."

Lori, in turn, expressed her concern and sympathy. Rae thanked them and explained that he wasn't a model patient.

Mrs. Price said, "I'm not surprised."

Lori asked, "Do you need to take the afternoon off."

Rae shook her head and said, "We may not have any patients."

They did have two cancellations that afternoon so Rae left early. She was glad because she was supposed to help Link move the heifers, but gosh, it was hot. Maybe Link had changed his mind, which certainly wouldn't make her mad.

She was surprised when she entered the barn and found Link saddling a big buckskin gelding. "Hi. Where's Zipper?"

"He's taking the day off. How are you?"

"Okay, I guess. I lost a patient today."

"What happened?"

"He had heart trouble, and even though the extraction went fine, he had a heart attack later."

"Old guy?"

"No, he was about your age."

"That's too bad. If you'd rather not go with me, I'll understand."

"No, I want to go. It'll help get my mind off Dale Smith."

Link flinched when she said Dale Smith, so she asked, "Did you know him?"

"No, I don't think so," he answered as he finished tightening the cinch.

"You're ready to go. I'd better get Maggie saddled."

"She's saddled."

They left the barn and headed north. It was so hot that it seemed to take all of Maggie's energy just to walk. There wasn't a leaf blowing, and heat waves shimmered across the dry brittle grass. Rae was glad she was wearing a hat and was thankful for the canteen on her saddle horn. Trying to get her mind off her misery, she asked, "What's your horse's name?"

"Buck. He's just green broke so don't be surprised if he does something crazy."

"Crazy like what?"

"He sometimes sees boogers that aren't there, or hears a monster and jumps sideways. He even decides to buck once in a while."

"What should I do if he acts up?"

"Hope that I can stay aboard."

"Why did you ride him?"

"He has to learn how to behave. Riding him is the only way to teach him."

They rode on, Rae watching Buck every step of the way. Even though she was watching, she couldn't believe how quickly he snorted and jumped sideways. Link just laughed and said, "You'll have to do better than that to unload me."

He snorted and shied a couple of times before they reached the pasture. Link acted like it was nothing unusual, but Rae was a nervous wreck. When they reached the gate, Link dismounted and swung it open. He was barely back in the saddle when Buck started pitching. Rae was horrified but Link rode like a pro and only suffered losing his hat.

Link finally got Buck under control and started to dismount to get his hat. Rae rode up, "You stay on that crazy horse. I'll get your hat."

Link laughed. "It's just a game. He won't buck any more. I'll get my hat, but thanks anyway."

Sure enough, he dismounted, picked up his hat, and mounted back up. Buck acted like nothing had happened as they continued on.

They found some of the heifers standing under a large hackberry tree. The rest were cooling off in the pond. "I'll drive the girls out of the pond," said Link. "You start these toward the gate. Now don't get in a hurry. We don't want to get them hot."

Getting the heifers to leave the shade was difficult. They were hot and heavy with calves so movement was not what they had in mind. Finally, Rae got them started toward the gate. She turned in the saddle to see what Link was doing. He was in the pond flank deep swinging his rope. Slowly the heifers bunched together and started toward home. There was no trouble until they started across the creek. The girls wanted to stand in the shade in the cool water. Once again they had to harass and push to get them moving. By the time they arrived at the pasture near the barn, both horses and riders were wet with sweat. Tired and hot, the heifers waddled to the nearest shade.

Maggie was relieved to get the saddle and blanket off. Rae rubbed her down with a towel and then rinsed her off. Maggie loved the water. She even liked to drink from the hose. Rae wiped her down and took her to her stall. She was shocked when Maggie lay down and started rolling and said to her, "Maggie, I just bathed you. Now you look like a pig."

Link laughed and said, "She loves to roll in the dirt."

Rae fed and brushed her while she ate. “I’ll bathe you again tomorrow, piglet.”

Link was busy feeding the horses so she started putting out flakes of hay and fresh water.

“You don’t have to do that. I’ll get it in a minute.”

“I don’t mind. When will the heifers start calving?”

“According to my records the first baby should be here next Thursday. But with heifers you can never be sure. They have to be watched closely in case they have trouble.”

“What kind of trouble?”

“Sometimes one can’t have the calf without help, so I hook a chain on the baby’s feet and pull him out. If the calf is turned wrong I have to turn it around, or sometimes the head is turned sideways and has to be straightened. There’s usually one or two that don’t want their calf so they won’t let it suck unless you tie them up. I could go on for a spell but those are the most common problems.”

“Can I help?”

“Sure. Do you want me to call you at two or three in the morning?”

“If you need help, I’ll be glad to come at two or three in the morning.”

After the horses were cared for, Rae walked to her car. Lord, she was hot and dirty. She could hardly wait to get home and into the shower.

When she walked through the door, the phone was ringing. She answered and was greeted with, “This is Dean Smith, Dale’s father. I’ll be in your office at nine in the morning.”

Rae said, “Make it eight-thirty, Mr. Smith. My first appointment is at nine.”

“When I get through with you, you won’t have any appointments.”

“I’ll see you at eight-thirty.”

Humming to herself, she headed to the shower.

Rae arrived at the clinic at eight-thirty and was met by an angry Dean Smith. She greeted him cordially and invited him into her office. While he ranted about her carelessness and called her unkind names, she calmly made a pot of coffee. When he finished by threatening her with a malpractice suit, she handed him a cup of coffee and sat down at her desk.

After taking a sip of coffee, she said, "Sue, if you want. I probably would if I were you. However, Dale knew the risks involved and he readily agreed to the procedure. Had he not had the tooth pulled, he could have died from the infection. We tried to get him to calm down and give himself time to heal, but he wouldn't listen. Dr. Mackey was right beside me and observed everything I said and did."

"He wasn't beside you when you were in Dale's room. What did you do then, and why was he so upset?"

"I removed the gauze packing and checked to see if the bleeding had stopped. He complained about the taste in his mouth, so I rinsed his mouth with saline solution and replaced the gauze. Evidently, as soon as I left the room, he removed the packing even though the nurse told him not to. He went into a rage that resulted in the heart attack. I am sorry, Mr. Smith, but your son's death was not my fault. I felt that I should talk with the family, but Dr. Mackey said he would since he knew you personally. Now, if you'll excuse me, I have patients waiting."

"You'll be hearing from my attorney," he said and spun on his heel.

"That's fine if that's what you feel you need to do. But let me ask you a question."

He hesitated and asked, "What is it?"

"If you were so concerned, why weren't you with him?"

He stormed out the door without answering.

Mrs. Price was coming in as he went out. "What did he want?"

"To sue me for malpractice."

"He's a windbag. Don't worry about it."

"I'm not worried. Want a cup of coffee?"

"No, thanks. Here comes our first patient and Lori. Bless her heart. She's getting as big as a barrel."

The day passed with business as usual, and there were no calls concerning Dale Smith. There were a few looks and whispers at lunch, which Rae ignored. Mrs. Price was ready to do battle, but Rae and Lori kept her in check.

Rae had forgotten about the interview with Margie, so she was quite unprepared when Margie and her mother walked into the office. She saw Aunt Emily's hand go to her mouth but didn't acknowledge she had seen the gesture. Mrs. Price introduced them to Rae. Rae asked her to have Lori come in so they could all visit.

Mrs. Tucker suddenly blurted out, "You seem familiar. Are you from around here?"

"No, I'm from Alabama originally, but I went to school in Florida."

"You remind me of my nieces, but I don't know why. They were blond with green eyes. They also had a mole on their lip, which you don't have."

"All of your nieces have a mole on their lip?"

"No, only Jane and Debra. They were identical twins."

Rae noticed the past tense but let it slide. "I'd love to be blond but I haven't the nerve to try. Where do your nieces live?"

"They lived here as youngsters, but after Jane's attack, they moved away."

"Oh yes, Mrs. Price told me about a young girl being attacked. That was your niece?"

"Yes, she suffered brain damage and had to be institutionalized. Then she disappeared from the hospital in Florida and hasn't been found. Debra was so depressed by Jane's disappearance, she committed suicide. I'm sorry, Dr. Roberts. I didn't mean to rattle on so. You just remind me of them."

"That's okay, Mrs. Tucker. Their poor parents. What's happened to them?"

"That's another shock. They divorced. My brother worked like a dog and tried to raise his daughters in a Christian home. Now, he's all alone, and his ex-wife is dating a police captain."

Rae almost gasped out loud. Her mother was dating Captain Stone? It was hard to imagine her leaving Dad. He usually managed to bully her into submission.

"We never know what people will do," Rae said.

"We certainly don't," Emily agreed.

Lori came in so they began interviewing Margie. After some discussion, Rae looked at Lori. Lori nodded in answer to her silent question.

Rae said to Margie, "You're hired."

Margie was so excited she wanted to start right then.

"Tomorrow morning will be soon enough," Rae said. "Be sure and wear comfortable shoes."

Mrs. Tucker remarked, "She isn't allowed to wear pants. Is that a problem?"

"No, it isn't a problem."

Lori and Mrs. Price were pleased. Lori said, "She needs to get out and about a little. Her life's too controlled."

"She's going to be easy to spoil," Rae said.

Mrs. Price spoke up, "You two are forgetting her mother will make her quit if she doesn't do what she's supposed to. Be careful you don't get her in trouble at home."

"Okay, we'll be careful."

The phone rang just as they were leaving. Mrs. Price answered and handed the receiver to Rae. It was Dean Smith's attorney. She talked with him for a minute and hung up.

Mrs. Price asked what was going on. Rae told her that Mr. Blackburn wanted to talk to her.

"Are you worried?"

"Not in the least. See you in the morning."

Rae thought about her mother on the drive home. All those years she had suffered and watched her daughters suffer because of her dad and his so-called religion. She wondered what Aunt Emily would think if she knew what he did on his truck driving trips. She hired a guy to follow him when she lived in Florida. Her good father had girlfriends in several places along his route. She was glad her mother left him.

J. B. greeted Rae when she got home but quickly returned to his wallow in the flowerbed. She scolded him for messing up her flowers but didn't make him move. The heat was awful. She couldn't blame the little dog for hunting a cool spot.

She toyed with the thought of going to see Maggie but decided it was too hot. After pacing around the house for thirty minutes, she knew she needed the friendship of the little mare. She changed her clothes and drove to Link's ranch.

Everything seemed in slow motion. All the heifers were standing or lying under shade trees or in the shade of a building. The horses stood with heads drooped, seemingly asleep. The only movement was a swishing tail or a stamping hoof to get rid of flies.

Maggie perked up a little when she saw her but didn't race to the barn as usual. Rae gave her a carrot and petted her, and then said, "Go back to the shade."

Link was in the barn cleaning stalls.

"Need some help?" Rae asked.

"I'm about finished, but thanks for the offer. Want to go out for dinner after I get cleaned up?"

"No thanks, but I'll take a rain check if that's okay."

"Sure."

Back home, she sipped iced tea and thought about the meeting tomorrow with Dean Smith's attorney. She couldn't afford to be anything but cooperative. An autopsy might get her into trouble, but only if the pathologist was on his toes. Potassium was hard to detect. Even if he suspected something it would be hard to prove since there were so many people around. She would play it cool and see what happened. Dr. Mackey and the nurses seemed to be on her side. That was a big help.

Sleep wouldn't come that night. She tossed and turned for hours. Finally, she reached for the magic bottle. The sleeping pill worked but she felt drugged the next morning. She hated feeling sluggish and slow, but couldn't work without enough rest.

The clinic was buzzing when she arrived. Mrs. Price, Margie, and Lori were getting ready for a busy day. Rae smiled as she watched Lori working with Margie. She would have her trained in a week, if not sooner.

They were busy all morning and Rae forgot that Mr. Blackburn was coming by at eleven. Mrs. Price took the attorney to Rae's office and then came to get her. She entered the office still wearing protective glasses and latex gloves. After introductions she said, "Get to the point. I have people waiting."

"Well, Doctor, my client feels that his son didn't receive proper treatment."

"Dale Smith had the very best treatment. He knew the risk and chose to take it. Dr. Mackey and I both talked with him. I did everything by the book. Unless you can prove otherwise, I suggest you leave this alone. Something that bothers me is the fact that not one member of his family was there with him. How concerned were they?"

"You have a point, Doctor. However, charges will be filed if Mr. Smith insists. He has mentioned an autopsy."

"Do whatever you think necessary, Mr. Blackburn, but I feel it would be a waste of time and money. Dale Smith, in a sense, committed suicide by losing self-control. Now, if you'll excuse me, I have work to do."

"Thank you for your time, Doctor. I may need to contact you again."

"I understand. Good-bye, Mr. Blackburn. Have a good day."

Rae returned to work feeling better. She would even close the office and attend the funeral. Two down, three to go. She still had a lot of work to do.

Margie brought her lunch, but the others convinced her to join them, their treat. The girl reminded Rae so much of Jane that her heart hurt. Rae wanted to take care of her and protect her, but she must be careful not to get too attached.

The afternoon zipped by. Mrs. Price offered Margie a ride home, but she declined, saying her mother was picking her up. She left with a happy, "See you tomorrow."

Lori smiled and said, "Sweet youth. She's not even tired, and I'm exhausted."

"You go home and get your feet up. Is there anything you need?"

"No, when I get home David will take care of everything. He's really wonderful."

Rae, on her way home, worried about Lori. She wanted to get Margie trained so Lori could stay home. Maybe she could train Margie herself, but she had a tendency to be a little harsh, which would probably demolish Margie. She'd keep a close eye on Lori and, if necessary, insist she stay home.

She hadn't been home fifteen minutes when the phone rang. She was surprised to hear Link's voice. "Hi, how are you?"

"I'm fine. How about you?"

"Actually, I'm in need of a favor."

"What can I do for you?"

"Well, since I'm stuck in a garage outside Dallas and my sometimes help is nowhere to be found, I was wondering if you might feed the horses and check the heifers for me,"

"I'll be happy to. Do you have any special instructions?"

"Nope. You know the routine."

"Do you need me to come and pick you up when I finish feeding?"

"No, I should be out of here in a few hours. Thanks. I'll see you later."

Rae changed clothes and headed for the ranch. After feeding the horses and giving them fresh water, she brushed Maggie and checked her hooves. Then she walked out to the nursery, as Link called it, to see about the heifers. They were all at the far end of the pasture except one. She was off by herself so Rae went to investigate. The heifer seemed uncomfortable and kept walking around. Rae kept her distance but stayed to watch her.

She was relieved when the heifer lay down. The relief was short lived when the heifer got right back up and started walking again. Rae walked around her to get a better look and was horrified to see a bag hanging from her back end. It had to be her water bag, which meant she was trying to have her baby.

She asked herself, "What should I do? Best get her to the barn."

Rae found that driving a heifer in labor wasn't easy, but managed to get her in a lot near the barn. By the time Link drove in, Rae was a nervous wreck, and the heifer was in hard labor.

Link said all they could do was wait, and if she couldn't have the calf, he would help her. Finally, the baby was born and the new mother licked the baby clean. The calf struggled to stand, only to fall down again. Rae was exhausted by the time it managed to stay on its feet. Then the little creature couldn't locate a teat, so he walked around the mother about thirty times. Just when Rae was ready to scream, he found the teat and started to nurse.

Link laughed and said, "We only have twenty-nine more to go. Think you can handle it?"

"Yep, I'll make it. Lord, look at the time. I may not make it tomorrow. Good night."

"Good night, and thanks for your help. I owe you."

"My pleasure, and you don't owe me anything."

Rae got up thirty minutes early the next morning to go by and see the new baby calf. He was nursing. She wanted to pet him but Link said he didn't think the new mama would allow that. Reluctantly, she went to work.

Margie greeted her with a cup of coffee and a cheery "Good morning, Doctor."

"Good morning, to you. You're in good spirits."

"I'm so happy to be here and have a job. I hope I can learn everything I'm supposed to."

"You'll do fine. Where are the other two?"

"They're in the back taking inventory."

"That's good. Well, shall we see if we can interest them in going to work?"

The morning went well. Margie was doing great and Lori seemed to be feeling okay. During a break Rae told them about the baby calf. They laughed at her because it was something they were familiar with.

"Just wait until you deliver a breech," Lori commented.

"You mean calves can be breech?" Rae asked.

"Oh, yes. You have to deliver quickly or the baby will suffocate."

"Thanks, you just made my day."

Mrs. Price returned from an errand with news. "Dale Smith's funeral will be Saturday afternoon at two o'clock. Are you two going?"

"I feel I should go, even though I don't want to," Rae said.

"I'm not going. Dale and I weren't best friends, to say the least." Lori said.

"Well, I guess I'll go if Doc's going," Mrs. Price said as she headed for the office.

"You can ride with me." Rae said.

"We'll just go to the church and not the cemetery, okay?"

"Fine, I'll be ready."

"I have to sing, so I'll be there," Margie said.

There were no more babies when Rae went by that afternoon, but Link had two heifers in the lot near the barn. They weren't in labor so Rae went to see Maggie. She had bathed her and was rubbing her dry when Link hollered for her. Rae hurried out to see what was happening.

He was trying to get a heifer into the lot, but the animal wouldn't cooperate. Rae went to help him.

"She fooled me," he said. "I checked this morning and she wasn't doing anything."

"Well, she's doing something now. Do you think she's going to be okay?"

"I'll keep an eye on her. You go ahead with what you were doing."

She brushed Maggie, cleaned her hooves, and had just finished combing her mane and tail when Link hollered.

Link said, "I think the calf has a foot turned under. I may need to push it back and straighten the foot. Would you get a bucket of soapy water and a clean rag for me?"

"Sure. What bucket do you want me to use?"

"There's a clean bucket in the utility room. The rags are in the second drawer on the right hand side of the kitchen cabinet."

Rae returned in a few minutes.

Link rolled up his sleeves and washed his arms and hands in the soapy water. Then he reached inside the womb and pushed the calf's head back and straightened the foot. When the heifer had her next contraction the baby's head and feet were in the correct position. After what seemed like hours, the calf was born and began searching for the milk supply.

"He'll be fine now." Link said as he washed his hands and arms, "I'd better go check the others before dark."

"I'll go with you."

This was Rae's favorite time of day, the last minutes before sunset. The western sky was filled with shades of reds and blues. Bobwhite quail called to each other so they could covey and go to roost.

Rae had the urge to reach and take Link's hand, but she didn't have the courage to make the move.

"Hello, anybody home?"

"Oh, I'm sorry. I was deep in thought, what did you say?'

He pointed to a heifer that was almost hidden behind a large oak tree. "We'd better get her in, she looks iffy."

Together they herded the heifer to the lot and turned her in with the mothers and their babies. The newest baby was lying down beside his mom.

Rae looked at Link and smiled. "He's a cute little guy."

"Yep. He's a good calf. Thanks for your help"

"No problem. I'd best be heading home."

"Bye. Have a good evening. See you tomorrow."

She was sorry she had said she would go to the funeral. She'd much rather help Link with the heifers and ride Maggie.

The next afternoon, Rae picked up Mrs. Price and drove to the church. She was surprised to find very few people there. Stephen Paul Morrison was one of the pallbearers. She watched him closely during the service, wishing she could have a few minutes alone with him. Margie's beautiful voice interrupted her thoughts and brought back memories of Jane.

Rae didn't view the body. She waited outside for Mrs. Price. They left before the family came out of the church.

Once home Rae changed into work clothes before driving to Link's. He was busy with two heifers that were in labor.

"Can I help?"

"Yep, I need a bucket of warm soapy water and a clean rag again. You know where everything is."

She got the requested items. He washed his hands and arms and then reached inside the heifer. "The calf's head is turned back and I can't turn it around. My hands are too big. Do you think you can do it?"

"I can try."

Rae washed as Link had. "I'm ready. Tell me what to do."

"Once you have your hands inside the heifer, feel around so you'll know how the calf is positioned. Locate both front legs and the head. If the head is not positioned on the legs, push the whole body straight back and turn it so it lays on the front legs."

"You make it sound easy. I feel the head and it's seems to be turned to one side."

"Try to push the calf back so you have room to turn the head."

Rae pushed the calf but it didn't budge.

"You can't be gentle, give it all you've got."

Rae pushed hard and was amazed when the calf moved. She turned the head but it slipped out of her hands. Then she had to wait through a contraction before she could try again. After three tries she managed to straighten the head. Once the calf was straight the birth took little time. Rae was exhausted and covered with slimy blood but excited that she had saved a life.

"You did a great job."

"Now I remember why I chose to be a dentist. I'm going to see Maggie and tell her about my experience."

She was brushing Maggie when Link came by and asked, "How about going out to dinner with me? A treat for saving me a vet bill."

"Okay. You've got a deal."

They were eating and talking when Stephen Morrison entered the restaurant. He was loud, arrogant, and a little drunk. Rae resented him ruining the lovely evening.

On the way home she thought about asking Link in but decided against the idea. After he left, she sat thinking about Morrison. She had to make a trip to Las Vegas and do some research. No sense in wasting time. She'd go next weekend. Maybe there would be talk at the café Monday and she could pick up a few tidbits. She might drive to Dallas tomorrow and see about a brown wig and fake identification.

Chapter Seven

Rae was up early Sunday morning preparing to leave when Link called to see if she could help with a heifer.

They weren't as successful this time; the calf was born dead. Rae was upset but didn't cry. She helped Link carry the calf to a spot where it was sandy enough to dig a shallow grave. When the task was finished, they walked back to the barn.

The little newborn calves were playing chase and worrying their mothers to death. Rae laughed at their antics. She forgot all about Stephen Morrison.

She spent the rest of the morning with Maggie and Link. She wanted to stay for the afternoon, but made herself go home and clean house.

Monday at lunch she overheard two guys talking about Morrison. They were saying he had a casino called Jacks or Better. She had no idea what Jacks or Better meant but she would find out soon.

The week passed with no unusual happenings. Margie soaked up her training like a sponge. Lori continued to grow larger. Rae sent Margie to the bank Wednesday so she could talk to Lori about Margie's progress.

"Do you think Margie is capable of handling your job?"

"Yes. She may have a few doubts but nothing you can't help her with. I'm kind of afraid to leave. You probably won't want me back."

"No way. You'll be welcomed back with open arms. I just want you to take care of yourself and have a healthy baby. Do you think we should give Margie a trial run without you Friday?"

"That's a good idea. Shall I tell her or do you want to?"

"Let's tell her tomorrow after work. Better yet, I'll tell her Friday morning. That way she won't be a nervous wreck Thursday night."

Rae went by a couple of times during the week to see Maggie and check on the little calves. They were growing like weeds and running everywhere. She would sit very still on a bucket in the middle of the pasture, and eventually curiosity would get the better of them. They would come up to her, but if she moved, they would scurry away like scared rabbits. She loved the happy little critters.

Friday morning she packed and put out extra food and water for J. B. She stopped by to tell Link she was going out of town. He was gone, so she left him a note.

Margie did such a good job on Friday that Lori decided to stay home until the baby was born. She would still be a consultant, if necessary.

Rae changed clothes at the clinic and drove to Dallas. She hoped this wouldn't take long because she would much rather be at the ranch helping deliver baby calves. She reminded herself she had a pledge to keep and she must stay focused.

Once in Dallas, Rae drove to Love Field Municipal Airport and parked her car. She hailed a cab and asked to be driven to the University of Dallas campus. After a few questions and directions, she located the favorite hangout of the college kids. It wasn't long before she had the name and address of Bob Sharp. Mr. Sharp was the best at making fake identifications.

It cost her five hundred dollars to become Pat Collins, but it was worth it. Now she had to buy a brown wig, change contacts, and book a flight to Vegas.

Rae arrived in Vegas Saturday about noon and found it unchanged since her last visit—bright, loud, and busy. She milled around watching people gamble. When a gentleman left a blackjack table, she took his spot. When she was down two hundred, she decided to get some sleep and try again later. While playing, she had learned jacks or better was a poker term, and poker was Stephen Morrison's favorite pastime.

After a two-hour nap she drifted down to the Jacks or Better Casino. It was nice, but just another casino. Hoping her luck would change, Rae sat down at a Blackjack table. She won two hundred back and quit.

Now she felt confident enough to try playing poker. Milling around she drifted into a room with several tables. She spotted a handsome older man standing watching a card game. She went to stand beside him and was soon getting her first poker lesson. He was watching Seven Card Stud. At another table, five men were playing Five Card Draw. He explained the rules of each game and how to ante and bet. Rae realized this was not entirely a game of luck and she was way out of her league. After watching a couple of hours, she decided her best bet was to find a tutor. She drifted over to the bar and ordered a Vodka Collins. As she chatted with the bartender, she learned Morrison was a master at poker and only a select few were invited to play at his table. His favorite poker game was Five Card Draw, jacks or better to open. She refused another dinner invitation and excused herself.

She wasn't ready to meet Morrison on his turf. This challenge would take time and planning. There was no need to stay in Vegas. She arrived home Sunday morning.

After a few hours of sleep, she ate and went to see Maggie and the babies.

Link was in a stall, feeding a calf with a bottle.

"Hi. Looks like you're pretty busy."

"Yep. Poor little guy's mother doesn't want him. I'll bottle feed him until Lucy has her calf."

"Why doesn't his mother want him and who's Lucy?"

"Sometimes when a heifer has a hard time calving, she doesn't want the baby, and Lucy is my milk cow. She gives enough milk for two or three babies and me. She'll be calving any day now, and I'll sneak this little guy in with hers."

Rae entered the stall, began petting and talking to the baby. She named him Leroy and promised to help take care of him. Link laughed, shook his head, and said, "I'm going to check the heifers."

"I'll go with you," Rae said. Then giving the calf a final pat said, "Bye, Leroy."

The heifers were fine so they went back to the barn.

"Think I'll go for a ride. Want to join me?"

"Sure. I'll saddle Zipper."

They rode along the creek and across the pasture enjoying the quiet of the evening and the lovely sunset. When darkness threatened, they turned toward home. Back at the barn they fed the horses. Rae groomed Maggie and went by to say good night to Leroy. Link walked her to her car.

"Do I need to feed Leroy tonight?"

"No. I'll feed him when I get up to check the heifers at one."

"Good. Call me if you need help."

Leroy was ready for breakfast when Rae arrived the next morning. She wanted to feed him but didn't have time to go back home and change clothes. When Link showed up with the bottle, the little guy forgot all about Rae. She laughed and left for work.

Margie and Mrs. Price were already in the clinic. The aroma of freshly brewed coffee greeted Rae and quickened her steps. They had a full schedule ahead and Rae was nervous thinking about not having Lori by her side. Margie was apprehensive at first, then settled down and worked like a veteran.

Lori called about closing time to see how things had gone. She was lonely and missed the activity of the office, but was glad there weren't any problems.

On the drive home Rae wondered if she could find a poker tutor in Dallas. Perhaps a desk clerk, bellhop, or bartender could give her some information. If she flashed enough cash, she would get results. A good book on cards would probably be a wise investment also.

Thinking about poker intently, she almost missed her turn. Link told her yesterday that he would wait to feed Leroy until she got there. Rae rushed home, changed clothes, petted J. B., and took off.

Link explained to her how to fix the bottle and then hurried to get a heifer into the lot. Rae went to the house and mixed the milk for the calf. Noticing how neat and clean the house was, she wondered if Link had a housekeeper. It took her a lot longer to fix the bottle than it did for Leroy to drink it.

She rinsed out the bottle and went to check on Maggie, who had been rolling in the dirt. Rae washed her off with the hose. She was about to start feeding when Link hollered for her to come see the new baby.

The little heifer calf was dark red instead of black. She was tiny and beautiful. Rae wanted to get into the pen and make a fuss over her, but mama cow wouldn't allow that. After the little one nursed and ran around, they left to care for the horses.

The rest of the week passed with more babies being born on the ranch, and Margie becoming very efficient at the clinic. The weather was getting cooler as fall approached so everyone seemed in a better mood. Rae found herself thinking that her life could be pleasant if she forgot her promise to Jane. Why couldn't she forget the whole mess and live like a normal person? Maybe have a family? No, a promise was a promise.

She drove to Dallas Friday and checked into the downtown Hilton as Pat Collins.

After dinner, she drifted to the bar for a nightcap and visited with the bartender. Twenty minutes and two drinks later she had the phone number of a wealthy gentleman who might be willing to tutor her. The bartender slipped a hundred-dollar bill into his pocket as Rae walked from the bar.

A man answered her call and asked her to hold. Buck Baldwin's voice was deep and southern, very sexy. She explained to him she was looking for a poker tutor. He expressed interest and said he and some friends were just starting a game, and she was welcome to come and watch. She asked for his address.

While Rae waited for her cab, she touched up her makeup and combed her wig. She jumped when the phone rang. It was the desk saying her cab had arrived. She climbed into the backseat of the vehicle thinking this might be a very interesting adventure.

Buck Baldwin met her at the door and welcomed her inside. He was a handsome man, probably in his mid-fifties, gray around the temples, and very tan. He had beautiful blue eyes, and white, even teeth. Taking her elbow, he ushered her into the game room where four gentlemen sat at a card table. All the men stood as he introduced Pat Collins. They welcomed her and invited her to watch and ask questions.

Buck seated her at his side and the game began. Each player started with five-hundred-dollars-worth of chips. Rae was fascinated and eager to learn how to play. When the game ended at five the next morning, she wasn't even tired. Buck agreed to tutor her on Saturday afternoons. Her first lesson would be this afternoon at four.

She returned to her room, bathed, ate breakfast, and fell asleep. Her wakeup call jolted her out of bed. She showered, dressed, and went down to grab a snack before time to leave. At three-thirty, her cab arrived.

The lesson was held in the game room. Buck explained the cards from low to high, the four different suits, and the joker. In most poker games only one joker is used and it can complete a straight, a flush, or count as an ace. Since she was interested in Jacks or Better, that's what they started with.

"This is a variation of five-card draw," Buck explained. "Each player antes and is dealt five cards. Before the game can continue, one of the players must have at least a pair of jacks or better, which is called openers. If a player has openers, he or she bets. The other players must call the bet to stay in the game. Each player may discard and draw more cards. The player who opened may bet again. The other players may call, raise the bet, or fold. The best hand wins the pot. After the hand is finished the person who opened must show openers. Okay, now that you know what it's all about, let's try a few hands."

Pat drew a pair of kings, a seven, an ace, and a five. She opened with a two-dollar bet.

"Must not have much if that's all you're going to bet. I call."

When they drew their cards Pat drew two, holding the kings and the ace. She drew nothing that would help her hand. Buck drew three cards.

"Now. Do I bet again?" Pat asked.

"If you want to and think you can beat me."

"I bet five dollars."

"I call."

Pat lost that hand to three tens.

They worked until eight o'clock. Rae wanted to pay Buck for her lesson, but he refused. He gave her two new decks of cards and told her to practice shuffling and dealing every day. She was to memorize the value of poker hands from the chart he gave her. She thanked him and smiled as he kissed her on the cheek. His limo would take her back to the hotel and pick her up Saturday afternoon at four o'clock.

Thoughts of Maggie, J. B., and Leroy prompted Rae to pack up and drive home Saturday night. It was after one when she got home, but she didn't care. She fell asleep thinking she had to wake up early so she could feed Leroy his breakfast.

Thunder, lighting, and heavy rain awakened Rae Sunday morning. She stretched and considered staying in bed. Then thoughts of a little black calf brought her to her feet. Leroy needed her, or at least she wanted to think he needed her. She dressed and went downstairs to make coffee. After breakfast she braved the rain and ran to the car.

Link was on his way to the barn when she arrived. He smiled and handed her the bottle.

"How is he?" Rae asked.

"He's fine. How are you?"

"I'm okay. And you?'

"Fit as a fiddle."

Leroy was ready for breakfast. He ran to meet her and started looking for the bottle. She held it out, and he latched onto the nipple. His little tail switched the whole time he was nursing. When he finished, she talked to him and brushed him. When he lay down for a nap, she went to visit Maggie.

Maggie raised her head when Rae walked in. Rae led her out into the hall and tied her to a post. Using a pitchfork she picked up the dirty hay in the stall. When all of the soiled hay was cleaned out, she spread fresh hay on the stall floor. Next, she took the water bucket and cleaned it, refilled it, and hung it back on its peg. Rae sat on the hay manger and petted Maggie. Rain pattered on the tin roof, and occasionally a horse would stamp or rattle a water bucket. The damp air intensified the odors of manure, mingled with leather, horses, and prairie hay. "This is a wonderful place, Maggie. Thank you for sharing it with me."

Link came in and said, "Come look."

She followed him to the end of the barn. In a stall stood a big black and white cow with a new black and white baby.

"This is Lucy, the milk cow who will soon be Leroy's new mama."

"She's huge."

"But gentle as a lamb and easy to milk."

"Can I try milking sometime?'

"Sure," he said.

They watched the baby get to its feet and start nursing. Lucy licked it clean. Rae watched for a while longer and then left for home.

The afternoon was spent doing laundry, cleaning house, and shuffling cards. The new cards Buck had given her were hard to control. Her first attempt to shuffle resulted in cards flying everywhere. She spent a couple of hours practicing shuffling, dealing, and playing fake poker hands.

As she practiced, she thought about Buck and wondered why he was so willing to help her. She was sure something would be expected of her, which was okay as long as it wasn't sex.

Monday was the usual first day back at work, long and busy. Margie, however, did a great job, and Rae found herself thinking about sending her to dental school. She would approach her with the idea one of these days when the time was right. Margie might not want to be a dentist, but at least she would have the opportunity for an education. It was too late to begin the fall semester, but working was good experience for her. She already seemed more self-confident.

Lori called and asked them to come to her house for lunch. Though Rae scolded her for being on her feet, she said, “We’ll be there in five minutes.”

Lunch was wonderful, and it was good to visit with Lori. She said she was feeling okay except for swollen ankles and twenty extra pounds.

Rae stopped by Link’s on the way home and found him delivering a baby calf. It was a difficult delivery, but both mama and baby lived. She couldn’t understand why he was cursing, so she asked what was wrong.

He replied, “Now isn’t the best time of year for cows to calve. They carry the calves through the heat of summer and then have to nurse them through the winter. The neighbor’s bull got in with these heifers while I was gone to a horse show. I went ahead and turned my bull in so they would all calve at the same time. I guess it’ll work out okay.”

“Were you upset with the neighbor?”

“Oh, a little, I guess. It’s pretty hard to keep a bull from going where he wants to go. Next time it may be my bull getting into his pasture.”

“I’m going home to change clothes. I’ll be back later.”

“Okay, I’ll be around here somewhere.”

The barn was quiet when she returned. Babies were lying next to their mamas and Maggie was eating supper. Link came by while she was brushing Maggie. “Want to go to a horse show with me Labor Day?’

“When is Labor Day?”

“Monday.”

“I’d love to go.”

Link seemed pleased that she was going with him. He told her to wear something cool and comfortable.

Saturday morning she cleaned house and prepared to go to Dallas. Although she was looking forward to her poker lesson, she dreaded the drive. Her car should be okay at the airport again this week, but next week she would find another location. If anyone tried to follow her they would have a difficult time.

At four o'clock the black limo pulled up in front of the hotel. She spoke to the chauffeur and got into the car. In a few minutes Buck greeted her with a grin and a kiss on the cheek.

"You look lovely," he said as he escorted her to the game room. "Have you had a good week?"

"No complaints, except for trying to shuffle new cards. Is there a secret to it?"

"Just lots of practice, and you'll soon prefer new cards."

She didn't argue but she had serious doubts.

The lesson went well and Buck was pleased she had been practicing. He asked her if she would like to join their game that evening. She eagerly accepted. He then asked if she would be his guest for dinner, which she also accepted.

Dinner was wonderful and Buck was a perfect gentleman. Many people in the restaurant came by their table to speak to him. He was evidently well known and respected in Dallas. Rae hoped to be long gone before they became an item.

The poker game that evening was held at Joe's. He was one of the men she met at Buck's. Joe greeted them at the door and directed them into the game room. Rae was impressed with the beautifully restored old house.

The men welcomed Pat, and then chips were bought and a new deck of cards opened. She watched carefully as the cards were dealt and reminded herself to keep track of the number of cards each player drew after the opening bet. The guys gave her pointers as they went along but never during a hand. If she won or lost, it was because of her own playing.

The game ended at two o'clock, and she played well enough to be invited to next week's game. Buck praised her on their way to his house.

When they pulled into the drive, he asked her to spend the rest of the night. Rae thanked him but refused, pleading the ever-helpful headache.

He smiled and said, "Perhaps another time."

She was exhausted by the time she arrived at her room. She locked the door and began removing her clothes. Shoes, slacks, blouse, hose, and bra decorated the floor from the door to the bed. She placed her wig on the wig stand and crawled into bed.

The phone woke her at noon Sunday.

Buck asked, "Want to play poker this evening?"

He explained this was a different bunch of guys and they played for blood. She would need at least two thousand dollars just to get started.

Rae jumped at the chance saying, "Just give me a time and an address."

He replied, "How about I pick you up at eight for dinner, and then we can go to the game."

Rae called Link to tell him she wouldn't be able to go to the horse show and to ask him to check on J. B. He sounded disappointed so she promised she would make the next one.

After eating she went shopping for a knockout outfit for the evening. She chose pale apricot slacks with a soft mesh shell to match. A pastel flowered jacket added the finishing touch.

When the phone rang at eight, she was ready and eager to go. Buck opened the limo door for her and complimented her on her attire. She, in turn, complimented him because he did look quite handsome in black slacks and a gray short-sleeved polo sweater.

Dinner was lovely, and Rae was surprised to be so hungry. Buck said she was just stocking up for the night. While they ate, he fired questions at her.

"What beats a full house?"

"Four of a kind, a straight flush, and a royal flush."

"Good girl. Remind me of what I told you last week about things to remember during a game."

"Watch the number of cards each player draws, avoid alcohol, act a little dumb, and use my looks to my advantage."

"By the time they figure out you know what you're doing, you'll be several thousand dollars richer, and I'll be laughing up my sleeve. I'll be your only real opponent at the table, and believe me, I won't cut you any slack."

"I'll beat you fair and square just like the rest."

Buck roared with laughter and asked for the check.

They arrived at the Epperson residence at ten o'clock sharp. A maid greeted them at the door and ushered them into the game room. Three gentlemen were smoking cigars and sipping brandy. Introductions were made, and the dealer was called from the kitchen.

Each player bought five-hundred-dollars-worth of chips. They decided to play Vegas rules, which meant no joker and no wild cards. The game agreed upon was Seven Card Stud. Rae preferred Five Card Draw, but she could handle stud okay.

Buck was right. The guys thought she was a dummy. They began to change their opinion when her stacks of chips started growing. At midnight they called for a break and left the table to have a snack.

When they headed back to the table, Buck gave her a wink to let her know she was doing well.

Rob, who had already lost quite a lot of money, was drinking heavily. He bet a hundred dollars with two hearts and the ace of clubs showing. Rae knew that even if he had two hearts in the hole, he still needed one more for a flush. She called his bet and raised him a hundred dollars. When the last card was dealt face down, he smirked and bet five hundred dollars. Rae had drawn a king, which gave her a full house, kings over eights. She called his five hundred. He laughed as he turned over his cards. Thinking she just had two pair, he reached for the pile of chips. When she turned over the other king, his face reddened and he said, angrily, "You cheated."

"How did I cheat?" Rae asked.

"I'm not sure, but you can't be that lucky."

She simply asked, "Need a loan?"

The other players laughed.

The game ended at three o'clock Monday morning. Rae was the big winner and was invited to play next month.

"I'll put it on my calendar," she said, "Thank you for a lovely evening."

Buck burst out laughing as soon as the car door closed. He said, "I've never seen old Rob so shook. It serves him right for underestimating you."

"That was fun. I could get hooked on poker."

"It's easily done. You're a natural. Few people have the skill and luck you have. I love the game, but I'll never be the player you'll become. You have the killer instinct."

"Right now it's new and fun. I may get tired of playing one of these days."

"Perhaps, but I doubt it. Would you like breakfast?"

"No, I just want to get some sleep. Thank you for a wonderful evening. I'll see you next Saturday."

"I'll be looking forward to seeing you."

He kissed her on the cheek and helped her from the car.

Chapter Eight

Tired but not sleepy, Rae called a cab and went to the airport. She drove out of the parking lot anxious to get home to a hot bath and a long nap.

She was fine until around five o'clock, when, as the night darkness turned gray, she could hardly keep her eyes open. She sang songs, rolled down the window, and even slapped herself once or twice. When she thought she couldn't stay awake another mile, a convenience store came into view. Hot coffee and a long stretch was a quick fix.

Still, she was immensely relieved when she pulled into her own driveway. J. B. ran to greet her.

"Hi boy, how are you? Do you need food and water?" Glancing toward his bowls near the backdoor, she said, "I see Link has already taken care of you."

After one more pat, Rae left J. B. and headed for the bathtub. The hot bath was wonderful, but even more wonderful was slipping between the sheets. She fell asleep immediately and slept until five o'clock that afternoon.

A rumbling stomach pulled Rae out of bed and to the kitchen. Scrambled eggs, bacon and toast satisfied the hunger pangs. Dressed and energy renewed, she went out to unload the car. J. B. ran back and forth, as if helping. Rather than going to Link's, she opted for a long walk. She would stop by his place after work tomorrow.

Tuesday morning Margie and Mrs. Price were so cheerful that Rae felt ashamed of herself. She just wasn't in the mood for bad breath and cavities. She would much rather be playing poker or riding Maggie.

She stopped at the grocery store after work. J. B. was out of food, and Maggie would probably like a carrot. She shopped quickly and drove home. Suddenly she was in a hurry to see Maggie and Link.

The little mare recognized Rae's car and ran to the fence to greet her. She eagerly took the carrot and thanked

Rae with a gentle rub from her velvety nose. Together, horse and woman walked to the barn. Link was filling water buckets.

Rae said, "Hi, how are you?"

"Hey, I'm doing great. How about you?"

"Oh, I'm fine. Glad to be home."

"Come to the house. I have something to show you."

She could tell he was excited so she left Maggie and fell into step with him.

"What are you up to?"

"Just wait and see."

When they walked into the den, she saw the trophy sitting on the coffee table. "You won! It's beautiful and so big."

"Yep, Zipper showed them how it's done."

Before she thought, she turned and gave Link a big hug. Grinning from ear to ear, he said, "I hope Zipper does as well at the next show."

Rae laughed and said, "I hope so, too."

Then feeling awkward, she walked over to examine the trophy. It was a bronze replica of a cutting horse and rider working a calf.

They walked back to the barn to feed the horses. When she went to see Leroy she was surprised at how fast the little guy was growing. He was too busy to be bothered. Maggie was munching hay. Reluctantly, Rae said goodbye and headed home.

She fixed a salad, sliced some cheese, and poured a glass of wine. Taking her supper out to the back porch, she ate and watched the sunset. The quiet countryside was wonderful. Surely there was no other place like this. Right now life was great. Maybe she should forget her promise. No, that meant Jane's death was for nothing. She would finish what she started.

Her thoughts drifted to Link. She asked herself, "Why did I hug him? It seemed so natural, but I'm not usually an affectionate person. I really like Link. He is different from any other man I know. It felt good to be in his arms. I wonder what it would be like to kiss him."

Taking her wine glass and bowl, she walked to the kitchen, saying, "I must be crazy. There can never be anything between Link and me."

She wondered how some people find their mate, marry, and raise a family without hassle or regret. Lori and David came to mind. They seemed so happy and were kind to each other. Maybe it was all just luck, like drawing a winning hand. Thinking about Lori, she picked up the phone and called her.

Lori answered the phone.

"How are you feeling?" Rae asked.

"Big, big, and bigger. I think I may explode if this goes on much longer. Are you sitting down?"

"Yes, why?"

"We have a surprise."

"What is it?"

"I'm going to have twins. We weren't sure until the last ultrasound so I didn't mention it before."

"You're kidding."

"No, a girl and a boy."

"That's wonderful Lori. How did David and Jake take the news?"

"They're both so excited I can hardly stand them. We've picked names. Want to hear them?"

"Certainly."

"Rae Jean and Joe Bob. We'll call them Jean and Joe."

Rae was so stunned she couldn't speak for a minute. "The names are great, I like them."

"Come over for lunch tomorrow. Bring Margie and Mrs. Price with you so I can tell them the news."

"Okay, we'll be there, but we'll bring lunch."

She poured a glass of wine and went out to sit on the porch. She pondered over her situation and scolded herself for letting others get close to her, "You idiot. You must keep your mind on your objective. Nothing or no one can interfere with your plans. From now on, keep a safe distance and watch what you're doing."

Rae went to work feeling sluggish from the sleeping pill she had taken. Despite Margie's cheery hello and Mrs. Price handing her a cup of coffee, she was not in a good mood. Hopefully she could make it until noon.

Lunch was a happy affair and Rae enjoyed herself. Lori was big and uncomfortable, but her attitude was terrific. Mrs. Price and Margie were thrilled with the news that twins were expected and began plans for a shower. Lori protested, saying she had Jake's things and they would manage. Rae doubted that Mrs. Price would be defeated that easily. Well, she'd better get busy because the little ones were due in a couple of weeks.

After work that afternoon, she handed Mrs. Price a check for three hundred dollars. "This is for a baby bed, bassinet, and whatever else you think Lori might need. If it isn't enough, let me know, and I'll give you more."

"Gosh Doc, I think that's plenty, but what will the rest of us buy?"

"Diapers, baby bottles, clothes, whatever. I just want to make sure Lori has what she needs. There's no reason for anyone to know about this, okay?"

"My lips are sealed."

"Margie, do you think we can turn the storage room into a nursery? Mrs. Price can schedule appointments and look after the babies, you can take over the front, and Lori can assist me."

"Do you think the babies will bother the patients?"

"No. We'll just make this temporary. When they get older, Lori may want to stay home with them."

"What a wonderful idea," Mrs. Price said, "I'll start cleaning right now."

"I'll go home and change and come back to help. Margie, would you like to go with me? I'll even take you to meet Maggie."

Margie's eyes lit up like Christmas lights. "Oh, I'd love to go if Mother will let me."

"Give her a call and ask. Tell her I'll bring you home at whatever time she says."

Fifteen minutes later they were driving to Rae's. Margie was so excited she couldn't sit still and chattered the whole trip.

While Rae changed clothes, Margie explored the house and yard. Rae couldn't believe how little it took to make Margie happy. She even enjoyed J B.'s lickings.

Link greeted Margie warmly and grinned at Rae. Rae found herself grinning back and knew she should be pulling away. She couldn't help liking him. He was such a nice man.

Margie fussed over Maggie and, like Rae, fell in love with the little mare.

Rae asked, "Have you ever ridden?"

"No, but I'd like to. It might be hard to manage in a dress, but I'd give it a try."

"What if you had some jeans here to change into? Would that be acceptable?"

"No, but I'll do it anyway. If I ever get out of that house, I'll do a lot of things I'm not supposed to."

"I don't want to cause trouble, but I'll get you a pair of jeans so you can ride. I don't think Link will say anything."

"Not me," he assured her when they told him what was up. "Do you reckon Maggie will squeal?"

They all pitched in and fed, watered, milked, and cleaned stalls. Then the three drove to the clinic to begin work on the nursery. They laughed and joked all the way to town. Rae couldn't remember having had a better time.

Mrs. Price was already there, working like a trooper. Link moved the heavy things to another room while the women scrubbed. The room was large enough for two baby beds, a chest of drawers, and a desk for Mrs. Price.

Link said, "I'll come by tomorrow and put a stove in, and a coat of paint wouldn't hurt."

Margie piped in, "Pink or blue?"

After a hamburger at the Dixie Quick, Link and Rae drove Margie home. She was unusually quiet. Rae knew how she felt and wanted to rescue her but now was not the time.

Link invited Margie to come back to the ranch, and she accepted.

Rae said, “Think about when you might be able to ride and we’ll talk about it tomorrow.”

That seemed to cheer Margie up a little.

Rae and Link talked and laughed all the way back to the ranch. He walked her to her car and opened the door for her. When she leaned out the window to say goodnight, he bent down and gently kissed her. She was so surprised she didn’t have time to do anything except kiss him back. Then he was saying goodnight and walking toward the house.

“So much for safe distance,” she thought. “In one short day I’ve jumped from a hug to a kiss. A baby was being named after her, and she was setting up a nursery in her clinic. Add adopting Margie and she had a recipe for trouble. She should win Citizen of the Month, which was exactly the image she needed.”

J. B. ran to meet her as usual. She petted him, and they walked to the porch together. She said, “You’ll get a treat if you wait right here.” She returned with his doggy biscuit and a glass of tea for herself.

As she drank her tea, she found herself remembering the feel of Link’s lips. She had been kissed before, but never like this. He was so gentle, like the feel of a rose petal on her fingertips or the brush of a baby’s hair against her cheek. She prepared for bed, mumbling, “Stop this nonsense.”

By the end of the week the nursery was finished. Lori was flabbergasted and relieved when Mrs. Price called and told her what they had done. She didn’t want to leave the babies with a sitter and she really needed to work.

When Saturday morning rolled around, Rae wanted to stay home. She struggled with packing and getting dressed to drive to Dallas. This would be her fifth lesson and hopefully her last.

Her thoughts drifted to Link as she drove the now familiar route. She had been nervous all week wondering what was going to happen next. Link hadn’t made another move to kiss her or touch her. He was certainly different from the few other men that she had dated. Maybe he didn’t want to get close either. She wondered if he was hiding something.

Rae left her car in a hospital parking lot near the hotel. Taking her luggage, she entered the hospital's lobby and found a phone. In five minutes her cab pulled up, and she was on her way to the hotel. Her room was ready so she went up and unpacked. At three-thirty the phone rang. Buck was sending a car for her. He sounded excited, but wouldn't tell her what was going on.

Buck greeted her at the door with a hug and a kiss on the cheek. Thoughts of Link flashed through her mind, but she dismissed them. Taking her hand, Buck led her to the den and sat down beside her.

"There's a big game tonight that I can get you in. The host set me up in a game many years ago. I've been waiting for the opportunity to return the favor. There will be four players, and all are good."

"Do you think I'm good enough?"

"Yes. If I didn't, I wouldn't have mentioned the game. Besides I'll stake you and any winnings are yours. All I care about is that you beat Jack. He likes pretty women. Your looks will distract him."

"What if I lose?"

"You won't. Jack's cocky, arrogant, and a good player, but not as good as you."

"Thanks for the compliment, but I haven't had much experience with pros."

"You are lucky, bright, and you have nerve. You'll do just fine. Play like you did last week. Will you do it?"

"Yes."

"One other hitch. The game is in Las Vegas. My private plane is waiting so, if you're game, let's go."

"Do we have time to go by the hotel so I can get some things?"

On the drive to the hotel, Rae questioned Buck about how he got her invited to the game.

He said, "I have friends in the right places."

A limo met them at the airport and whisked them to Caesar's Palace. Buck explained that he had a suite reserved, so they could rest until game time. Not only did he have a suite, he had also purchased Rae a new black outfit to wear that evening. He smiled as she examined her new clothes and said, "Why don't you try it on?"

She looked at the size, "It'll fit, but I'll wait until later to put it on. Thank you."

The poker game was going to be held at a private residence later that evening. After dinner, Rae excused herself to shower and dress. When she returned wearing the sleek black pantsuit, Buck whistled softly, "Pat, you are absolutely stunning. Jack doesn't have a chance."

At nine o'clock there was a knock on the door. Buck answered the door and invited a tall muscular man inside. He introduced Rae to Andrew Smith, her chauffeur and bodyguard for the evening. If she wanted anything, she need only ask Andrew.

Buck gave some last minute advice, "Don't start out like a house afire. Lose a few hands on purpose, but don't get caught. Have Andrew bring you a Vodka tonic often. It will be water. The game will break every hour for a stretch, so don't worry about drinking water. Use your head, your skills, and follow your gut feelings. I'll see you later. Good luck."

Buck kissed her on the cheek and handed Andrew an envelope containing fifty-thousand dollars.

Andrew announced their arrival in the speaker at the large double gates. The gates swung open, and they drove up a long drive to a beautiful stone house. Rae thought, "This is like a movie." Andrew pulled into the circle drive and parked at the front door. He escorted her to the door, telling her he would see to the car and return immediately. She panicked for a minute, thinking he might not return, but was saved from further thoughts when the door opened. A handsome older gentleman asked her in and introduced himself as Jack Peace.

It was evident he was impressed with her. His eyes swept up and down her, not missing a detail. She didn't like him. She was ready to begin the game. It would be a pleasure to beat Jack Peace.

He led her to the game room where three gentlemen were seated having drinks. They stood when Rae entered and Jack made introductions.

Dirk Cherry said, "It's going to be difficult to take money away from someone as beautiful as you."

Rae smiled and said, "Don't start counting yet."

Rae watched the dealer and decided he was honest. A player could call for a new deck of cards whenever they wanted to.

Dirk sat on her left and smoked one cigar after another. Rae was determined not to act annoyed. Finally, Larry said, "second hand smoke is killing me. How about giving us a break, Dirk." Dirk put the cigar out and only smoked occasionally after that.

The first couple of hours were spent feeling each other out. Rae didn't play well and allowed Dirk to bluff her out of a five-hundred-dollar pot. After losing a hand, she would ask Andrew for a drink. She knew they didn't consider her a threat, and she was ready to make her move.

By two o'clock Dirk was drunk and sloppy. Larry wasn't drawing well, but Pete and Jack were playing very good poker. She had lost a considerable amount but wasn't worried. The worm was going to turn.

Within an hour the guys were beginning to notice that she was raking in a lot of chips. Dirk nearly had a stroke when she bluffed him out of a thousand-dollar pot. He was in serious trouble.

Jack and Pete continued to play well, but Rae was beating them. By four o'clock Dirk was chain smoking and Larry was jiggling his poker chips. The final blow came when Jack had three kings and an ace showing. Rae had a seven of clubs, eight of clubs, six of hearts, and jack of spades showing. She had a nine and ten of clubs in the hole. Following her gut feeling, she called Jack's bet making the pot fifteen thousand dollars. Pete folded after the second king had been turned. When the final card was dealt, Jack bet five thousand more. Rae considered the situation. He might have four kings. There hadn't been any kings dealt to the other players before they folded so it was possible for him to draw one. When she drew a jack of clubs, it didn't make any difference. She had a straight flush. Smiling, Jack pushed ten-thousand-dollars-worth of chips to the center of the table. Rae calmly counted out ten thousand and raised him five thousand more. Jack laughed and said, "That's an expensive bluff, Pat. I call."

He wasn't laughing after she turned her cards over, showing a jack high club straight. Nor was he laughing when the chips were traded in for cash. The four men were dumbfounded when the cashier handed her seventy-five thousand dollars.

Jack walked her to the door. He raised her hand to his lips. "It's been a pleasure and a good lesson. For some reason, I feel that I have been set up. If we should meet again, I'll take you more seriously."

Andrew whooped and hollered when they got out of hearing range. "You're one cool poker player, lady. I sure would hate to play against you."

Buck wanted a play by play of the game. He laughed and congratulated her on a job well done. When she handed him the money, he handed back all but ten thousand back. "Buy yourself something nice. You've made me a happy man."

It was noon by the time they got back to Dallas. Rae went to the hotel and crashed until five o'clock. She drove home richer and no longer in need of Buck. He would be expecting her Saturday and would probably try to locate her but she was ready to go it alone. Now all she needed was an invitation from Stephen Paul Morrison. She would fly to Vegas in a couple of weeks and see what she could find out about him.

Time passed slowly that evening, and she found herself wanting to call Link. Deciding that calling wasn't a good idea she turned on the television to see if there was a good movie showing. Instead of a movie, she tuned in to a weather alert. The county was under a storm warning so she walked out onto the porch to look at the clouds. There was only a slight breeze, but to the south, dark clouds loomed and lightning streaked across the sky. Wisps of clouds were moving in an easterly direction but the clouds from the south looked very angry. They moved slowly toward her, stretching across the sky with blue showing underneath.

Occasionally part of the large cloud would dip lower than the rest and then rejoin the main body. Since it wasn't a real threat yet, she sat on the porch and watched the storm approach. In a short time the wind was rattling the shutters and blowing leaves off the trees. Distant lightning was accompanied by rumbling thunder. Suddenly, lighting flashes streaked in all directions and the thunder became deafening.

The first splattering drops of rain were huge. They hit the dry earth and porch with a splat. Soon the rain poured down, and the wind became severe enough to blow rain onto the porch and send Rae in the house. Maybe this would cool things off.

The phone rang. A frantic Mrs. Price said. "There's a tornado on the ground headed for Decker. I'm going to the cellar; you get in a hall closet or the bathtub."

She went to the closet under the stairs and climbed inside. Thinking of J. B., she ran to the door and called the little dog. Soon the two were secure in the closet, waiting for the storm to cease.

Fifteen or twenty minutes passed. Rae heard cracking sounds and chairs being blown off the porch. J .B. jumped into her lap when something slammed against the side of the house. "It's okay, boy, this will be over in a minute," Rae said, hoping she was right because she was getting cramped, and J.B. didn't smell too great. Finally the wind died down and she came out. J. B. rushed ahead of her. She tripped over him causing him to yip and her to reach for a light switch. There was no electricity. Carefully she made her way to the kitchen and located a flashlight. Not sure how long the batteries would last, she searched for candles and matches.

She picked up the phone to call and check on Mrs. Price, but the line was dead.

Flashlight in hand, she went to the front porch. In the dim light all she could see were scattered chairs and broken limbs. Thoughts of Lori, Link, and Margie flashed through her mind. She hoped they were okay.

The storm had passed but it was still raining. With nothing else to do, she went to bed. Thunder rumbling in the distance and intermittent lighting flashes had a hypnotic effect that soon put her to sleep.

The lights downstairs came back on at five in the morning, jerking her awake. She got up to turn off the lights and tripped over J. B. again. He had been asleep on the rug beside her bed. Petting him, she said, "Sorry, boy. Go back to sleep."

A soft rain was falling, bringing welcome relief from the heat. Sleep was impossible, so Rae made a pot of coffee and went to the porch. About daylight J. B. scratched on the door wanting out.

Later Rae tried the phone and found it was still dead. She dressed and drove to town. Decker was without power. The storm, which by-passed the city, caused serious damage to power lines and transformers.

Rae checked on Mrs. Price and Lori before going by the clinic. There was nothing she could do in town, so she went to see about Link and Maggie.

The storm had made a mess of the large pecan trees that were scattered over the property. Link was busy picking up tree limbs. She offered to change clothes and come back to help, but he said he had hired a guy.

When Rae turned to go to the barn, she saw a woman coming from the house. Rae decided to hang around for an introduction.

The lady's name was Karen Allford, the woman she had seen Link with before. Not in the mood for a friendly chat, Rae said hello and left to visit Maggie. Maggie welcomed her but Rae didn't stay long. She didn't like the idea of Karen Allford, so said goodbye and returned home.

Rae had several limbs blown down in her yard. She changed clothes and, with J.B.'s help, began cleaning up the mess. She was pitching the last limb on the pile when J. B. started barking. Link was riding Buck up the driveway, leading Maggie.

He rode up to her, tipped his hat, and said, "Howdy, ma'am. Would you like to go for a ride?"

"Where are you headed, cowboy?"

"To check some cows west of here. It's a far piece, but we should be back before sundown."

"Step down and have a cold drink while I change into my riding gear."

"Hold that dog. I'd hate to get licked to death."

She laughed and went to get Link a glass of iced tea. When she came back, he had tied the horses to a fence post and was playing with J. B. She handed him the tea and left to change. It was cloudy and cool so on her way out she grabbed a jacket and her hat.

"I'm ready"

"Okay, let's mount up and hit the trail."

J. B. wanted to go so they let him. It was only a mile or two to the pasture, and he was in good shape from running around all the time.

Cool, fresh air blew softly from the south, and puddles of water were everywhere. The horses were frisky and eager for exercise. It was a wonderful afternoon to ride.

They rode side-by-side, laughing and talking. Link explained that he usually drove and hauled a horse to check these cows but just had the urge to ride today. Besides, Buck needed a good workout.

"Well, if he bucks you off, you'll have a soft landing."

"He might as well try to get rid of his tail."

Buck behaved pretty well, only shying at something unexpected now and then. Maggie, as usual, was a perfect lady.

Two miles down the road they stopped at an orange gate. Link dismounted, unlocked the padlock, and swung the gate open. Rae, Maggie, and J. B. walked through the gate and waited for Link to mount up.

The hay shed that stood near the gate was minus a roof. He was worried about how much hay would be ruined from getting wet. Maybe he could get a crew out tomorrow to fix the roof. They rode on, amazed at how many tree limbs were down. After riding thirty minutes or more, they hadn't seen a cow.

"I hope a tree hasn't taken down the fence. If so, my cows may be in the next county."

J. B. relieved Link's worry when he started barking at a black bull and his girlfriends concealed in a thicket of trees. Rae helped drive the animals out of the thicket so Link could make sure they were all there. Two cows were missing. After a short search they found them grazing peacefully by a pond.

Rae was surprised when Link didn't start back toward home after they found all the cattle. Instead, he rode toward another stand of trees. She was glad because she was having a great time. Weaving in and out of dense timber, they had to practically lay on their horses' necks to avoid low hanging limbs. Suddenly, they broke through into the open on a plateau. The view was breathtaking.

"This is beautiful!" Rae exclaimed.

"I think so. I have dreams of building a house here someday." Link dismounted and said, "Step down and stretch your legs."

Link removed Maggie's hackamore, put on a halter, and tied her to a tree. He did the same with Buck, and then loosened the cinches so the horses could rest comfortably.

Rae was standing at the edge of the tabletop hill looking across the valley. A stream wound its way down the edge of the meadow, and low hills flanked the other side. The grass was turning brown, but it was still beautiful.

Link walked up behind her and put his arms around her. Without hesitation, she leaned against him and placed her arms and hands over his. They stood for a long time savoring the surrounding beauty and the warmth of each other. Remembering Karen, she asked, "What about Karen?"

Link replied, "Karen is a close friend but there's no commitment. We both see other people."

Rae made no comment. She was too content to worry about Karen.

Link said, "I have a surprise. Stay right here and don't peek."

"Surely you don't expect me not to peek. I can't stand suspense."

"J.B., stand guard. If she peeks, bite her."

After what seemed like an hour, he came back to her and turned her around. She was delighted to find he had brought a picnic complete with Asti Spumante and glasses.

"What a nice surprise."

They sat on a large rock overlooking the valley, sipping wine and eating cheese. Rae was a little light headed, but she wasn't sure it was from the wine. They were jolted back to reality by a clap of thunder.

Laughing, they scurried to gather up the picnic supplies and head home. Link bridled the horses and tightened their cinches. Rae packed the saddlebags and put on her jacket. They left the beautiful hilltop at a brisk trot, vowing to return soon.

They managed to get through the trees and across the open pasture before the rain became heavy. Half a mile from Rae's, it began to pour. They put the horses in a long lope and headed for the barn.

Horses, riders, and dog were drenched. Link apologized for not being better prepared.

Rae laughed and said, "A little rain isn't going to hurt me. I had a wonderful time."

They unsaddled the horses, wiped them down, and stalled them in her barn. Rae went to change into dry clothes while Link carried water to Maggie and Buck. She was going to drive Link home and bring back feed and hay for them. Link would bring the trailer and take them home tomorrow.

After a hazardous drive to the ranch, Rae was grateful when Link said, "Wait until I change and I'll follow you back home."

When they arrived back at Rae's, it had stopped raining. Together they carried feed and hay to the horses. Then she got the wine and glasses and asked, "Do you want to finish our picnic?"

"Throw in the cheese and crackers, and you've got a deal."

They ended the day watching a cloudy sunset and sharing a long goodnight kiss.

Chapter Nine

Rae was basking in the afterglow of being in Link's arms and enjoying his kiss when the phone rang. It was Mrs. Price telling her the power had been restored in town. They chatted about how they were going to reschedule today's patients and decided to come in an hour early and stay an hour late for the rest of the week. Mrs. Price agreed to call enough patients to start early tomorrow, and Rae was going to call Margie to see if she could come in early.

Once business was taken care of, she headed for the bathtub. She soaked and thought about Link. He was so different from the men she had known, not that she was greatly experienced. Sex had never appealed to her, even though she had been intimate with a couple of guys. Both times amounted to an experiment so she would know what to do and how to act. There was never any feeling on her part, but she could fake well.

She knew that to live up to her pledge, she had to know the tricks that lured men to her. Sex was one of the best. For some reason she thought it might be different with Link, but he was probably like most men--just interested in one thing. She must get Link out of her head and focus on Morrison.

There wasn't much time for Link or Maggie the next four days. Rae almost lived at the clinic. By the end of the day on Friday, everyone was a little cranky, even the bubbly Margie. They managed to get Monday's patients worked in, so that was a relief.

She stopped at the store and on impulse decided to invite Link for dinner. If he accepted, this would be the first meal shared at her house.

When she turned into the driveway, she saw Link working Zipper in the arena. He was so intense, he didn't notice her. Rae walked to the fence and watched until he took a break. She called to him and he came over to her.

"Would you like to come over for dinner later?"

"Sure. What time shall I be there?"

"Is eight good for you?"

"That's great, I'll get my feeding done and come on over."

"How do you like your steak?"

"Pink, but not bloody."

Rae prepared the salad and put the potatoes in the oven to bake. She waited until seven-thirty to fire up the charcoals. Everything was going well so she relaxed on the porch with a glass of tea. Link arrived and together they went inside. While he poured the wine, she put the steaks on the grill. They sat on the porch and talked until the steaks were ready.

Dinner was a success. She was surprised since she hadn't cooked in such a long time. Not that this was really cooking. Full and relaxed, they retired to the porch swing and enjoyed the crisp night air.

When Link pulled her into his arms, she didn't resist. She turned and made herself more comfortable. Link kissed her, and she returned his kiss. She kept telling herself she should stop this nonsense, but she didn't. She felt wonderful and, for once, was not afraid of that feeling.

Link kissed her once more. "I really care for you, Rae. You're beautiful, wonderful, and you scare me to death."

"Why do I scare you?"

"You are so perfect. I'm afraid I can't measure up to you."

"Perfect? Are you crazy? I'm far from perfect. You're the perfect one."

"No, I'm not. There is a lot you don't know about me."

"I'm listening if you want to tell me."

Just as Link started to speak, the phone rang. Rae started to ignore it, but then for some reason, changed her mind and answered. David was calling to tell her he was taking Lori to the hospital.

"I'm on my way," she responded.

She explained to Link, "David's taking Lori to the hospital. I told him I'd be right there."

"I'll go with you."

They put the dirty dishes in the sink and headed for town. The previous conversation was forgotten.

Lori was not in a good mood, but she smiled when Rae walked into the room.

Within ten minutes she was whisked to the delivery room. David donned cap and gown and went with her. Link and Rae drank coffee and paced the floor. Rae thought to call Mrs. Price and Margie. Mrs. Price was so excited she could hardly talk. Margie didn't have a way to town so Link went to get her.

Link and Margie had just returned when David came into the waiting room saying, "The babies are fine. You'll be able to see them in a little bit."

How's Lori?" Rae asked.

"Tired but otherwise okay. She should be back in her room soon."

They gathered at the nursery window and watched Dr. Good examine the babies. Satisfied that they were okay, she held them up for everyone to see. They were so tiny. Jean had black hair like David. Joe's hair was light brown like Lori's.

Dr. Good returned the little ones to their beds and waved the visitors away. Jake was upset because he couldn't hold the babies. David explained that he could hold them later.

Link drove Rae home, walked her to the door, and kissed her goodnight. She was tempted to invite him to spend the night, but there was no way she could allow this to go farther because eventually questions would be asked. She could never reveal any of her past, and she couldn't hide her physical identity forever. Why was she letting this continue?

The nightmare came in the early morning hours causing Rae to awaken drenched in sweat. She dreamed about the time her dad saw her talking with a boy after school. They were standing close together looking at a math problem and discussing how to solve it. Her dad called her a whore and demanded to know the boy's name. Jane finally convinced him to leave the boy alone. If that weren't enough, she dreamed she was playing poker with Tom Snodgrass, Dale Smith, and Stephen Morrison. Link was the dealer.

She walked onto the balcony and shivered in the cool morning air. She made coffee because sleep wasn't going to happen.

Rae picked up Margie at ten a.m. and they drove to the hospital. Lori was still tired but doing fine. Lori asked a nurse to bring the babies to her. When the nurse handed Joe to Lori he just squirmed and made squeaky sounds. Jean yelled like a banshee. Though nervous, Rae took her and rocked her. The baby stopped wailing and went to sleep.

Lori smiled and said, "I think you've made a new friend."

Rae treated Margie to lunch and then asked, "Ready to go riding?"

"Oh, yes, I can hardly wait."

"Let's go."

When they reached the dirt road, Rae asked Margie if she knew how to drive. Margie said, "No."

As she slowed to a stop, Rae said, "Well it's time you learned."

Following Rae's instructions, Margie drove to Rae's and then to Link's. After they stopped at the barn, Margie said, "I was scared to death but now I think I've got the hang of it. Thanks for letting me drive."

"You're welcome. You did well."

Like everything else, Margie took to riding like a duck to water. She started riding Maggie first and then Link brought in a gentle mare named Annie for her to ride. The three of them took the heifers and their calves to the north pasture. The cows weren't any trouble, but the babies were constantly doing something. Rae laughed at two little new ones who couldn't find the gate. Bawling, they ran up and down the fence. Finally, a cow went through the gate and the calves scurried after her.

Later, Link told Margie to come back any time and ride. She promised she would. They had to rush to get her home in time for evening church. Letting her out at home was difficult to do, but Rae knew she must.

Rae and Link had plans for dinner that evening, but by the time she returned from taking Margie home, her head was pounding. She called Link and explained that she wasn't feeling well.

A hot shower helped, but her head still hurt. Although she was hungry, she didn't have the energy to cook. J.B. hadn't been fed but she didn't think she could walk that far. The couch seemed like her safest bet so she stumbled toward the living room. The doorbell rang just before she reached the couch. Link was at the door with a pot of soup. Rae asked him in and then proceeded to lie down. In a few minutes, Link was serving soup and hot tea. She felt better eating but still had a headache. Link picked her up and carried her upstairs to bed. He left after getting her a glass of water, kissing her goodnight, and promising to feed J.B.

She slept well that night and was anxious to be up and about the next morning. After a good breakfast and a walk with J. B., she called the hospital. Lori answered the phone. She and the babies were fine.

The natural thing to do, it seemed, was to go see Maggie and to thank Link for caring for her last night. Maggie was happy to see her, but Link wasn't around. She brushed Maggie before saddling her and heading out to check the heifers. She met Link on the way.

He had already checked the heifers and was on his way to another pasture to check the fences. Rae rode along with him.

When they returned to the barn, she helped Link feed and water the horses and then went home to clean up. Link was going to take her out to dinner that evening.

As they were driving to town, Rae told Link about holding Jean so he headed for the hospital to hold a baby. She was amazed at how gentle and calm he was with baby Jean. The baby snuggled up against him and seemed content. Rae held Joe and then older brother Jake so he wouldn't feel left out. Lori and David were generous with their children. David said he knew who to call when they needed a baby sitter.

Link took Rae to a steakhouse in a nearby town. While they were waiting for their order to be served, Link asked, “Would you like to go to the horse show in Oklahoma City in November?”

“I’d love to go. I need the date so I can close the clinic.”

“You mean you’re actually going to shut down for the whole week?”

“Will you be performing every day?”

“No. I’ll probably have a couple of breaks, but I don’t know when they’ll be.”

“Well, we’ll just see what happens. I may have to close for the week. I’m not going to miss watching you and Zipper win the championship.”

That evening they sat in the swing and talked. Link said, “I want a bunch of kids.”

“I’m not sure I want any.”

“You’ll change your mind after you’ve been around the twins for a while.”

“They are cute, but I’m not sure I’m the mothering type.”

When Link left she sat and thought about a family. She decided it was great for some, but not for her. She went to bed with plans for a trip to Las Vegas forming in her head.

Monday morning Rae called the airlines to make reservations for a Friday night flight to Las Vegas. She wasn’t sure what she was going to do when she got there, but she was going.

Lori and the babies left the hospital on Wednesday. David was taking his vacation so he could help out until Lori was feeling better. Both grandmothers were going to help, so Rae wasn’t worried Lori would overdo.

She stopped by Link’s Wednesday after work. He asked her to go out Saturday night. He didn’t say anything when she refused, but she could tell he was upset. She didn’t go by to see him Friday before she left to catch her flight to Las Vegas. Time was tight and she had to take care of J. B. and pack before driving to Dallas.

The flight was uneventful except for the eccentric old man who hit on her. She finally lost her patience and called the flight attendant. When the flight attendant insisted that he change seats, he glared at Rae but complied.

She checked into the hotel, ate dinner, and strolled the strip. It was one a.m. when she walked into the Jacks or Better Casino. There was a vacant chair at the stud table so she joined the game. At six she left with several hundred dollars. A big breakfast and hot bath enabled her to go to bed and sleep soundly the rest of the day.

Saturday evening the poker tables were full so she drifted up the strip and played the slot machines and blackjack for a couple of hours. When she returned to the Jacks or Better, she found an open table. Luck was with her. She was winning and attracting attention, but not the attention of Stephen Morrison.

She left, but the poker thirst had not been quenched. Okay, a hand or two of blackjack, and then she would call it a night. At four a.m. she was back at Jacks or Better seated at a poker table. She had not seen Stephen Morrison and didn't dare ask about him. When six a.m. rolled around, she cashed in her chips. She hadn't done as well this session, but that was okay. There would be another day.

She slept until eleven which meant she was rushed to catch her flight. She dozed on the flight, but couldn't rest. When she started home, the car began cutting out. Time to get something new and comfortable, like an El Dorado.

J. B. ran to greet Rae when she pulled into the driveway. He wiggled and barked, making her ashamed of herself for leaving him alone. "Sorry little guy, but this is something I have to do. With a bit of luck maybe this won't take long."

Link called Sunday evening to see if she was okay and give her an animal update. Leroy had gotten out and had quite a romp. She rocked with laughter as he described how the little calf raced up and down the barn hallway and ran to Zipper thinking anything black was a friend. Link had to turn Lucy out so she could rescue Leroy. After they hung up, she realized he had not asked any questions about where she had been.

Margie was quiet all Monday morning. Rae asked her if something was wrong, but she wouldn't talk. At lunch Rae asked Margie if she would like to go horseback riding after work. Margie brightened up and said she would call home and ask permission.

That evening instead of turning toward home, Rae turned in the direction of Lori's, "Margie, we'd better check on the little ones, hadn't we?"

"Yes, I bet they've grown already."

"Surely not, they're only nine days old."

"You'll be surprised."

Rae was surprised at how the babies had filled out. They were less red, and their perfectly formed hands and feet amazed her. Lori was thrilled they had come to visit. She thanked Rae for all the nice gifts.

Jake wanted to go with Rae and Margie, so they took him. He was never around Margie's parents so the secret about her riding clothes was safe.

When they all drove up to the barn, Link was getting ready to work Buck. Margie and Jake were mesmerized as they watched him ride the beautiful buckskin. Jake allowed that he wanted to be a cowboy just like Link.

While Rae and Margie saddled up, Jake roamed the barn. Rae found him in the pen with Lucy the milk cow and her babies. She decided she'd better keep him within arm's reach.

They left the corral, with Margie riding Annie, Rae riding Maggie, and Link riding Buck, with a small wormy boy behind him asking a million questions. When they returned to the barn, Jake fell right in, helping feed the horses and clean stalls. Link got him a bucket to stand on and let him brush Zipper. It wasn't long before Jake was sitting on Zipper brushing away.

Rae felt like she had been run over by the time she dropped Jake off at home. He was delightful, but a little too lively for someone who was not used to children.

On the drive to her house, Margie told Rae her father wouldn't let her go to college. He didn't think women needed an education, just a husband. He even had a man picked out for her. Rae was horrified for the girl.

"What if I paid for your education?"

"He still won't let me go. It's a control thing."

"What if you moved out of the house?"

"They would disown me. I would never be able to go home."

"If you need me, I'll help, but you have to decide what you want to do. I don't want to cause problems for you."

"You are wonderful to me, Rae. I want to be just like you someday."

"No, Margie. Be your own person, but thanks for the compliment."

Friday arrived and Rae managed to get away early. She asked Link to check on J. B., and then drove to Dallas in search of a Cadillac dealership.

In a short time she found what she wanted. The salesman almost fainted when she paid in cash. She felt like a new woman driving to the airport in a hunter green El Dorado.

The flight to Vegas was rough because of stormy weather, so she didn't get much rest. She wasn't sleepy, but would have enjoyed peace and quiet. At least, she thought, I'm not being aggravated by some dirty old man.

Once in her room, she tried to take a nap. Unable to sleep, she dressed and went out to dinner.

Slot machines and blackjack helped pass away three hours before she went to the Jacks or Better to play poker. All the tables were full so she decided to try her luck at craps. It was fun to throw the dice, but it wasn't fun to lose money.

When a seat opened at a poker table, she took it and played until five a.m. She didn't play well. This was her first experience with bad luck, and she didn't like the feeling. Maybe tonight would be better. Even breakfast wasn't as good as usual; and to add to her frustration, she couldn't go to sleep.

Saturday evening was a repeat of Friday. Rae left Las Vegas tired, frustrated, and several thousand dollars poorer.

The flight to Dallas was nice and smooth so she did manage to take a nap. The bright spot was her new car.

As she drove, she rehashed the horrible weekend. She had been distracted with thoughts of Link and babies. Next weekend would be different because she intended to isolate herself all week, especially from Link. He wouldn't understand her behavior, but it must be if she was to achieve her objective.

J. B. was happy to see her. She petted him and asked, "Want to help?"

After the luggage was taken into the house, mistress and dog went for a walk to the pond. When they returned, she gave J. B. fresh water and filled his food bowl, and then said to herself, "Don't even think about calling Link."

The week was long and difficult. She stopped at Link's only after checking to see if his pickup was gone. Maggie seemed puzzled that she only stayed for a short time. Leroy couldn't care less if she came by, at all. Even though it was good to see the animals, Rae found herself hoping Link would appear.

When the phone rang Thursday evening, she hurried to answer. Link's familiar voice said, "Hi, how are you?"

Although her heart was beating rapidly, she answered, "I'm fine. How are you?"

"Lonely. I miss you."

"Sorry, I've been busy."

"Give me a call when you have some time."

"I will," was all Rae could say.

When Rae drove away from Decker Friday, she had only poker and Stephen Morrison on her mind. By the time she arrived at the airport, she could hardly wait to get to Las Vegas. A short nap on the plane gave her a new burst of energy so she went straight to her room to freshen up for dinner. The call of the blackjack table was strong, making Rae rush through her meal.

Lady luck was with her. She felt like her old self and could hardly wait for time to march along. In the early hours of morning, she went to the Jacks or Better to find a seat at a poker table. By four a.m. she was stacking up a nice pile of chips. At six a.m. she left her money in the casino safe and went to her room.

Something told her Morrison would be around tonight so she dressed with extreme care. The sleek turquoise blouse with black slacks looked, and was, expensive. Diamond studs, a gold bracelet, and a matching gold necklace added just the right touch.

Heads turned as she walked into the casino at one a. m. Sunday morning. She found a seat at a table and asked for chips.

Cool, calm, and with skill, her chips multiplied. The dealer couldn't believe her luck. One by one, the other players dropped out. She was getting ready to call it a night when a man said, "Ms. Collins, will you join me at a private table?" Rae looked up straight into the eyes of Stephen Morrison.

"I suppose I could play a few hands."

"Good. I'm Stephen Morrison, the owner of this establishment. I hear that you are some poker player. How would you like to play in a private game upstairs?"

"Mr. Morrison, your challenge is accepted.

"Please call me Stephen."

"Okay, Stephen it is. How many will be playing?"

"Five."

Stephen Paul Morrison. At last we meet, Rae thought as she walked to the poker table. Morrison told her to make herself comfortable while he went to find Jack and Freddy.

Rae fixed herself a glass of ice water and walked around looking at the pictures of celebrities that covered the walls. She was beginning to tire, but once the game began she would forget the day, year, and hour.

The men returned and Morrison made introductions. Jack, Freddy and Jarrod all looked like gangsters. Each wore a pinstriped suit, white shirt, black tie, and black loafers. Rae would have bet a thousand, a frisk would produce a gun or two, but she really didn't care who they were as long as they had money and could play cards.

Once the players were all seated, Morrison explained the game was jacks or better to open, and the joker counted only as aces, straights, or flushes. Rae reminded herself to stay aware of the joker.

They played until five a.m. Sunday morning with no one winning or losing much. Rae was relieved when Jack said, "Let's call it a night and get some sleep."

Freddy asked, "Would you like to join us for a game later this evening?"

"I would like to, but I already have an engagement."

Morrison walked her to the door and asked, "Ms. Collins, would you join me for breakfast?"

"Please call me Pat, and yes, I'd love to have breakfast with you."

Five minutes later they were in his penthouse suite, Rae having coffee, Morrison drinking mimosas. They had breakfast in the sunroom overlooking the city of Las Vegas. He was a very attentive and attractive host. One would never picture him a rapist.

Time passed quickly, and Rae realized that she must get ready to catch her plane.

"I've had a lovely time but I must pack and get to the airport."

"Where are you off to?"

"Dallas."

"Please stay. I'll furnish you a room and fly you home in the morning."

"You tempt me, but I really can't."

As they walked to the elevator, Morrison asked, "Can you play next weekend?"

"Yes, I'll be back Friday evening."

"Good. I'll have a room ready for you. What's your favorite color?"

"Blue. Why?"

"Just curious."

As she started to leave, Stephen asked for her phone number.

"It's better that you not call me at home. How can I reach you?"

In a flash he produced a business card and wrote his private number on it.

"When is the best time to call?"

"Anytime. Promise you'll call as soon as you get home."

"I'll call as soon as possible. Thank you for a lovely breakfast."

He bent to kiss her, but she just brushed his lips and said goodbye. For the first time all weekend, thoughts of Link flashed through her mind.

"Do you really have to go?"

"Yes, I really must."

She kissed his cheek and pushed the elevator button. Once in her room, she dashed to the bathroom to brush her teeth and wash her face. Allowing Morrison to touch her took much effort, but she could do whatever she had to do to get close to him.

Rae had collected her bag and was almost to the door when the phone rang. There was only one person that could be calling. Sure enough, it was Morrison. "I couldn't resist calling. I hope you aren't upset."

"Why would I be upset?"

"Can you stay for dinner?"

"No, I must get home. Maybe I can stay longer next week."

"Wonderful. I can hardly wait."

Rae hung up, grabbed her bags, and rushed to the airport. Maybe she could catch a few winks on the plane. On the other hand, it would be wiser to stay awake so she could sleep tonight.

Once she was home, J. B. barked and ran in circles until she sat down and petted him. Together they made trips from the car to the house until everything was unloaded.

Exhausted, but not ready for bed, she walked with the little dog to the pond. She sat and watched the moonlight reflect on the water and thought about Link. She had not seen him for a week and she missed him. Deciding she was a total fool, she walked to the house and dialed his number. After five rings she hung up and checked the kitchen for something to eat. A grilled cheese sandwich on stale bread was all she could manage. She got ready for bed thinking she had probably just poisoned herself.

Chapter Ten

Rae didn't even question taking a sleeping pill. She knew she had to sleep and wouldn't without help so she took two. Monday morning she had a hung-over feeling. She was almost late to work because she couldn't seem to get going. When she arrived at the clinic, she felt as if she had already put in a day's work.

Mrs. Price scolded Rae, "You need to get more rest, and I bet you aren't eating right."

Even Margie seemed concerned about her, saying, "Gosh, Doc, did you stay up all weekend?"

"Okay, get off my case. Who's the doctor around here? Where's my coffee and who's the first patient?" Rae grumbled, only half kidding.

There was little time to think or rest all morning. By the time noon rolled around, she was exhausted and starving. She went to her office while Mrs. Price ordered lunch.

Margie said, "You need to go home, eat, and then take a nap."

"I think I will."

She did feel better after she ate and rested for thirty minutes. Somehow she managed to make it through the afternoon.

When she got home, she fixed a glass of iced tea and sat on the porch. J. B. lay near her with his head resting on her feet. She said to him, "I would like to see Maggie and Link."

He whined as if to say he understood.

The feel of autumn was in the air. She had been too busy to notice the days were getting shorter and the nights cooler.

At the first hint of darkness, she went to bed. She had eaten a bowl of soup and taken a hot bath so she felt very relaxed. She was out almost as soon as her head hit the pillow.

Tuesday was a better day. She felt rested, and the patient load wasn't as heavy as the day before. Mrs. Price commented, "You look better today."

"I feel better, but I may need more rest. Let's close the clinic on Mondays for a while."

"Starting when?"

"Next Monday. Can you reschedule the patients?"

"I'm sure I can."

Margie wasn't happy with the closing, so Rae told her to come in and clean the days they were closed.

That afternoon after work Rae went to see Lori. Lori was feeding the babies. When Rae offered to help, Lori handed her Joe and a bottle. Dry and full, they were soon fast asleep. There were great differences in them besides gender. Joe had blue eyes and brown hair like his mother, but Jean had brown eyes and black hair like her dad.

Jake came bounding in, excited to see Rae and anxious to tell her about school. She was amazed that the little ones slept right through the noise and even a kiss from their older brother.

On the way home she stopped to see Maggie even though Link's pickup was there. Maggie nickered when she saw Rae bringing her a carrot. Rae was petting her when Link walked up. His greeting was cordial, but cool. They seemed like two strangers trying to find something to talk about. He didn't ask any questions, but she felt the need to explain. She said, "Link, I'm gone on the weekend because I have to be, not because I want to be."

She could almost see the relief he felt. He looked at her and said, "I miss you, and Maggie misses you. This place is much better when you're here."

"I may have to be gone a few more weekends, but believe me, I'd much rather be here."

"Make it quick. I have several good shows coming up, and I want you with me."

"Okay, I'll try my best."

They walked to her car and all seemed right with the world again. Link kissed her and held her close. She wanted to stay and enjoy the comfort of this wonderful man, but knew she couldn't. Having feelings and caring for others interfered with her plans.

Wednesday was a great day. Work went well and everyone was in good spirits.

Rae went grocery shopping after work with plans to invite Link over for fried chicken that evening. He wasn't at home when she stopped so she left him a note. When she hadn't heard from him by seven, she fixed dinner. He called at nine. "I'm sorry. I had to meet Doyle Jones to try out a horse. Do you have any leftovers?"

"I think there's a chicken leg. Would you like me to save it for you?"

"I'll be right there."

Rae sat at the table and drank tea while he ate. He told her all about the horse he had gone to see. "He's a classy looker and has a great disposition. I think I'll buy him."

"Is he better than Zipper?"

"Not yet, but he will be as good or better with lots of work. It's always wise to have a horse or two to fall back on if one gets sick or hurt."

"What about Buck?"

"It may be two or three years before I get him lined out. He has the talent but not the want to. But he's young. If he ever figures out he's having fun, he'll be hard to beat."

Together they cleaned up the kitchen and then retired to the porch. The evening was chilly and invited the opportunity to snuggle. Having Link's arms around her and feeling the steady beat of his heart made her feel secure and safe. She knew this was a mistake, but couldn't break away.

He left at midnight. She wanted to ask him to stay, but didn't. She longed to be close to him, to feel him inside her, and to sleep in his arms. Perhaps the time would come.

For now, she had a job to do and she was going to do it. Morrison was going to die. Then she would find the other two. She had not been able to find a trace of them yet, but she would eventually.

Rae called Margie's mother just before quitting time Thursday afternoon. She said, "Mrs. Tucker, this is Dr. Roberts. I'm calling to ask if I may keep Margie for a while after work today. I'll have her home by nine o'clock."

"I suppose it'll be all right. Her father isn't home so I'll give my permission."

"Thank you. Good-bye."

Rae stopped at a pay phone on her way back from the bank. She had promised to call Stephen. He answered on the third ring, "I thought you had forgotten me!"

"No, I haven't. I've just been extremely busy."

"You're going to be here tomorrow, aren't you?"

"Yes, but it will be late."

"Late doesn't matter. Come straight to the casino. I'll be waiting for you. Better yet, I'll meet you at the airport. Give me your arrival time."

"I'm not sure what flight I'm going to take. I'll just grab a cab." She thought she would never get off the phone.

Margie was waiting for her mother when Rae got back to the office.

"Guess what, I talked to your mother and you get to spend the evening with me."

"What are we going to do?"

"We're going to visit Lori."

"I'm going to hold Jean just as soon as I get there," Margie stated as she got into the car.

"No, I'm going to hold Jean, you can hold Joe."

They fought over choice of babies all the way to Lori's. Actually it was just a game because they didn't play favorites.

Lori met them at the door with hugs and a fussy baby.

"Jean has not had a good day. I think she ate too fast and has a bit of gas." Margie took the baby.

David and Jake were changing Joe's diaper. Once the chore was finished, David handed him to Rae.

Margie said, "I can't believe you gave her my baby."

"Gosh Margie, haven't you been taught to share?" Jake asked.

They all laughed, and Rae explained that Margie was only kidding.

Lori and David fixed dinner for Rae and Margie. After a good meal and lots of baby holding, they prepared to leave. Jake was unhappy that they were leaving so Margie took time to read him a book.

Once on their way, Rae asked, "Have you decided what you would like to do with your life?"

"Yes. I want to go to college."

"I didn't think you were going to college. What changed your mind?"

"Dad has started asking Bob over for dinner so we can get acquainted. I like Bob, but I don't want to marry him. I'll leave home before I'll marry someone I don't love."

"I would too. Have you decided on a major?"

"I think I would like to be a dentist."

"Have you told your folks how you feel?"

"No, and they'll never forgive me. I'll have to do this on my own."

"I'll help you. We'll get you enrolled next semester. It'll be hard for a while, but your family will eventually change their minds and even be proud of you"

"You don't know Dad."

"No, and I'm not sure I want to. He sounds an awful lot like my dad."

"Was he strict?"

"Very. He made life miserable for me."

Margie thanked Rae for being such a wonderful boss and friend. Rae told her not to worry, that all would be okay. On the way home she made up her mind to set up a trust fund for Margie. She would see that her first cousin was cared for.

Friday morning she had a slight headache. She took a couple of aspirin, but they didn't help. Maybe a cup of coffee would cure the problem. It didn't. She went to work feeling miserable, but managed to make it through the morning. However, by one o'clock her head was hurting so badly, she was nauseous. By two o'clock she was almost to the point of screaming. Mrs. Price wanted to call Dr. Mackey, but Rae refused. She said she would close the clinic and go home.

Margie drove Rae's car. Mrs. Price followed so she could take Margie home.

Once home Rae went straight to bed. The light was killing her so they hung blankets over the windows to darken the room. She was waiting for the pills Margie had given her to take effect when she started throwing up. Fortunately, she had a wastebasket near the bed. Concerned, Margie called her mother and asked permission to stay with Rae. Mrs. Price went to town to get groceries for the patient and her nurse.

Saturday morning Rae was still very ill so Margie called Dr. Mackey at home. He came to the house and gave Rae a shot to relieve the pain and nausea. Margie had been up all night so the doctor suggested that she go home and get some rest.

Rae slept until Saturday evening. When she awoke, she heard Margie and Link in the kitchen. They were fixing supper and talking about horses. Link came to check on her and was surprised to find her awake. He hollered at Margie to bring the soup. She managed to sip a cup of tomato soup and drink a little tea. When she tried to get up to go to the bathroom, Link picked her up and carried her. She protested, but he paid no attention. He waited outside the door and carried her back to bed.

She took the pills the doctor left for her and was soon fast asleep. She slept until Sunday morning. Margie had gone home to go to church, but Link was still with her. When he found she was awake, he fixed breakfast for her. Link served her breakfast and sat on the side of the bed while she ate.

"I'm going home to feed but will be right back."

"You've done enough. I'll be fine now."

"I'll be back anyway."

Rae felt one hundred years old. Slowly she got out of bed and made her way to the bathroom. Her eyes were hurting. She was surprised and relieved to see her contacts were still in place. She locked the door, removed her contacts and bathed her eyes. A shower would feel wonderful, but she didn't think she could stand up that long.

Monday afternoon Rae called Stephen and explained that she had been ill. He wasn't happy but seemed to accept her explanation and made a date for the following Friday.

Morrison didn't seem nearly as anxious to see her as he had been before. She shouldn't be surprised. He probably had women falling all over him. Well, she would get him interested this weekend, but the delay meant it might take longer to win his confidence.

Tuesday was a beautiful cool day. Rae left work fully intending to go home and clean house, but on reaching Link's driveway, the car simply turned in. His pickup was there but she couldn't find Link. Buck was not in his stall so that meant Link was riding.

She returned to her car and hurried home to change clothes. Then she rushed back to saddle Maggie. They headed north across the open pasture but saw no sign of their friends. She soon quit looking for Link and just sat back and enjoyed the fresh air and the beautiful country. Riding Maggie was as comfortable as sitting in a rocking chair. When she returned to the barn, Link was unsaddling Buck.

"Hi, looks like you're feeling better."

"Much, thanks to good care."

"I was worried. You were awfully sick."

"I'm fine. Just a little weak."

Rae unsaddled Maggie, brushed her, and put her in her stall. Suddenly she was very tired. She sat down on a bale of hay. Link came over and sat beside her.

"I think I'd better get home."

"Are you sure you're okay?"

"I'll be fine."

"Go to bed. I'll be over later and fix you something to eat."

"I can manage."

"I know you can, but I'd like to spoil you a little."

"I'll leave the door unlocked."

She drove home, swallowed a pill, and went to bed. When Link got there an hour later she was asleep. He covered her with a blanket and left quietly, locking the door on the way out.

Wednesday evening she had Mrs. Price, Margie, and Link over for dinner. It was a gesture of thanks for taking care of her. It required special effort on her part because she didn't like to cook.

She left Decker Friday determined to get rid of Morrison so she could stay home and enjoy life. She had to be careful not to get in a hurry. How many times had a killer been caught because of one little slip? Well, she wasn't going to slip or get caught. But she really wasn't a killer, more an avenger.

Rae called Morrison from the airport. When she arrived in the lobby of the casino, he was waiting for her. They exchanged greetings and took the elevator to the tenth floor. Morrison warmed a little during the ride.

The suite was beautiful. The walls were white and soft blue plush carpet covered the floor. The furniture was luxurious blue leather. Fresh flowers were everywhere.

When they walked into the bedroom, the first thing Rae saw was the white canopy bed. On the bed lay a set of blue lounging pajamas.

"This is absolutely lovely."

"I want you to be very comfortable. I'll leave and let you freshen up for dinner. Shall we say eleven?"

"That will be fine. Are we playing poker later?"

"I'm ready to take your money."

"You can try."

Dinner was wonderful but she was anxious to play cards. Finally they were seated at the poker table at twelve-thirty. Jack, Freddy, and Jarrod were back and ready to play. She reminded herself about the joker as she began to deal the cards.

Lady luck was with her tonight. She won several thousand dollars by four a.m. Around five, Freddy was out of money and ready to call it a night.

Stephen invited her to his suite for breakfast. She accepted but wanted to go to her room and freshen up first. Truth was, she wanted to check and see if her luggage had been searched. She had taped a piece of thread so if her bag had been opened, the string would be disconnected. Sure enough, the thread was only taped on one side.

It was a good thing she had placed her syringes inside the tubes that usually held tampons. She had removed the plunger and needles. Then she had taken out a couple of tampons, cut out the middle, and replaced them with the syringes. The top and bottom ends of the tampons were placed back in the tube, and the tube was placed back in its plastic wrapper and the end glued. You couldn't tell it had been opened.

A vial of Valium was hidden in a jar of cleansing cream. It didn't appear to have been touched. Thinking a camera might be hidden in her room, she was careful not to reveal she was checking for anything.

She had worked up a big appetite and ate a hearty breakfast. Morrison did more drinking than eating but didn't seem to be getting drunk. He had consumed a large amount of Jack Daniels last night while playing cards, or maybe it just looked like Jack Daniels. If she got a chance, she would have a little taste tonight.

She thanked Stephen and started to leave, saying, "I hope I can sleep. I sometimes have trouble unwinding."

"I'll help you unwind, if you'll stay. Sex is a perfect stress reliever."

"You're probably right, but I think I'll pass this time. I want to be fresh and rested so I can show you a good time."

"I can wait for that. Just a minute. I know what you need." He left, then returned and handed her a bottle of pills. "Take one of these and you'll sleep like a baby. I'll call later. Would you like to catch a show tonight?"

"I'd love to."

"Okay, sleep well."

She allowed him a kiss and then left to get some sleep.

Rae was almost certain the room was bugged. She had an eerie feeling someone was watching her, which meant she couldn't remove her wig. That was going to present a problem. Surely they hadn't bugged the bathroom. Just to be safe, she went into the bathroom and turned on the hot water in the shower.

When the room was fogged over good she removed her clothes and got in the shower, then she removed her wig. Perhaps she should have her hair dyed before her date.

The blue satin sheets were a luxury she could get used to. When she awoke at two o'clock, she ordered a salad and iced tea.

Three p.m. found her in a health spa getting a massage and making an appointment for a manicure and a hair-do. Rae watched carefully to be certain she wasn't being followed. Still she asked her beautician for a station in the rear of the salon. At six p.m. she came out of the salon with brown hair and a nail job.

The phone was ringing when she entered her suite. Stephen was calling to arrange their evening schedule. He planned an early show, dinner, and then meeting the guys for poker. Rae had an hour to shower, dress, and put on her make-up. The last touch of eyeliner was going on when the doorbell rang.

She opened the door and Stephen's eyes lit up. "You are absolutely beautiful."

"Thank you, and you're very handsome. Would you like to come in for a drink before we leave?"

"No, thank you. We'll have one before the show."

The evening went well. Morrison was interesting and a gentleman. Rae almost enjoyed herself.

The cards were in Morrison's favor that night. He was getting obnoxious. Jarrod was angry, Sam was silent, but Rae was being patient, waiting for the tide to turn. At last she began to draw some decent cards and added a few chips to her stack. Morrison wasn't as happy and loud now. When they took a break at four-thirty, Rae managed to take a sip from his drink. He was drinking iced tea.

When the game resumed, the cards were still favoring Rae. She won back what she had lost and a little extra. Sam and Jarrod were the big losers. She wondered why they played because they rarely won anything. When she beat Stephen's two pair with three of a kind, he threw up his hands and quit.

He asked her to join him for breakfast, and she accepted. When he excused himself to take his insulin shot, she was happy that she had stayed. Insulin would be a very helpful tool. They ate on the balcony and it was nice but Rae thought of home and wished she were there. She jerked herself back to the present when Morrison poured his third mimosa and asked, "What do you do in Dallas?"

"I'm an unhappy housewife."

"Oh, so you're married."

"Yes, but not for long. I hired a lawyer two weeks ago. Are you married?"

"No, never have found the right woman."

She moved to him and leaned down for a kiss. "Would you like to take a nap with me, say in thirty minutes?"

He smiled and nodded his head. "I'll be there in thirty minutes."

She rushed to her room and checked the refrigerator and liquor cabinet. There was an abundance of champagne and orange juice, just what she needed for mixing a mimosa. She found the pills Morrison had given her. Remembering there might be a hidden camera, she took her overnight case to the bathroom along with her new pajamas. After the shower steamed up the room, she took a small bottle that contained pulverized Valium pills and placed it under a towel. Stephen would have a long nap because she wasn't in the mood for a sexual encounter yet.

After a short shower she hurried to mix two drinks. Carrying one to the bathroom as if she was sipping it, she poured out some of the contents and added the Valium.

When the doorbell rang she met Stephen with a kiss and a drink. They sat on the sofa and chatted while they finished their drinks. Stephen became aggressive and suggested moving to the bed. Rae excused herself to go to the bathroom and when she returned, Morrison was asleep.

Stephen slept until late evening. He awoke intent on resuming where they left off. When Rae pleaded hunger, he relented and went to his suite to get ready for dinner.

While at dinner Rae left the table to go to the restroom hoping there would be a maid in the restroom, and there was. She gave the woman her pager number and a crisp one hundred-dollar bill with instructions to page her at six a.m. She stressed the point that she would likely need her services again and it was very important that she make the call. After going over the instructions one more time, she returned to the dinner table.

After dinner they returned to the Jacks or Better to play poker. Not wanting to burn the guys out too early, Rae lost several pots on purpose. She won enough to be a challenge but didn't walk away with much money. Stephen asked her to his suite for breakfast.

When they finished eating, he took her hand and headed to the bedroom. Rae was greatly relieved when her pager went off. She begged forgiveness and went to her suite to make some phone calls. Rae then called Stephen and told him an emergency had come up with her mother and she had to leave. Morrison was upset but said he understood. Rae promised to call him the next day.

Rae had her plans made for Morrison by the time she got home. All she needed were a couple of vials of insulin. She stopped and called him from a pay phone outside of Dallas. He was pleased to hear from her and asked her to meet him for dinner on Wednesday. She explained that her husband would suspect something so they would have to wait until the weekend.

Home was a welcome sight. She felt as if she had been gone for a month. J. B. ran out to greet her. She petted him and went to the kitchen to get him a treat. He ate his treat and watched as she unloaded the car. When she finished, she sat on the porch and told him about the weekend.

Tuesday Margie and Mrs. Price fussed over her and complimented her on her new hair color. She was almost relieved when the first patient came in.

Lunch-time brought Lori and the babies. Lori wanted to try working half day for a week or two before trying a full day. Rae agreed. At one o'clock there were babies asleep in the back and three women making excuses to check on them. Jake was spending the afternoon with his grandfather.

Rae left Lori in charge of cleaning and went to find a pay phone to call Stephen. He wasn't home so she left a sweet message. I wonder if he really believes all that hogwash, she thought as she walked back to the office. Lori was almost finished so Rae checked her work and said, "You haven't lost your touch. I couldn't have done better myself."

After work she hurried to the grocery store and then home. She planned to change clothes and go for a ride before dark. The cooler weather was very nice, but shorter days meant less time for Maggie. Link wasn't home, which was a disappointment. She brushed Maggie and was saddling her when he walked into the barn and said, "Hi, stranger. How are you?"

"I'm fine, how are you?"

"No complaints. Want some company?"

"Sure."

"I'll saddle up and be right with you."

Link came back in a few minutes leading a pretty sorrel gelding.

"Who is this?"

"This is Sampson. I'm riding him for a friend. Pretty, isn't he?"

"He's beautiful. Is he a cutting horse?"

"No, he is used for team roping and jerk down steer roping. I'm keeping him in shape until John gets back on his feet. He broke his left ankle in a tractor accident last week."

They mounted up and started across the countryside, talking and laughing. Rae could feel the tension drain from her body. Riding was the best stress relief she had ever found, and having Link riding beside her was a great comfort.

He asked her to stay for supper, but she didn't want to be close to him just yet. She needed some space after the weekend with Morrison. Link didn't deserve this but she couldn't change things right now.

Later that evening she sat on the porch and thought about the coming weekend. She needed to act soon because she had a feeling that Stephen didn't want any ties. After a few rolls in the hay, he would tire of her. He was always getting calls or someone was dropping by to conduct business, which made her think the casino was a front for a much bigger operation. For her plan to work, she needed to get him away from Las Vegas.

The week was gone before she knew it, and by Thursday she had a perfect plan for the weekend. She had called Morrison every day and he was peaches and cream. Friday afternoon she called him and told him her husband was acting strange. "I think he smells a mouse, and if so, he will be watching me closely. After next week it won't make any difference, but I must be careful until the papers are served. Ralph knows I go to Vegas so I thought a change might be in order. Would it be possible for you to meet me in Tahoe Saturday?"

"Let me do some checking and see if I can get away. Can you call me back in a couple of hours?"

"Yes, I'll call you at three-thirty, okay?"

"Okay."

She was in the middle of filling a tooth at three-thirty but managed to get to a phone a little before four. He was waiting for her call and was upset because she was late, but said he would be in Lake Tahoe Saturday afternoon. He would reserve a room at Harrah's under the name Bill Smart. After a few sweet nothings and a request that he leave his buddies at home, Rae hung up and went back to work.

She saw one more patient and helped Lori load Jean and Joe to go home. Once everyone left, she gathered the Valium and other supplies she needed.

She hadn't planned to stop at Link's, but changed her mind. She could drive to Dallas later tonight. After talking with Maggie for a while, she watched Link work Zipper in the arena. When she hollered "Got to go, cowboy," Link rode over and kissed her goodbye.

The drive to Dallas enabled her to go over her plans for Morrison. If all went well, she wouldn't be making this trip again for a long time. She reached Dallas around eleven p.m., ready for a good night's sleep and looking forward to tomorrow.

Chapter Eleven

Rae checked and made sure the syringes and needles were secure in the tampon box. A small bottle of pre-prepared smashed Valium and a vial of insulin were hidden in her cleansing cream jar. Now all she needed was opportunity. She left for the airport singing a happy tune.

She arrived at Harrah's and used a pay phone to call Stephen to find out the room number. When she arrived, he greeted her with a kiss.

The door was barely shut when he started devouring her.

"Whoa, how about dinner?" Rae asked.

"We can eat anytime. I'm hungry for you. We'll have something sent up later."

He couldn't keep his hands off her. She moved away from him. "Stephen, I'm hungry! I'll be much more fun if you feed me."

"Okay. What would you like? I'll order while you fix drinks."

"I'd like a T-bone steak, medium rare, and a salad with vinegar and oil dressing."

They ate and chatted. Stephen drank throughout the meal. When they had finished eating, Stephen became amorous again.

Rae played along temporarily, then said, "Let's take a bath in that spacious tub."

"Great idea. I'll mix the drinks," Stephen said.

"I'll mix them. I want to get my bubble bath. You fill the tub."

While Stephen sang in the bathroom, Rae poured a healthy dose of Valium into his drink and gave it a good stir. She carefully wrapped a napkin around each glass, tucked the bottle of bubble bath under her arm and headed to the bathroom. Getting into the tub with him was almost impossible but she did it.

"Pat, you're the best."

"What do you mean?"

"You know how to relax a guy and get him in the mood for a delightful evening."

Rae smiled as she washed his back. When he began to slur his words and slid down in the tub, she said, "Let's go to bed."

She managed to keep him awake long enough to get most of another drink down him. Once he was out, she washed the glass she had used and placed it back on the shelf. Then holding his glass with a napkin, she rinsed it out with Jack Daniels and refilled it.

A check of Morrison's pulse assured her that he was heavily sedated. Rae pulled on latex gloves, unwrapped a syringe and retrieved the vial of insulin. Once the syringe was filled, she opened his mouth, lifted his tongue, and injected the drug into a vein. She located his shaving kit and the bottle of pills she knew would be there, took out all the pills but five and dropped the bottle beside the bed. To be safe, Rae used a towel and wiped the surfaces she might have touched.

She dressed in blue jeans and a sloppy shirt and checked on Morrison again. He was dead. "Enjoy hell," were her last words as she grabbed her bag and left the room. She paused long enough to hang the Do Not Disturb sign on the doorknob.

The early morning flight was on time and left with a happy, but jittery, woman on board. Arriving in Dallas, Rae caught a cab to the hospital where she had left her car. Relieved to be on home ground, she headed for Decker.

Once home she unloaded the car and visited with J. B. She ate a bite but was too wired to sleep so she went for a long walk.

Rae asked J. B., "I wonder when they'll find him? Probably not until Monday. Some of his goons will be looking for Pat Collins, but they won't find her."

Exhaustion finally overcame her and she went to bed. No spirits haunted her so she slept well and was fresh and alert Monday morning. Then she remembered she had the day off. Wonderful! Rae listened to the news while she dressed, but there was no mention of a death in Tahoe. She could spend the day with Maggie and Link.

By ten a.m. she was walking into the barn at Link's ranch. There were all kinds of activities going on. Several men were unloading horses out of trailers. Link was saddling Sampson.

"What's going on?" Rae asked.

"We're bringing the cattle in to be wormed and vaccinated. Want to help?"

"You bet. I'll get Maggie."

"No hurry. I have to get all the supplies loaded. Did you have a good weekend?"

"Oh, it was okay. I'm glad I'm home."

"Me too."

Rae hurried down the hall to get Maggie saddled. She was excited to be part of a big adventure, or it was big to her anyway.

Thirty minutes later four horsemen and one horsewoman rode to the west pasture to begin a day of hard work. She rode beside Link and he filled her in on what they were going to do. She forgot that Stephen Morrison lay decomposing.

The news of Morrison's death reached Decker on Wednesday. Evidently, it was Monday afternoon before anyone checked the room. The news stated it looked like an accidental death caused by mixing drugs and alcohol. However, foul play had not been ruled out. The police were asking anyone with information to please contact them. Fat chance, Rae thought.

Later she heard Lori and Mrs. Price talking. Lori commented, "Morrison makes the third one to die of the five who attacked Jane Hayes. I'm beginning to think this is a little more than coincidence."

"It does seem a bit strange." Mrs. Price agreed. "I wonder if the other two have heard."

Margie bounced in and the conversation ended. Rae entered after Margie, and everyone went back to work. Morrison's name never came up again.

September ended, and October brought cool weather and signs of an early winter. This was perfect weather for horseback riding so Rae rode almost every afternoon.

She rode alone most of the time because Link was fine-tuning Zipper for the National Quarter Horse Show that would be held in Oklahoma City in November.

Rae felt herself slipping into a closer relationship with Link. She realized this was not the thing to do but couldn't help herself. Her deep distrust of men could not keep her from caring for this kind and gentle man. She thought about a home and a family, and told herself to stop. She couldn't marry Link and have a family. She didn't want kids even though she liked Jake and the twins very much. Sure, she might be able to hide the truth for a time, but eventually she would be found out, or the fact she was hiding something would be discovered. Now, how was she going to call this off gracefully? She would wait until after the horse show.

Margie wanted to start college in January. Rae and Lori promised to help her tell her family and then stand by her. Rae placed a sizable amount of money in a trust fund for her, and Lori agreed to oversee the trust. Margie wouldn't have to worry about finances.

Joe and Jean were more active now, and Rae couldn't believe how much she enjoyed them. Just knowing they were going to be at the clinic made going to work more pleasant. Jake came by after school sometimes and made himself at home in Rae's office. Many times she found colored pictures in her desk drawer.

It was the night before they were to leave for the horse show when the demons came. Rae went to bed and dreamed of Link and the trophy he was going to win. Suddenly the faces of Stephen, Thomas, and Dale appeared in place of the faces of the calves. Link was riding Zipper and unaware of the hideous faces looking at him. Then they broke away from the herd and started running toward her. She called for Link, but he didn't hear her. Rae woke wet with sweat and shaking. She changed pajamas and went back to bed, but every time she closed her eyes, the faces appeared. Unable to sleep, she got up, dressed and waited for Link.

They arrived in Oklahoma City about noon and found their way to the fairgrounds where the show was being held. Once Zipper was unloaded and stalled, they left to eat lunch and check into their rooms. Link asked, “Are you sure you won’t stay with me? I promise I’ll be a perfect gentleman.”

“I’m sure you would be, but this is the wrong time of month and I would be uncomfortable.”

“Okay. Are you feeling alright?”

“Just a little tired. I’ll rest while you check on Zipper. Do you mind coming back for me, or would you rather I go with you now?”

“You rest. I’ll pick you up about four.”

Link was to compete at seven that evening so they ate a light dinner and went to the fairgrounds. Rae had never seen so many beautiful horses and riders. She could tell Zipper had his work cut out for him, but there wasn’t a horse that was any prettier than he was. Link walked her to her seat, kissed her for luck, and then returned to get Zipper warmed up and ready to show. The calf roping competition was in progress, and Rae was soon caught up in it.

There were many entries in each event so even though they started early, it was late by the time Link finished. Zipper worked great and they advanced to the next round of competition, which would be held the following day.

She slept that night and was bright and cheery when Link came for her the next morning. Link was quiet as they walked down to breakfast.

Rae asked, “Are you upset with me?”

“Not at all. All things happen in due time, if they’re meant to be. I’m just tickled to death you’re with me.”

They spent the morning walking through the barn and shopping at the various booths around the arena. Rae sat in the stands while Link saddled Zipper for his two o’clock competition.

Zipper worked well and made it to the next round, which would not be until Tuesday evening. Link thought he and Zipper would be happier at home, so they loaded up Sunday and headed for Decker.

Rae didn't return with him Tuesday but promised she would go if he made it to the next step. A jubilant Link called late Tuesday evening to say they had made it to the finals, and he would be home very late but would call her Wednesday.

Everyone was so excited for Link. They all decided to go watch the finals Saturday evening. Rae rode with Link but loaned her car to David so he could drive Mrs. Price and Lori. Jake and the twins were staying with Lori's parents. Rae met them at the grandstand entrance at seven-thirty. The whole clan was going to stay at the Holiday Inn after the show.

Zipper and Link won the reserve champion trophy Saturday night. Rae was disappointed for them, but Link was very pleased. He hadn't expected to do that well. Several people came by to congratulate him, and some wanted to buy Zipper. Link wouldn't even consider selling him. Sunday, the happy crew headed home.

Rae closed the clinic three days for Thanksgiving. She planned to cook and have Link over for Thanksgiving dinner. He never mentioned any family so she assumed he would be alone. The only question he had asked about her family was where her parents lived. She told him they were dead.

Thanksgiving dinner was a big success. They had turkey, dressing, and all the trimmings. Link ate too much so they went for a walk. Then he was hungry and ate again.

That evening they started a fire in the fireplace and talked about horses and ranching.

Friday was a cold sunny day. Braving the cold, they rode out to check the cattle. Their route took them back to the hill where Link wanted to build his dream house. The view was just as beautiful in fall as it was in summer. Rae had never felt such peace and happiness. The rest of the holiday weekend was spent riding and being with Link. All was wonderful until Sunday night.

Happy but tired, Rae went to bed early, but she jerked awake when Jane's voice repeated, "You promised, you promised."

Rae muttered, "I haven't forgotten, I'm just taking a break."

When she drifted back to sleep, the three men she had killed and Jane appeared at the foot of the bed. They were all pointing at her. Unnerved she got up and made a pot of coffee.

"You're right, Jane, I haven't attempted to find Jim Garrett or Jackson Cooper. They haven't been mentioned nor have I seen anything regarding them in the paper. Looks like I'd better get busy."

Margie and Mrs. Price were putting Christmas decorations in the clinic window. Rae helped them for a few minutes and then went to help Lori unload the babies. Jean laughed when Rae picked her up. Rae hugged her close and kissed her little cheek.

Link came by after lunch and played with the babies. He even changed Joe's diaper, which earned him a star with Lori. Rae laughed at his diapering job but praised him for his effort. Before he left, he asked, "Would you like to go Christmas shopping with me this evening?"

"I'd love to. I'll stop by after work."

"See you then."

Quietly, she asked Margie what Lori might need or like for a gift, and then she asked Lori about Mrs. Price. As for Margie, she was taking her shopping Saturday and buying her a new wardrobe to begin her college career. The babies and Jake would be given money for a start on their college fund.

She caused a patient to yelp when she thought about a gift for Link. Apologizing for the pinched lip, she decided she'd better concentrate on the task at hand.

When she stopped by Link's on her way home, she found him waist deep in a mud hole. A water line had burst and he was in the process of fixing it, but he needed a connection. While he dipped water out of the hole, Rae jumped back into the car and headed to town to buy what he needed. Mr. Johnson was locking the door but opened for her. Once she had the connection, she hurried back to Link's.

By the time he finished, Link was wet, cold, and covered with mud.

He asked Rae, "Would you mind getting me a towel?"

"Not at all. You want some dry clothes too?"

"No, I'll rinse off a little and then go in and shower."

When Rae returned, Link had his shirt off and was trying to hold the hose and wash off at the same time.

"Here, let me hold that for you."

When Link turned to hand her the hose, she saw a jagged scar on his right shoulder. Quickly, he turned away.

It was too late to go shopping. After going to see Maggie, she went home to fix supper while Link cleaned up and took care of the animals.

As Rae peeled potatoes and chopped onions for stew she wondered what kind of accident caused such a horrible scar. She wasn't going to ask, even though Link knew she had seen it.

By the time Link arrived, the stew was done and a fire was burning in the fireplace. During dinner the subject of Christmas came up.

"What did you do for Christmas when you were a kid?" Link asked.

"Not much. We spent most of our time at church."

"Did you have a tree and presents?"

"No tree and usually just one gift. How about you?"

"We always had a big tree with lots of decorations and presents. Christmas was a real fun time at our house. Tell you what. Tomorrow we'll cut a tree and decorate it."

"I don't have any decorations."

"I do. You don't worry about a thing. This is going to be fun."

Link left, promising to be back tomorrow so they could go find the perfect tree.

Rae worked hard the next day, anxious to be finished and free to go Christmas tree hunting. She couldn't believe her excitement but allowed herself to enjoy it. To be part of the norm felt good. In the past, Christmas had not been a happy time.

When Mrs. Price went home for lunch, Rae asked Margie, “Would you like to go shopping with Link and me Saturday?”

“I doubt Dad will let me. Besides I really don’t have anything I need to shop for.”

“You already have all your Christmas shopping finished?”

“We don’t celebrate Christmas like most people.”

“Well, you could go just to humor Link and me.”

“You know I love to be with you and Link. I’ll go if Dad will let me.”

It was an overcast dreary afternoon, but Rae forgot about the weather when Link arrived. He greeted her with a big hug. They decided to drive instead of going horseback since it looked like it might rain. They found a small cedar that was well shaped. Link cut it down and put it in the back of the pickup.

Rae was right beside him while he built a stand and attached it to the tree. Later that evening they would decorate it.

They had a wonderful time hanging icicles, ornaments (all horses), and lights on the tree. The final touch was a beautifully wrapped gift with Rae’s name on it. She shook it, turned it over, and begged Link to tell her what it was.

“No,” he refused, “You have to wait until Christmas.”

Picking up her gift when he started to leave, he said, “You’ll have this opened in two seconds if I leave it, so I’d better take it with me.”

“No, I promise I won’t.”

Link put it back under the tree. She hoped she could live up to her promise.

Friday was a hectic day filled with Christmas carols, fussy babies, and lots of patients. When the last patient left, Lori, Rae, and Mrs. Price sat down exhausted. Margie, still full of energy, was excited about going shopping. Rae and Link would pick her up in the morning.

Rae went straight home to fix dinner, expecting Link to call when he finished feeding. He called and said yes to dinner. When he arrived, dinner was ready, a fire burned hospitably in the fireplace, and the Christmas tree was lovely. A perfect setting for a perfect evening.

Saturday, Link joined Rae for coffee before they left to pick up Margie. The three sang Christmas carols all the way to Dallas. Margie's beautiful voice reminded Rae of Jane and depressed her momentarily.

Margie was first on the list to shop for and was the highlight of the day. She was so appreciative and excited, Link had tears in his eyes. Rae spent more than she intended, but Margie was worth every penny.

Next was Link, so Rae had Margie lure him away while she bought his gifts. After lots of looking, she picked out a leather jacket and a pair of lizard boots. Margie returned without Link, saying he would meet them at the car in an hour. That gave Rae time to have his gifts wrapped and shop for Lori and Mrs. Price. She was glad Margie was there to help her because she had no idea what to buy.

After stowing their purchases in the trunk, the three shoppers walked down the street singing and trying to find a restaurant. Margie started singing "Silver Bells" and everyone on the street stopped to listen. She finished the song and received a hearty round of applause. Many of the listeners remarked on her beautiful voice. Rae began to doubt she would be a dentist, but that didn't matter as long as she went to school.

They dropped Margie off at home but kept her new clothes for her. Margie didn't like hiding things from her parents, but she realized her father wouldn't let her keep the gifts.

Link had hired a neighbor to feed so he wouldn't have to hurry home, but he stopped by the barn to check on a sick mare. The mare was better, and all the other animals seemed quite content, so the weary travelers went home to spend a quiet evening in front of the fireplace.

While Link gathered kindling and logs for the fire, Rae went to change into something more comfortable.

When she returned, Link had a small fire going and was slowly adding more wood. Rae grabbed a couple of pillows and a throw from the sofa and put them on the floor in front of the fireplace.

Once the fire was going well, Link pulled off his boots and stretched out bcsidc Rae. For several minutes they lay without talking, then Link gently pulled Rae to him so that she lay in his arms with her back against his chest. Tenderly he massaged her arms and caressed her face.

At first she was nervous and thought to herself, Find an excuse and get up. Then as if this were the most natural thing in world, she began to want more.

Rae turned to face Link and welcomed his kiss. He kissed her lips, her cheeks, her eyelids, her neck, causing her to hold her breath and hope this feeling wouldn't go away. Where were these feelings coming from? She had best get up before she lost control.

When Link's tongue sought hers, she responded. Without asking, he slipped his hand under her shirt and massaged her back. Ever so slowly he made his way forward until he reached her abdomen. When he touched the smooth area beneath her breasts she was unprepared for the sensation she felt. Her skin tingled and goose bumps popped up all over her.

Anticipation held her spellbound as Link's hand moved to her breast. Should she remove her bra? As if he read her mind, he reached behind her and released her now taut breasts. She had been touched, but never like this.

She gasped as Link's mouth sought and found her nipple. Rae was on fire all over. "Don't stop, please don't stop," she begged as her hands roamed over Link's body. Her fingers traveled through the hair on his chest and played with his nipples.

Clothes flew in all directions. When Link slipped his hand between her thighs, she experienced a stirring in her loins that demanded attention. Boldly, she grasped him.

Link said, "I don't have any protection, but I promise I don't have any diseases."

Rational thinking was gone. Rae simply said, "I believe you," and without further hesitation, guided him to her. Link gasped as he drove deeply into her and felt her tightness. In a frenzy she wrapped her legs around his hips and arched her back to better accommodate him. It was a strong and lengthy coupling that ended with Rae withering in delight and Link lying spent with her wrapped in his arms.

Later, when they had the energy, they showered and went to bed. Most of the night was spent talking and loving.

Rae couldn't believe the joy she was experiencing. Now she understood why people in love made complete fools of themselves. She spent the day looking forward to seeing Link. She kept telling herself that this had to stop but made no attempt to change.

Mrs. Price talked Rae and Link into going to the Christmas program with her. Rae managed to stay through "O Holy Night" this time. Margie truly had a gift, and Rae found herself wishing she would seek a career in music.

Christmas morning, Link got up before Rae and started a fire in the fireplace. He was making coffee when she bounded into the kitchen. "I can't stand it any longer. Let's open presents."

Rae didn't know what to say when she unwrapped a box to find a beautiful western suit. Her next gift was a pair of boots. The gift that had plagued her for so long was a pair of leather riding gloves. Link loved his leather jacket and boots.

Together they fixed breakfast, ate, and cleaned up the kitchen. Then they went to the barn to feed the horses and give them their Christmas treats.

The holidays were fun, but Rae was ready to get back to work. Margie was getting nervous about going to school but was determined to go through with her plans. Rae and Lori constantly reassured her they would always be on standby.

Link and Rae were very happy. Rae kept reminding herself that she needed to slow things down, but couldn't seem to do it. She knew that Link wanted marriage and a family. She couldn't make that commitment and knew the day would come when she would have to hurt him.

Jane began visiting Rae to remind her that she wasn't keeping her pledge. Rae was plagued by her inability to locate Jim Garrett and Jackson Cooper. She was happy and enjoying life and didn't want to change, but knew she must.

The Friday after Christmas, Rae took Jake with her to see Maggie and Link. Link wasn't home so Rae and Jake brushed Maggie and then Rae took Jake home. Lori was busy fixing supper. Rae sat at the table and visited with her while she cooked. "What do you think about closing the clinic during spring break and doing some cleaning and rearranging?" Rae asked.

"I think that's a great idea. Exactly what do you have in mind?"

"I think we should paint the reception room and maybe wallpaper one wall, clean the carpets, and give all the dental equipment a good scrubbing. Can we do all of that in one week?"

"Let's get Margie to come home and help. She'll probably be on spring break. I'd love for her to stay with us. She's such a great kid."

"Sounds like a good plan to me. Let's do it."

Rae got up to leave saying, "I'd better get home and feed J.B.," but was distracted by a crying baby. She followed Lori to the nursery. Jean was asleep but Joe was fussing. Lori scooped Joe up and hurried from the room before he woke Jean.

Noticing a yearbook on the coffee table, Rae picked it up and began thumbing through it. She was shocked when she saw a picture of herself and Jane in the group of seniors.

Taking the book, she walked back to the kitchen where Lori was warming a bottle for Joe. Lori laughed when she saw Rae with the yearbook.

"David dragged that out last night to show Jake what we looked like when we were young. You can have a barrel of laughs looking at it."

"Let's see if I can find you without looking at the names. Is this you with short hair and wearing a pink sweater?"

"Yep, that's me."

Rae looked for Jackson and Jim Garrett. She found Jackson but there wasn't a senior picture of Jim. As she searched, she tried to recall what he looked like. What she remembered most was that he had a gap between his front teeth, light brown hair and hazel eyes. She was looking through the sports section when she saw a picture of the track team. Jim Garrett was a member of the team and qualified for state in the mile. A close up of him in his tracksuit revealed a large scar on his right shoulder. She almost dropped the book when she recalled that Link had a scar on his right shoulder.

Placing the yearbook on the table, she said, "I've got to get going. I'll see you Monday."

Chapter Twelve

The drive home was a blur. She couldn't believe Link was Jim Garrett. There just was no way Link could be a rapist. It was possible that two people could have a scar in the same place. Not likely, but possible.

He couldn't be Jim Garrett. Link didn't have a mean bone in his body, plus there was no gap between his teeth. The scar had to be a coincidence. She would do some checking and see what she could find out about Link's past. Her mind wouldn't rest until she knew he was innocent.

She asked herself, "Where and how do I begin? Maybe I should start at the high school. I'll have to think of some way to get into the old records without asking questions. There's never been any mention that Link went to school here. I have to be wrong."

Rae was a nervous all weekend. Link had gone to a horse sale, thank goodness. It was going to be hard to act normal around him until this was settled. How could she check him out without causing suspicion? Monday morning she went to work feeling like she hadn't slept at all.

Mrs. Price met her at the door, took one look, and said, "Honey, have you had another headache?"

"Yes, as a matter of fact I have. Do I look bad?"

"Well, you don't look good. Let me get you a cup of coffee, maybe that will help."

"Thanks, I'm sure it will."

She made it through the day but was too tired to go by and see Maggie. Actually she didn't know how she would react if she saw Link. Staying calm and acting natural was the only way to deal with this. Someway she would find out about Link. She had to come up with a plan.

The voice began about two o'clock the next morning. First there was just a lot of confusion and then Jane spoke, saying, "You are smarter than Link. Go to his house and find what you need. Just think you were considering marriage to a rapist. I've told you all along to stay away from him."

"Okay, okay, I'll see what I can find. Leave me alone and let me sleep."

Rae suffered through the long day and was afraid there would be more. She was very tired but stopped by to see Maggie.

Link met her with a hug and a kiss. "I've missed you. How are you?"

"I'm fine, just a little tired. How are you?"

"Oh, I'm fine. Getting ready to go to a show this weekend. You interested?"

"I'm always interested in what you and Zipper are doing, but I'd better stay home and catch up on my domestic chores."

"If you'll go, I'll help you when we get back."

"You're sweet, but I'll stay and take care of things around here and at home."

"Sure you want to feed? I can call Clyde."

"I'll be happy to feed for you. How's Maggie?"

"She's fine."

Rae knew Link was confused when she didn't ask him over for dinner and to spend the night. She gave a lame excuse about a meeting and being tired. Link kissed her good-bye and said, "I'll see you tomorrow."

Rae was certain that this man could not be one of the five. The scar was a fluke. She would find out for sure this weekend and prove Jane wrong.

The rest of the week was horrible. Rae avoided Link and wracked her brain trying to come up with a plan. Lori and Mrs. Price both cautioned Rae that she needed to go to the doctor but she refused. Little did they know that she was on a mission and that was all she could think about. She was so distracted that she wasn't doing a good job on her patients.

Lori finally questioned her, "Rae what's wrong? You're not yourself. Are you ill? Can I help?"

"I don't seem to have much energy. I'll rest this weekend."

"Rae, come stay with me this weekend and let me fix you some of my magic soup."

"Thanks, Mrs. Price, but I'll be fine."

Saturday morning Rae drove to Link's. She met him at the end of the driveway.

"I'm sorry I forgot to tell you that I'd have time to feed this morning."

"That's okay. I want to see Maggie anyway. Have a good trip and bring home the gold."

"Thanks. We'll do our best. I'll call you when I get home. Honey, are you okay? I've hardly seen you this week and I sure miss you. If I've done something wrong, please tell me so I can fix it."

"You haven't done anything wrong. We'll talk when you get back. Be careful."

Rae walked to the barn. Better give him some time. He may have forgotten something. After thirty minutes had passed, she went to the house. The extra key was in its usual place. Once inside, she wasn't sure where to start.

The office seemed like the logical place. Pulling on surgical gloves, Rae started sorting through papers, but found nothing incriminating. Noticing an address book, she scanned through the alphabet, nothing under Garrett or Wood.

After searching the desk, Rae went to Link's bedroom. A search of his dresser revealed nothing but the fact that Link was a very neat cowboy. From the dresser, she went to the closet and there she found a safe, which, unfortunately, was locked. I bet the combination is here somewhere, but where? She looked in all the places she thought it might be but didn't find anything.

Rae removed the gloves and stuck them into her pocket. She shut the door, made sure it was locked, turned to leave, and ran right into Link.

"What are you doing here?" Rae blurted.

"I was about to ask you the same thing. Are you okay? You look like you've seen a ghost."

Rae started to laugh. "You just surprised me. I had to borrow your bathroom. I hope you don't mind."

Link laughed. "Of course I don't mind."

"What are you doing back so soon?"

"I had a flat on the trailer and had to unload Zipper before I could change the tire. Evidently, he lost a shoe in the trailer so rather than risk crippling him, I came home.

"Is he okay?"

"He'll be fine as soon as Tom comes out and puts the shoe back on."

"Will you have time to make it to the show?"

"No, I'm going to call and withdraw."

"That's too bad."

"Just part of the game."

Glancing at her watch, Rae said, "I'm not getting my cleaning done, so I'd better get going."

"Want some help? I'm a good cleaner."

"I know you are, but I can handle it. I'll call you later."

Rae was sweating by the time she got in the car. Man, that was close, she thought. I'm not sure he was convinced that I had to go to the bathroom. The stool lid is probably up and he'll know I was lying.

She went to work cleaning house. Link called while she was waiting for the kitchen floor to dry so she could wax.

"Could a guy interest you in going out to dinner?"

"Yes, but I'm too tired and I'm a mess."

"We could grab a burger, bring it home and watch a movie."

"Sounds like a plan to me, if you'll pick up the burgers and movie and bring them here."

"You got it. I'll see you in a bit. Any special movie you'd like to see?"

"No, you choose."

Rae stood with the phone in her hand, wondering why in the world she had agreed. What was she thinking? Or was she thinking at all?

Maybe I'll just casually ask the combination to the safe or make things simple and ask if he's also known as Jim Garrett? This is going to drive me crazy. I have to find out.

By the time Link walked in with a bag of burgers, fries, and drinks, Rae had showered and changed clothes.

"Boy, the house looks great and smells nice. You've been working hard."

"Yes, I have and my body knows it."

They moved to the coffee table to spread out the food. When everything was ready, Link started the movie. Food and entertainment took the place of conversation so they quietly ate and watched the movie.

When Link moved to take her in his arms, she slid away from him saying, "I'm not in the mood."

"Honey, I only want to hold you. Why are you so uptight?"

"I have a lot on my mind. Everything will be okay in a day or two. Can you bear with me until then?"

"Sure. Give me a kiss and I'll get out of your hair."

"I guess I can manage a kiss, maybe two."

Sunday morning was dismal. The cold cloudy day made Rae restless. She paced for a while then put on her coat and headed to town. The clinic needed a good cleaning.

She spent the day cleaning and going through her inventory. While she was busy, she came up with a plan to check Jim Garrett's high school records. She would give it a try first thing in the morning.

Instead of going to the clinic Monday morning, Rae drove to the high school. When the bell rang, she entered the principal's office and said hello to Susan Day, the secretary. "Hi, Doctor Roberts, how can I help you?"

"Well, if possible, I would like a copy of Margie Tucker's transcript. I'm applying for a scholarship for her at the University of Florida where I graduated. This will be a surprise for her if she qualifies."

While they were talking, students began to line up, waiting to talk with Mrs. Day.

"I'll be glad to get Margie's records for you if you'll give me thirty minutes."

"Actually, I need them now because I have to get them in the mail this morning. The application form must have gotten lost in the mail because I didn't receive it until Friday."

"Just a minute and I'll help you."

Mrs. Day left the room but returned shortly with another lady.

"Mrs. Anson, this is Doctor Roberts. Doctor Roberts needs a copy of Margie Tucker's records. Would you mind opening the vault?"

"Do you have a release from Margie or her parents?"

"No, I didn't have time and this is a surprise for Margie. I hoped to be able to send in all the information without her knowledge. A scholarship would make things easier for her."

"We can't give out personal records without consent from the person. I'm sure that you understand our position, Doctor."

"Yes, of course."

"Oh, Edith, you know Margie wouldn't object. I'll handle this if you'll help the students."

"Okay, I'll take care of the front."

"Come on, Doctor."

Rae and Susan walked behind the desk into a room joining the principal's office.

"Here we go," Susan said as she opened the door to a steel vault. Looking around she selected one of many large books that contained records of former students.

They were flipping through to Margie's name when Mrs. Anson came to the door. "Susan, Mrs. Jones is here and she refuses to talk with anyone but you."

"Oh no! She can be a real problem. Stay with me, Edith."

"Okay. We'll just be a minute, Doctor Roberts."

"Go ahead. I'll be just fine."

The minute they left, Rae found the year she graduated and flipped to Jim Garrett's name. The name listed was James L. Garrett. He had transferred from Fresno, California, and was an average student. The only other thing she noticed was his birth date.

When Susan returned, Rae was patiently waiting.

"Here we go," she said as she found the page with Margie's information on it. Now let's go make you a copy."

"Thanks so much."

"No problem. Margie was always one of my favorites. She deserves the very best, as far as I'm concerned."

Rae left the office with a copy of Margie's grades and not much else. Besides not getting any information on Jim Garrett, she was late for her first appointment.

Mrs. Price met her at the door saying, "Mr. Harkey is not happy."

"I don't blame him," was all Rae said as she pulled on her lab coat and mask.

"Hello, Mr. Harkey. I'm sorry I'm late. I've had one of those horrible mornings where everything went wrong. Have you ever had one of those?"

"Not often, but yes, I've had them. I'm just worried that I'll be late to an important meeting that is scheduled for ten."

"I'll have you there on time or you won't have to pay me. How's that?"

"Sounds fair to me."

Mr. Harkey paid before he left.

Weeks went by and Rae still was no closer to finding the combination to the safe. She had checked in the tack room and horse trailer but had no luck. It was probably obvious and she was just overlooking it.

Link continued to be attentive and affectionate and, even though he didn't say anything, she knew he was confused. They hadn't had sex since she saw the picture of Jim Garrett in the yearbook. She missed him and wanted their old relationship back. Maybe she would find some answers soon.

The coming of spring was a welcome change. Rae walked to the March Kiwanis meeting. She was unprepared for the rain that blew in as she started back to the clinic. All she could find was a newspaper to hold over her head. When she opened the door, Sheriff Davis spoke from behind her.

"Hey, Doc, can I give you a ride?"

She didn't like him, but she also didn't like the thought of getting soaked, so she said, "Thanks, I'll take you up on the offer."

"Stay right here and I'll bring the car around."

He pulled the car right in front of the building and got out carrying an umbrella. Rae was escorted to the car without getting even a little wet. Once in the car, she asked questions about all the gadgets. Sheriff Davis was happy to explain in full detail what everything was for. When they arrived at the clinic, he got out and walked her to the door.

"Thanks, Sheriff. I appreciate your kindness."

"You're most welcome. Call on me anytime."

As he turned to walk away, Rae called out, "Hey, Sheriff, could I ride around with you sometime when you're working?"

"You bet. I'd enjoy your company. Give me a call and I'll pick you up."

Rae was wondering why she had come up with that hare-brained idea when Lori brought in Mrs. Palmer. Work put Sheriff Davis on the back burner.

Friday, when Rae left the clinic, Sheriff Davis was parked outside.

"Hey, Doc, want to go for a ride?" he asked from the car window.

"Maybe a short one. I'm pretty beat." Rae got into the car asking, "What's up?"

"Nothing, but something could happen any minute. I live life on the edge."

Rae laughed and said, "I've noticed that you are always in peril."

They cruised around the countryside for about twenty minutes without a call coming in.

"Well, Sheriff, it's been fun, but I'd better get home and check on my dog."

"Would you have dinner with me?"

"No thanks. Don't you go home for dinner?"

"Sometimes. Depends on my mood."

Deciding to change the subject, Rae asked, "What kind of shotgun is this?"

"A sawed off twelve gauge pump." He pointed to a nearby building and said, "One shot could blow a good sized hole in that wall."

"Do you use it often?"

"No, but it's a comfort to have it handy."

When they pulled up to Rae's car, Sheriff Davis said, "Maybe next time we'll have some excitement."

"Maybe so. Thanks for the ride."

Rae drove home wondering what she was doing, but convinced she would find a use for Sheriff Davis. He was charming, handsome, and entertaining. She knew, of course, what he was after, but that wouldn't happen.

The first warm Saturday, Link called Rae and asked, "Want to ride with me and help check fences?"

"I'll be there in ten minutes."

"Better bring a coat and your gloves. The weather may change before we get through."

"Okay. Do you want me to fix some sandwiches or something?"

"I have our lunch packed and a canteen of water so get your pretty self over here."

Rae could hardly wait to climb into the saddle. She had ridden some during the winter but only short trips.

They enjoyed a wonderful day, and again Rae tried to push thoughts of Jim Garrett from her mind. She told herself to drop Garrett for now and look for Jackson Cooper. So far she hadn't heard one thing about him.

Link didn't ask her out Saturday night, which was a relief in a way. She couldn't blame him if he was seeing someone else. He probably had a date with Karen, or he might call and ask to come over later.

Link didn't call Saturday night. Sunday morning Rae went to see Maggie and check to see if he was home. He wasn't and the horses hadn't been fed. That meant he had stayed out all night. Rae fed the horses and was cleaning Maggie's stall when he came in.

"Good morning. You're up early," he said.

"Hi. I want to ride if it warms up enough. I'm afraid if I don't, I'll be sore tomorrow."

"Good thinking. I'd join you but I have to take Zipper and get his shoes reset. Hey, thanks for feeding. You didn't need to do that."

"No problem," Rae answered as she brushed and curried Maggie.

Link left the barn and went to the house. When he returned a little later, Rae noticed he had shaved and changed clothes. He led Zipper from his stall and loaded him in the trailer. Coming back to the barn door, he said, "Be careful if you go riding. I'll call you tonight."

"I'll be careful. Bye."

When Link left, Rae headed for the house. She locked the front door, and then went to the kitchen and unlocked the back door and screen. If he should return while she was in the house she could sneak out the back without him seeing her. Once that was done, she went into the bedroom. He had forgotten his wallet. It was lying on the dresser. There wasn't much in it except his driver's license, credit cards, and some cash. She wrote down his birth date and license number, and then locked the back door and went out the front. He might return to get his wallet.

She was saddling Maggie when she heard his truck coming up the driveway. As she rode out of the paddock, he was coming out of the house.

"I forgot my wallet. Now I'm going to be late. See you."

"Be careful."

Another close call, but he should be gone for a while now. Just to be safe, she rode in the arena for fifteen or twenty minutes. Then she took Maggie back to the barn and tied her in the hallway.

Her heart was racing as she went back to the house to try the safe. Once again she locked the front door and unlocked the back door. Pulling on latex gloves, she went to the safe. She reached to clear the lock when she remembered that to save time people sometimes dialed in the first two numbers so they only had to turn to the last one. The dial was setting on five so she would make sure to return it to that position. If Link did have it set maybe he would just think he messed up.

She tried three-seven-one first, and then three-seven-zero, which were numbers in his birth date. When those numbers didn't work, she tried his license number forward and backward. None of the combinations worked. Maybe she should try left, right, left, instead of right, left, right.

That didn't work either. Leaving the dial on five, Rae went back to the barn.

Maggie nickered as Rae approached. She didn't like to be tied when she could be in her stall eating hay. Rae unsaddled her and led her back to her stall. She was walking from the barn when Link drove in.

"Did you go for a ride?" he asked.

"Yes. Is Zipper okay?"

"He'd better be. We have three shows coming up soon, plus maybe a new girlfriend."

"I thought you weren't going to breed any more mares."

"I wasn't until I saw this mare. She is perfect, and I get part ownership of the foal. Even better, I get to train and show the youngster."

"Sounds like a great deal. When is all this going to happen?"

"As soon as she comes in. I'm going back over next week to take Zipper's papers. You want to go with me and meet a beautiful lady?"

"Yes. I'd best check this new gal out."

"I'll give you a call."

"Great, I'll be waiting. See you later."

"How about dinner tonight?"

"Okay."

"I'll pick you up at seven."

"I'll be ready."

Rae and Link had a good time Sunday evening. Link lingered at the door when he took her home. Rae kissed him good night but didn't invite him in.

Sometime in the night, Jane appeared at the foot of Rae's bed. Gone was the blank stare. Her eyes sparkled with life, but the determined look on her face told Rae she was not happy. Rae reached for her but Jane backed away saying, "You've forgotten your pledge." Before Rae could speak, Morrison appeared. In his cocky manner, he said, "I can't believe you're letting your sister down." Jane linked arms with Morrison as if they were best friends. Rae spent the rest of the night struggling with what she needed to do to appease Jane.

Monday afternoon Rae left the clinic with thoughts of a long nap. She was almost to her car when someone said, "Hey, Doc, got time for a ride?"

She turned to see Sheriff Davis parked across the street.

"Sure," Rae said as she walked to his car.

They were cruising around when a call came in about a domestic disturbance. Rae was excited until they arrived on the scene where two police officers were trying to subdue a large man. He was throwing them around like rag dolls. Sheriff Davis joined the brawl and the three, finally, managed to get him on the ground and handcuffed.

When the sheriff came back to the car, Rae asked, "Are you all right?"

"I've got a few bruises, but I'll survive. We always have a fight on our hands when Alice calls for help. Thank heavens, Brett doesn't drink very often."

"What did he do?"

"He got drunk and slapped Alice, that's his wife. She won't file charges so we'll have to let him go. At least we can keep him until he sobers up. He'll be fine for months then go on another binge. This has been going on for years."

"Alice must be pretty tough."

Sheriff Davis laughed and said, "She's about half your size, but quite a fighter. The time she slapped old Brett upside the head with a ball bat once, knocked him out cold, I thought he might straighten up, but he didn't."

They headed back toward the clinic. Rae asked, "Do you ever get a day off?"

"Yes, I take Tuesday afternoon and evening off. I only take calls on my private line. No dispatchers, no sirens, and no radios."

"What do you do?"

"I fish or work on one of my antique cars."

"Do you live in town?"

"No, I live about two miles north of you."

"It's nice to know you live close."

"Feel free to visit anytime."

"What does your wife do?"

"Ruth's a hair stylist and bingo fanatic. She always plays on Tuesday so I'm footloose and fancy free."

He handed her a card and a pen. "Here, write down my number in case you need to call me."

"Thanks, I'll do that."

The phone was ringing when Rae walked through the door. She wasn't going to answer, but then changed her mind. It was Link with good news.

"Come see the new foal that was born this morning. He's a dandy."

Rae was a sucker for a baby of any kind, "I'll change and be right there."

The colt was black, just like his father Zipper. Link was strutting around like he was the father. Rae suggested that he name the baby Clothespin or Button. Link was leaning toward Snap or Velcro.

"Would you like something to drink?" Link asked.

"I'd love a glass of water."

They walked to the house. Link brought Rae her water and sat down across the table from her.

Completely out of the blue, he said, "Rae, will you marry me?"

She was so shocked she didn't know what to say. Finally, when she came to her senses, she said, "I'm not ready to get married. I care for you more than anyone I've ever known, but I need more time."

"Okay, I'll wait. It's just that, at times, you seem so distant."

"I know. I'm a strange bird."

Rae didn't get much sleep that night. Jane visited and insisted that Rae get to work on finding out about Link. Every time Rae closed her eyes, there was Jane or Link. She was almost glad when the alarm went off.

Friday morning Sheriff Davis stopped by the clinic. Rae agreed to speak with him between patients.

"Doc, I have a prisoner with an awful toothache. Will you see him?"

"Sure. Talk with Mrs. Price and have her arrange a time for you to bring him in this afternoon."

"Thanks, Doc."

Mr. Robbins and Sheriff Davis came in just before closing time that afternoon. Rae examined him and found that he had a badly infected tooth plus a gum disease. She wrote him a prescription for an antibiotic and treated his gums. When she finished, she spoke with Sheriff Davis.

"I'll pull that tooth as soon as he's over the infection. It's pretty bad so I'd better write him a prescription for a painkiller. Will someone see that he takes his medicine properly?"

"Yes, we're all pretty fond of Judd. He's a frequent visitor. Thanks, Doc."

"You're welcome."

Rae left the office, looking forward to rest and relaxation for a couple of days.

Chapter Thirteen

Saturday morning Rae ate breakfast, drove to the clinic, and gathered the items she needed to treat Mr. Robbins' gums.

Sheriff Davis wasn't in, but one of the deputies took Rae to see her patient. He was feeling better. Rae treated his gums and supplied him with toothbrushes, floss, and toothpaste. When she finished, she reminded him to continue his antibiotics.

She was chatting with the deputy and gathering her supplies when Sheriff Davis walked in.

"Hi, Doc. I didn't know you made house calls."

"Only in certain situations," Rae replied.

"While you're here, would you mind signing some forms so we can pay you?"

"No problem."

Rae followed the sheriff into his office and sat down while he searched through his desk. He had just found the forms, when the phone rang.

"Excuse me," he said as he picked up the receiver.

"This is Sheriff Davis." After a couple of minutes he said, "How can I help you, Captain Stone?"

Rae almost fell out of her chair. Maybe it was another Captain Stone.

"Yes, I remember the case. Terrible thing to happen to a young girl."

"Yes, I heard she disappeared and the sister committed suicide. No, there hasn't been anyone show up here that looks like Jane Hayes. Her mother thinks she's still alive? You're just trying to ease her mind. I see. No, there wasn't anything suspicious about Smith's or Snodgrass's death.

"I heard about Stephen Morrison on the news. He wasn't what you would call an upstanding citizen. I'm not sure where the other two are that were supposedly involved.

Last I heard, Jackson Cooper married Tom Snodgrass's first cousin and lives in Argentina. I have no idea what happened to Garrett. If I see anyone who looks like Jane Hayes, I'll contact you first thing... No problem, Captain."

Rae had sat calmly through the entire conversation, but her heart was beating twice its normal rate, and she could feel the moisture under her arms and between her breasts. She wanted to jump up and run from the room. Instead she asked, "Do I sign all three?"

"Yep, one's never enough for City Hall."

Somehow she managed to sign her name. "Well, I'd better get. Have a good day, Sheriff."

"You too."

Rae thought she would never get to her car. When she reached for her keys she dropped them. Once in the car her hands started shaking and her legs felt like butter. She drove to the clinic, went inside, dropped everything on her desk and sank into her chair. After a few deep breaths, she got control of herself and began to think rationally. There was no way Captain Stone could have a clue about her or what happened to Snodgrass, Morrison, and Smith. I just have to continue to plan carefully and leave no evidence, she thought.

Back in control, Rae got up to leave. She was almost to the door when she noticed Sheriff Davis turning the corner. She went out the back door and down the street to the café. He was becoming a pest.

After a cup of coffee, Rae walked back to her car. She went to Link's. Nothing cleared her head like a long ride across the countryside.

But today was an exception. What-ifs tormented her all afternoon, beginning with what if Captain Stone came to Decker? What if Sheriff Davis realized that she was a newcomer and close to the same age Jane Hayes would be? What if Link was Jim Garrett and she had to carry out her promise?

That evening she did laundry and cleaned the house, which left her physically exhausted but she couldn't sit still. She went back to Link's. He wasn't home so she went to the barn and began cleaning tack. When she left the barn early the next morning, the tack room was spotless.

A glass of wine and a hot bath did the trick. She was still asleep when Sheriff Davis called Sunday morning.

He greeted her with, "Hi, Doc sorry to bother you but Judd's carrying on something awful."

"No bother, I'd better come in and see what's going on."

After the exam, Rae determined that the infection wasn't responding to the antibiotics.

"I think he needs to be in the hospital so we can get an IV going and get this infection under control."

Sheriff Davis put Robbins into the car and took him to the hospital. Rae followed and discussed his case with the doctor on duty. It was twelve o'clock by the time she left the hospital.

Not sure what she wanted to do, she went by Lori's to see the kids. They weren't home. To make matters worse, it was clouding up, which meant she couldn't ride that afternoon. She spent the afternoon cleaning out closets and dresser drawers.

Sunday night she dreamed Captain Stone arrested her and threw her into the cell with Robbins. Morrison and Snodgrass laughed at her and called her stupid. Jane paid her bail so she could go on with her promise. Monday was a long day.

Link called Tuesday and asked Rae to go with him to see the paint mare Wednesday. They agreed to meet at the clinic, since going home would be out of the way. Rae took a change of clothes with her to work Wednesday morning and was ready when Link came by.

Link asked, "Did you have a good day?"

"Not bad. How about you?"

"Good day. Wait until you see the baby that was born this morning."

"Another foal?"

"Yep, a little filly, and she's a beauty."

"Is she black?"

"No. She's a bay like Maggie."

"Then she has to be pretty."

They had driven about an hour when Link turned onto a blacktopped road. Large pecan trees lined the road leading to a beautiful colonial style house.

"This is quite a place," Rae said.

"Yes it is. Wait until you see the barns."

There were several large barns, but Link drove to the long one in the middle. The barn was immaculate and filled with horse stalls. Mr. Lucas met them and gave Rae a guided tour of the facility. They ended the tour at the stall housing a gorgeous gray mare. She was every bit as pretty as Zipper.

"Oh, what a pretty baby they'll have," were the first words out of Rae's mouth.

While Mr. Fred Lucas and Link discussed bloodlines and breeding, Rae looked at pictures and awards that lined the office walls. They were getting ready to leave when she noticed Zipper's registration papers on the desk. She picked them up and asked Link, "Do you need these?"

"Yes, thanks."

As she handed them to him, she noticed the registration number. The first three digits were 941. She knew immediately that she had the combination to the safe.

The ride home was a blur. She tried to act excited about the foal that would arrive next year, but she could only think about getting to the safe.

Link asked, "Is something wrong?"

She replied, "No, I think I'm just tired and hungry."

"We'll stop at the first place I can find. I'm sorry I took so much time with Lucas."

Rae was more sociable after eating. She told Link goodnight and promised to see him the next day.

Rae stopped by Link's the next morning on the pretense of seeing the new Maggie look-alike. She was really checking Link's schedule so she could get into the house, but he didn't seem to have plans to be away anytime soon.

Sheriff Davis brought Robbins in Friday afternoon so Rae could pull his tooth.

As they started to leave, the sheriff asked, "Want to chase bad guys with me when you get off work?"

"Can I wear a gun?" Rae asked.

"I don't think so."

"Well, maybe I can turn on the siren."

"Now, that you can do."

Rae found herself looking forward to riding around, chasing bad guys. She was a bit disappointed when nothing exciting happened. After about thirty minutes, she asked the sheriff to take her back to her car.

Saturday morning she went to Link's hoping he might be gone. He was keeping a close eye on a mare that was in labor. Rae groomed Maggie and cleaned her stall. She headed home, wondering if she was ever going to get a chance at the safe.

Link called later to report the birth of a stud colt and to ask her out to dinner. Rae accepted the invitation if they could go to Roy's Steak House. She knew it was Link's favorite place to eat.

The phone rang early Sunday morning and Rae answered with, "This had better be important."

"Is a sick mare important enough?" Link asked.

"Who's sick?"

"Jessie. She seems very uncomfortable and won't eat. She isn't due to foal for another three weeks. I think I'd better get her in for an ultrasound. Do you mind feeding for me?"

"Not a bit. I'll be over shortly."

"Doc's waiting at the clinic, so I shouldn't be gone more than an hour or two."

"No hurry, just take care of Jessie."

Rae dressed in jeans and a sweatshirt. The digits 9, 4, 1 ran through her mind as she picked up a pair of latex gloves.

"Should I feed first or go for the safe," she asked herself as she headed out the door.

Link was gone when she got to the ranch, so she headed for the safe. I can always make up an excuse for being late with the feeding, but I wouldn't be able to explain going through his safe.

She pulled on latex gloves, cleared the lock then turned the dial right to nine. Turning to the left, she passed four the first time, but stopped on it the second time around.

Last she turned back right to one. Holding her breath, she turned the handle. The door opened. Exhaling softly, she sat back on her heels and peered inside.

Carefully, she sorted through papers making sure she kept them in order. She was almost to the bottom of the stack when she saw something near the back. Her heart stopped and sweat ran from her face as she picked up the locket. Tears pooled in her eyes but didn't fall until she opened it and saw the images of herself and Jane. Jane was wearing the locket the evening of the attack. Tears began to fall as she replaced the locket and then the papers.

She had to get out of the house before she threw up. Once out the door and away from the house, she regurgitated until there was nothing left. Weak and sick at heart, she slumped to the ground and leaned her head against a fence post.

"I tried to tell you", Jane's voice said. "Now what are you going to do? You're always talking about revenge, let's see some action. Are you too chicken to keep your promise? Do you love him more than me?"

Rae pulled herself up and walked to the barn. A slow burning anger crept through her as she methodically filled feed buckets. When she thought about having sex with Link, who might be Jim Garrett, she got sick at her stomach again. Well, he would pay big time for that roll in the hay. She knew what she must do, but how to do it was the puzzle. A plan would come if she gave it time.

When she finished the chores at the barn, she left Link a note saying she needed to run some errands. She didn't want to see him for fear of what she might do or say. He must not suspect that she knew about his past.

Rae spent the rest of the morning sitting on the porch. Her mind was spinning in a dozen different directions. It was hard to believe that Link was capable of rape, but the evidence was in his possession. Maybe he found the locket or someone gave it to him. Just having it didn't prove that he was Jim Garrett. She should have dug a little deeper. The locket threw her off guard.

"Well, I guess it's back to the safe to finish what I started," she told herself.

Link called later to thank her for feeding.

"How's Jessie?" Rae asked.

"She's going to be fine, just a little touch of colic. Doc cleaned her out good."

"I'm glad she's okay."

"Can I see you tonight?"

"Let me call you back. Lori said something about a girl's night out, but I haven't heard from her."

"Okay. Give me a call."

Activity is what I need, Rae told herself, but she didn't move.

She called Link about five and asked him to dinner. Over dinner they talked about horses and horse shows. Rae realized that she was comfortable with him because she'd shifted to the same mindset she'd employed to trap her other victims.

Everything functioned on automatic pilot for the rest of the week. Rae went to work, stopped by Link's, and went home. She rode Maggie a couple of times but even that didn't lift her heavy heart.

Sheriff Davis stopped by on Friday to report that Robbins was well and a free man. When he started to leave, he asked Rae to go with him to serve some papers that evening.

"How long will we be gone?" Rae asked.

"About two hours. It's a pretty drive. You'll enjoy the scenery."

"Okay. Pick me up at five fifteen. I'll have to wear scrubs."

"That's okay. You look good in them."

Sheriff Davis was waiting when the clinic closed. Rae was surprised that Mrs. Price didn't say something when she left. She knew she wanted to, but didn't have the nerve. Lori did make a comment about her seeing a lot of the sheriff. Rae laughed it off.

Sheriff Davis said, "Hi, Doc, how was your day?"

"Long. How about your day?"

"Nothing exciting. Just the usual drunks and petty stuff. There have been several burglaries in rural areas so be sure and lock up as best you can."

"What are they stealing?"

"Mostly electronic equipment and guns. Of course, cash and jewelry are always big favorites."

"Do you have any leads?"

"Not really. Lots of times these guys are from other places. They case the country late at night and come back in the daylight to check if anyone's home. They clean a place out in fifteen minutes."

"You're kidding."

"Nope. They know where to look for valuables and only take things that are easily accessible."

The countryside was beautiful. Rae didn't tell the sheriff that she'd once taken this route to and from school. They drove to a house far back in a wooded area. Rae was a little uncomfortable when Sheriff Davis left her in the car and went to the door of the decrepit shack. Old car bodies and air conditioners littered the yard. She couldn't imagine living in such a mess.

"Does someone really live here?" she asked when the sheriff returned.

"Oh, yes. About seven head in fact."

"Seven people live in that little shack!"

"Yep. Mom, Dad, and five little ones, plus I noticed a couple of coonhounds under the table."

"Good lord. Are they in trouble?"

"Dad isn't paying child support for his first three kids."

"Does she really think he will?"

"No. Just wishful thinking."

On the way back to town, Rae asked, "Remember the call you received when I was in your office one Saturday morning? I believe it was from a policeman asking about a girl who is missing."

"Yes, I remember. He was asking about Jane Hayes."

"Has she been found?"

"I doubt it. I haven't seen her. He was just trying to ease her mother's mind."

"Do you remember the case?"

"Yes. It happened my first year in office. Some boys gang raped her. It was a bad deal, but I didn't have any evidence or witnesses, just a suspicion. Suspecting and proving are two different things. The Hayes bunch was weird, could have been some of their own that did it."

"Are you serious?"

"They're a strange family."

Good way to ease your conscience, Rae thought. "Things like that don't happen often, do they?"

"No. Thank goodness. Want to stop and grab something to eat?"

"I'm starved."

"Okay, we'll stop at Jim's. He has the best barbecue in the state."

The food was excellent, but Rae was glad when they got back to Decker. She drove home, wondering just how much it had taken to buy off the sheriff. She knew there was a new vehicle involved and no telling what else.

Home brought no comfort. She paced the floor and fretted about Link's safe and finding Jim Garrett. By midnight she had the beginning of a horrible headache, so she took a painkiller and went to bed.

Chapter Fourteen

Much of the weekend was spent with Link. Instead of distancing herself, Rae seemed to need to be as close to him as possible. They quibbled over names for the new foals and rode out to check the cattle. She was disappointed that she didn't get back into the safe, but knew an opportunity would present itself eventually.

Link called her at the clinic Wednesday afternoon. Rae left a patient to take the call.

"Hi," Link said, "I'm sorry to bother you, but I wanted to tell you that I'll be gone this afternoon. Do you mind checking the horses for me?"

"I'll be glad to."

"Mr. Lucas is bringing the mare over Friday, so I'm taking Zipper for a check-up."

"I'll stop by and check on things on my way home. Is there anything else you need me to do?"

"Not that I can think of. I'll call you when I get home."

Rae was out of the office as soon as her last patient left. She drove straight to the ranch and hurried to the safe. Pulling on gloves, she opened the safe and sorted through papers. There was a legal looking document at the bottom of the stack. Rae opened it cautiously, like it might contain an explosive. The document stated that James Lincoln Garrett had legally changed his name to James Lincoln Wood. She carefully returned everything to the safe and locked it. Once outside, she took a deep breath and wiped the tears from her eyes. Nothing to cry about. She knew the truth when she found the locket. She just didn't want to believe it.

Maggie whinnied when Rae walked toward the barn. She went to the fence and petted her. Together they headed to the barn and into Maggie's stall. Maggie stood patiently as Rae wrapped her arms around her neck and sobbed into her mane. When she regained control, Rae saddled Maggie and rode for about an hour. She would have ridden longer but she didn't want to see Link.

While riding, Rae pondered her options. Perhaps she should confront Link and give him a chance to explain. But if she did, she would have to explain herself, and she couldn't do that. She really didn't have a choice if she kept her promise. Take your time, she thought. This has to be a perfect accident. Perfect enough to fool Sheriff Davis, which shouldn't be too hard. He'd probably be glad if something happened to Link.

J. B. met Rae at the car when she got home. Realizing that she had neglected him lately, she bent down to pet him. He rolled over so she could scratch his belly. When she started to the house, he trotted along beside her. The phone was ringing when she opened the door. It was Link telling her Zipper passed inspection. She was friendly but did not invite him over.

That evening she was sitting on the porch thinking of a plan when Jane spoke, "Kill them both."

"What do you mean?"

"I mean get rid of Link and the sheriff at the same time."

"How am I supposed to do that and not get caught?"

"You'll think of something. Don't let me down."

"Okay. Okay. Get off my back."

By Friday Rae had come up with a plan. She needed Sheriff Davis to come by and take her for a ride so she could put her plan into action. Sure enough, he came by at closing time.

They'd been driving around for about ten minutes when a robbery was reported at a house five miles west of town. They drove to the scene and the sheriff got out to investigate. While he talked with the owner, Rae took two shotgun shells out of a half full box and put them in her purse. The sheriff returned to report that the door had been busted in, but nothing was missing. Someone must have scared the burglar off before he had time to steal anything.

"Let's drive around the country roads and see if we spot a strange car."

"Okay."

They drove around but didn't see any strange car or unusual happenings so Rae asked, "Do you mind taking me to my car?"

"I mind, but I will."

When they got to her car, she opened the door, turned to Sheriff Davis and asked, "Are you going to be home Tuesday evening?"

"As far as I know. Why?"

"I thought I might come by and look at your antique cars."

"That would be great."

"I'll call before I head your way."

"Okay. I'll give you the grand tour."

"Thanks for the ride. I'll see you Tuesday."

Saturday morning brought sunshine and a gentle breeze. The need to be outside pulled Rae to the ranch and Maggie. The little mare seemed as eager as she to enjoy the beautiful day.

Link wasn't around so Rae saddled up and rode away from the barn. The recent rains and warm temperatures had put everything into bloom. Every shade of green could be seen if you looked long enough. Birds were singing and insects buzzing. Rae enjoyed the moment and tried to store every experience. She realized she would be leaving soon and she wanted to remember this special day. Even if she came back nothing would be the same. She was returning to the barn when Link came galloping toward her.

"Hey, isn't this a wonderful day?" he asked.

"Beautiful day. What are you doing?"

"Checking on some heifers. Want to go with me?"

"Lead the way, cowboy."

They rode and talked for a couple of hours. Both were half starved by the time they got back to the house. The lunchmeat in the refrigerator had a dull green cast, so they settled for peanut butter and crackers.

Saturday evening Link took Rae to dinner. They returned to her place to watch television. Rae was sad when he left. She was still having trouble believing he was guilty of rape. All the times they'd been together, he never once tried to force her to do anything. He was a wonderful lover. Maybe he had a side that she hadn't seen, or another woman who satisfied his kinky sexual appetites.

The demons came in the night, reminding her she had made a promise. Morrison, Snodgrass, and Smith badgered and heckled her about being a coward. Jane just hammered away with, "Don't let me down."

When Sunday morning dawned, Rae had slept little. She dragged out of bed and made coffee. It was another beautiful day, but she didn't have the energy to enjoy it. A short walk with J. B. was all she could manage, but that made him happy.

When the demons started Sunday night, Rae got up and took a sleeping pill. She slept better but still woke up hours before the alarm went off.

Rae called Margie from the clinic so they could all visit with her. Margie was doing fine and loved school. She was looking forward to spring break so she could help spruce up the clinic.

One of Margie's first questions was, "How's Link and Maggie?"

"They're fine. We went riding Saturday."

"I can hardly wait to ride."

After chatting awhile, they said good-bye.

Rae took a sleeping pill Monday night. The pill wore off after about four hours. Every time she closed her eyes, Morrison and Smith leaned over her and laughed.

Tuesday after work Rae drove by to see Maggie. When Rae left her friend, tears trickled down her cheeks. She was glad Link was working Buck in the arena. She waved at him as she drove away.

Once home, she changed into casual clothes and boots. She took the shotgun shells out of her purse and loaded them into her twelve-gauge semi-automatic. Next, she took a piece of string the length of the gun barrel, tied a wad of cloth on one end and a safety pin on the other. She rolled the string up and put it into her pocket. Just before dark, she took the shotgun and drove back to the ranch.

Link was in the house when she drove to the barn. He stuck his head out the door and Rae told him, "I've lost my prescription pad. I bet it's in Maggie's stall. I'll be back in a minute."

"Do you need me to help you?"

"I don't think so. If I don't find it, I'll holler."

When he went back into the house, she took the gun and hurried into the barn. She went to the back door and set the gun behind a stack of hay near the door. Climbing up on the hay bales, she put on gloves, unscrewed the light bulb, and shook it so that the filament broke then put it back. Taking a deep breath, she ran to the front door of the barn and hollered for Link.

He opened the door and she said, "I think someone's in the barn."

"Get out of there. I'll get my gun."

In just a minute Link came running to her. "Did you see someone?"

"Yes, near the paint mare's stall."

"Oh, God. I can't let anything happen to that mare. You wait here while I check this out."

"No, I'm going with you."

They returned to the barn and began looking around. Finding no one, they relaxed a little and talked softly. Slowly, Rae worked her way to the back of the barn. Link went with her.

When they got to the hay, Rae said, "I'll take this side. You look over there."

"Okay, but be careful."

When Link turned to look behind the hay bales, Rae picked up the gun and pushed the safety off. Making sure hay bales shielded her, she said, "Link, I think he's outside."

Link worked his way to the barn door. He walked outside and was gone for a minute. When he stepped back inside, Rae shot him. He fell against a bale of hay and the doorjamb. The shot upset the horses and they were restless in their stalls but Rae didn't have time to comfort them. She pulled a bale of hay in front of Link's body, picked up the spent hull, grabbed the shotgun and ran to the house.

Dialing Sheriff Davis's private number, she held her breath and waited for him to answer. After three rings he picked up.

"Sheriff, can you come over to Link Wood's ranch? I think something's wrong. The lights are on in the house and the barn, his pickup is here, but he's nowhere to be found... I didn't go all the way into the barn but I did holler for him. He has a very expensive mare here. I'm afraid someone may be trying to steal her... Okay, I'll stay in the house... You're probably right, but I'd still like for you to check."

As soon as she hung up, Rae returned to the barn and picked up Link's .357 semi-automatic pistol. She placed his hat on the floor near the back door. Then she arranged bales of hay so she could see the sheriff when he walked toward the hat, but he couldn't see her. Now all she had to do was wait.

Link's body lay close, and she climbed over the hay to keep from stepping in his blood. She didn't look at him, just stayed focused on what was about to happen, but couldn't keep her mind from whirling. What if he decides to come to the back door first? I'll be in plain sight. He's too big a coward to walk around in the dark. He'll come through the front.

After what seemed like hours, she heard a car stop near the front of the barn. Once in a while she caught a glimpse of the sheriff as he checked stalls and corners. He was carrying his shotgun and a flashlight. Her heart was beating rapidly and she imagined that he could hear her breathing. Slowly he worked his way through the barn. When he spotted Link's Stetson, he shined his light all around before cautiously approaching the hat. He bent over to pick it up. Rae stood up enough to shoot between two hay bales. When the sheriff raised up, he was hit in the chest by a .357 slug. He landed flat on his back and didn't move.

Rae put the hay back in place, picked up the spent shell casing, and ruffled the place where she had stood. She approached the sheriff and retrieved Link's hat. After placing the pistol in Link's hand, she aimed out the door and pulled the trigger. She laid the hat where it had fallen after she shot Link. Satisfied that all was okay there, Rae went to the sheriff and placed the dropped shotgun in his hands, pointed out the door and pulled the trigger. The hallway was covered with loose hay so there were no boot tracks to be found. When she was sure everything was in place, she went to the house to call the police.

Once back in the house, Rae removed her gloves and stuck them in her boot. She scrubbed her hands and then called the sheriff's office.

"Hello, this is Doctor Rae Roberts. I need someone to come to Link Wood's ranch... I'm not sure what the problem is. I came over about dark and all the lights were on in the barn and the house. Link's pickup's here, but Link isn't around. I called for him and looked around, but then I got scared and called the sheriff. He had given me his private number. Sheriff Davis told me to stay in the house and he'd come over and check out the barn. I just heard shots and nobody has come out of the barn. Please send someone to help me..."Oh, good...Yes, I'll stay in the house until a deputy knocks on the door. Please hurry."

Hanging up, Rae pulled on fresh gloves and went to the safe. She dialed the combination, opened the safe, and removed the locket and the document with Jim Garrett's name on it. She placed the locket in her bra and the paper in her boot.

Picking up her shotgun, she ejected the shell from the magazine, and took the string from her pocket. She dropped the safety pin down the barrel until it was visible in the magazine. Grasping the safety pin, she pulled the string through the barrel. She repeated this procedure another time then wiped out the magazine. Taking a paper towel, she wiped the gun and took it to her car, put it in a leather scabbard and locked it in the trunk.

She was returning to the house when she heard the sirens. Two police cars sped up the driveway as she closed the front door. Quickly Rae flushed the string and paper towel down the toilet. She put the shotgun shell in her pocket, pulled out her shirttail and pinned the safety pin to the waistband of her jeans. Another pair of gloves went into her boots.

It seemed like hours before one of the deputies came to the house. She opened the door as soon as he stepped on the porch. "What's going on?" she asked.

"We don't know for sure, Doctor Roberts, but it's bad."

"What do you mcan, it's bad? Where's Link and Sheriff Davis?"

"They're both in the barn."

"Okay, good, I'll go out there."

"No, you'd best stay here. It looks like they accidentally shot each other. They're both dead."

Rae screamed and fell to the floor. The deputy tried to comfort her but didn't have much luck. Desperate, he asked, "Is there someone I can call?"

"Call Lori. Please call Lori."

"Lori who? Do you know her number?"

"Lori Farmer, 555-2007."

The deputy walked to the phone and called Lori. "She'll be right here, Doctor Roberts."

"This is my fault. I called Sheriff Davis and asked him to come over here."

"You couldn't know what was going to happen. We'll get some people out here to figure this out. You try to remember everything that happened so you can talk with the investigator."

Rae nodded her head.

The deputy stayed with her until Lori and David arrived. The place was beginning to fill with various law enforcement people. Rae sat on the couch and shredded tissues. Once the bodies were removed, Rae was allowed to go home.

An officer walked them to Rae's car. "Do you think you can come to the station in the morning, Doctor Roberts? We need to know exactly what you saw and heard."

Rae nodded and got into the car. Lori talked with David and he agreed that she should stay with Rae.

When they got home Rae excused herself to go to the bathroom. Once out of Lori's sight, she hid all of the extra articles she'd been carrying around. She walked the floor and cried until Lori called Doctor Mackey. He came and gave her a shot to knock her out. She woke up the next morning with a severe headache, swollen eyes, and no desire to go to town. Lori called Mrs. Price and told her to cancel the appointments for the rest of the week. Then she called the sheriff's office, and the investigator agreed to come out to the house.

When he arrived Lori fixed coffee and served him while Rae made herself presentable. Lori sat next to Rae and held her hand while Rae told Mr. Harwell what happened. "I stopped by Link's after work to see Maggie."

"Who is Maggie?" Mr. Harwell asked.

"A bay mare that I dearly love. I spent some time grooming her and must have dropped my prescription pad out of my pocket. When I got home and changed clothes, I noticed that it was missing. I didn't feel that it was too urgent, so I did a little cleaning and ate a sandwich. I thought about calling Link and asking him to go look, but decided to go myself and surprise him. When I got to the ranch, Link's pickup was there and the lights were on in the house. I called out to Link, but he didn't answer. Thinking he might be in the shower, I opened the door and called to him again, but there was still no answer. I looked through the house, no Link. I became frightened even though I've been to the ranch many times by myself. I went to the barn and called to him. He didn't answer. I really became frightened and called Sheriff Davis. He told me to stay in the house, lock the doors, and he would be there in a minute. I heard his car drive up. I was watching out the window when he went into the barn. He was gone a few minutes and then I heard shots. I didn't know what to do, so I waited and watched. No one came out of the barn. I called the sheriff's office and asked for help."

"Do you think someone else was in the barn?"

"I don't know. It's possible, I guess. Someone could have used the back door and I wouldn't have seen them."

"What was your relationship with Mr. Wood?"

"We were good friends. More than friends. Link asked me to marry him."

"What's your relationship with Sheriff Davis?"

"He was a friend. I rode patrol with him a few times. He gave me his private phone number in case I needed him on his day off."

"How did Link feel about you riding around with the sheriff?"

"He didn't carc. Link wasn't jealous."

"Where do you think Link was when you called to him?

"I don't know, unless he had walked out in the pasture to check a mare. He certainly didn't hear me or he would have answered."

"Would he have walked out the back door to check on the mare?"

"It's possible."

Mr. Harwell got up to leave, "Where is Mr. Wood's family?"

"I don't know. He never mentioned his family."

"Can I call Clyde and ask him to take care of the horses?"

"Who's Clyde?"

"A neighbor who works for Link."

"I think that would be okay. If you think of anything else, give me a call. Even if this appears to have been an accidental shooting, you'd best hang around until we wrap this up."

"I'm not going anywhere."

Friday, Rae went to Link's graveside service at ten a.m., and Sheriff Davis's at two p.m. She was relieved to get it over in one day.

Mr. Harwell took the safe in hopes of finding a will or someone to contact. So far, none of Link's family had shown up, so Rae hired Clyde to take care of the ranch.

Rae returned to work two weeks after the accident. Her intention was to hang around until she could learn the exact location of Jackson Cooper. The problem was, she couldn't ask a lot of questions without attracting attention. A simple solution finally popped into her head. I'll go to the bank and visit Mr. Morrison on the pretense of opening a special account to help care for Link's horses. If I'm lucky, he'll have a picture of his grandchildren on his desk and will be willing to discuss their ancestry.

Rae began the meeting in a businesslike manner. She stated her concern about Link's finances possibly being in probate, and if so, Clyde would have trouble buying feed for the horses. Mr. Morrison assured her that an account could be set up to take care of the ranch.

After her business was finished, Rae picked up a picture saying, "What lovely children."

"Thank you. Those are my grandchildren."

"Tom's children?"

"Yes. Did you know Tom?"

"We were in Kiwanis together. I'm so sorry about his death."

"Thank you. It was a shock, I assure you. I still can't believe he's gone.

"How are the children?"

"They seem to be doing okay. My wife takes care of them a great deal of the time. She plans to take them to visit her family this summer. They haven't been to Argentina before, so this should be an interesting adventure for them."

"Your wife's from Argentina?"

"Yes. Her family has a large ranch located between the Andes Mountains and the Parana' River. Smack dab in the middle of the Pampas."

"Have they owned the land for many generations? Like you see in the movies?"

"Yes, the Francesca family has owned the La Casa de Francesca for years."

"Does most of the family live on the ranch?"

"Everyone but my wife and her younger sister, who also married an American. My wife's niece married Jackson Cooper, one of Tom's friends. He's a doctor and operates a clinic on the ranch."

"How interesting. I bet the ranch is beautiful."

"You'd have to see it to believe it."

"I'd like to. Thank you for your time, Mr. Morrison. I'd best get going."

"It's been nice visiting with you, Dr. Roberts. Perhaps you'll have dinner with me some evening."

"Perhaps, if your wife will accompany us."

Mr. Morrison didn't respond to the last comment.

Rae shook her head as she walked back to the clinic. No wonder Tom was such a jerk. He was raised by one.

A month passed and Rae announced to Lori and Mrs. Price that she was closing the clinic and taking some time off.

"What are you going to do, dear?" Mrs. Price asked.

"I'm not sure. I may just drive. There are many places I'd like to visit.

"Will you come back?" Lori asked.

"I'm sure I will. I'll probably open the clinic again. Will you and David take care of my place for me? You can live in my house if you want to and save paying rent."

"I'd love to live in the country. I'll talk to David about it. Even if we don't live there, we'll take care of the place for you. What about J. B.?"

"Clyde's keeping him. He'll be happy at the ranch."

"When are you leaving?" Mrs. Price asked.

"In a few days. There's some business I need to take care of."

A teary Mrs. Price asked, "Will you call once in a while and let us know that you're okay?"

"Of course."

It was a sad group that left the clinic that day. Rae knew she had to leave soon or she might change her mind.

Two days later, after securing the house and packing, Rae took J. B. to Clyde. Going back to the ranch was gut wrenching. Maggie whinnied when she saw Rae, which really tore at her heartstrings. She brushed the little mare and tried to explain that she had to leave. J. B. was busy checking the place out, but came to Rae when she called him. She petted him and left the barn. Tears flowed down her cheeks as she got into her car.

Rae called Lori and told her that she had opened a checking account for her so that she could pay the taxes on the place. There was also enough in the account for repairs or emergencies that might need to be taken care of. She didn't tell Lori that the place would become hers if anything happened to Rae, or if she didn't return in five years.

She withdrew enough cash to last until she finalized her plans. Once she was located, she would transfer money to a new account. Her financial status wasn't great, but she would worry about that later. She had enough to last three or four years if she were frugal.

Rae didn't look back when she left the house. No tears fell but a large lump in her throat made it difficult for her to breathe. Once she reached the highway, she felt better. She'd originally planned to drive to Los Angeles but changed her mind. She would go to Seattle. With map and pistol by her side, she headed northwest.

When Sarah Hayes Stone received the Decker paper with news of the sheriff's death, she was convinced that something strange was going on. Stone thought she might be right. He agreed to a trip to Decker so she could visit old friends and he could do some investigating. Four men who'd been involved with Jane's case were dead. That seemed more than coincidence. Jack and Sarah Stone arrived in Decker about the same time Rae reached Seattle.

While Sarah caught up on old times, Stone strolled around Decker. He found that most of the locals were quite willing to tell all they knew about the deaths of four of their citizens. Even Dr. Mackey talked to him at length and was certain that Dale Smith's death was his own fault. According to all accounts, Dr. Roberts was pure as fresh fallen snow.

There was a bit of a buzz when a key was discovered in Link's safe. The key was to a safe deposit box in a Dallas bank. After a court order and lots of red tape, the authorities finally got to look in the box. They found that Link changed his name from Jim Garrett the year he became twenty-one. His father, Lon Wood, bought him the ranch when he took back his birth name. Mrs. James Garrett, Link's mother, was located in London, England, but expressed no interest in coming back to Decker. Link's half-brother, Peter Garrett, did come and was staying at the ranch. Mr. Wood hadn't been located.

Captain Stone dropped by the sheriff's office and asked, "Did you dust the safe for prints before you removed it from the house?"

"No, looked like a cut and dried accidental shooting to me," Deputy Sheriff Hanks answered.

"You don't think someone could have set Link up and then lured the sheriff to the scene and shot him?"

"Why would anyone want to?"

"Good question. Can you think of anyone who might have a grudge against either man?"

"No, at least not enough to kill them. The sheriff had a few enemies, but nothing serious. Link wasn't that well known around town. Matter of fact, he rarely was seen in town."

"Do you think they were both in love with Dr. Roberts?" Stone asked.

"Link might've been in love with her, but Harley wasn't. He took her riding around with him because he enjoyed her company. Lord knows, she's a looker."

"What does she look like?"

"Tall and slender with auburn hair and brown eyes. Has a look-but-don't-touch air about her."

Stone didn't have one piece of evidence to go on and no authority in Texas. He was guessing that Dr. Roberts was the common link in the deaths of five men. If he could find anything to prove that fact, he could exhume the body of Debra Hayes buried in Florida. Her father had refused to allow an autopsy or her request for cremation. Later, after Stone and Sarah were married, he found that Debra broke her right arm when she was young. He would love to open that coffin and look at the corpse's right arm.

There were a couple of things he could do. He could take a trip to Las Vegas and see if Stephen Morrison was dating someone when he suddenly overdosed, and he could warn Jackson Cooper that his life might be in danger.

Seattle, like everywhere else that Rae had been, proved that enough money could buy what she wanted. It took two weeks to find someone who would get her a fake passport. Corrupt government officials don't come cheap. The passport cost her ten thousand dollars. A brunette wig cost two thousand dollars then it cost her another five hundred to hire a seamstress to sew the extra padding under the lining. The lady didn't know that the padding concealed Rae's real passport. She chose pale blue contacts, and her new name was Joan Estelle Bennett. Now she was trying to think of a scheme to get an invitation to visit La Casa de Francesca.

Rae booked a flight to Paris, France instead of to Argentina. She wanted to transfer her money to a bank in Paris. To look like Rae Roberts again, she would buy a brown wig and brown contacts once she reached Paris.

Transferring her money wasn't a big deal. She simply had it sent to one bank, then withdrew it and opened an account for Joan Bennett at another bank. Now she felt a little more secure and no longer needed her original passport. She would sell it. If anyone tried to find Rae Roberts, they would have a merry chase.

Her plan was to telegraph the ranch stating that she was a freelance writer researching cowboys in different areas of the world for a series of articles. Could she please come for a short visit and observe real gauchos in action? While she waited for a reply, she went to Switzerland and opened a bank account.

Captain Stone returned from Las Vegas fully convinced that Rae Roberts was the mystery woman who appeared at the Jack's or Better Casino. Pat Collins matched a description of Roberts except for hair and eye color. The lady was smart, no doubt about that, because not a fingerprint was found.

He called Mr. Snodgrass in Decker, Texas, and requested Jackson Cooper's telephone number. He claimed to be a cattleman interested in importing some beef from Argentina. Snodgrass was most helpful.

Stone called Cooper and explained that Tom Snodgrass, Dale Smith, Stephen Morrison, Jim Garrett, and Harley Davis, were dead. He explained further that he believed a woman was responsible for the deaths and that she might be looking for him. Not sounding overly concerned, Jackson thanked him for the warning.

Chapter Fifteen

Rae returned from Switzerland and anxiously waited for a reply from the ranch. A telegram arrived the following day, welcoming her to La Casa de Francesca. A private plane would be waiting for her at Cordoba if she would call the enclosed number and tell them when she would be arriving.

She left the next morning on a plane to Miami, Florida. After checking her flight schedule from Florida to South America, she called the ranch and gave them her estimated time of arrival in Cordoba. Three days later a weary Joan Bennett boarded a plane for the final leg of her journey.

A driver met her at the ranch's private runway and after a thirty-minute drive they arrived at the ranch headquarters. Carlos Francesca welcomed her. He escorted her to the guesthouse, where she would be staying while visiting the ranch, and introduced her to the staff.

"Send Maria to me when you arise in the morning, and we will visit about the article you wish to write. I hope you rest well, Senorita."

"Thank you. I'm sure I will."

Carlos excused himself and left her in care of the servants.

Rae slept well, but was still tired from many hours of flying. It was midmorning before she sent Maria to tell Carlos she was ready to visit with him.

Carlos requested that Rae meet him in the garden. When she arrived, he asked if she would like a tour of the grounds. She jumped at the chance. As they walked, he asked, "What is it you want to write about?"

"The everyday work on the ranch, with emphasis on your cattle operation."

"Can you ride?"

"Yes. I enjoy riding very much."

"Western or English?"

"Western."

"Very well, we will provide you a gentle horse and a western saddle. You can ride with the men whenever you want. I assure you that you will be shown the utmost respect. My only request is you get my approval before anything is printed."

"That isn't a problem. I'm so glad for the opportunity to get such a great story. Will it be possible for me to start tomorrow?"

"Yes. I'll speak to Juan, my foreman, and ask him to be your guide. He speaks English and can answer your questions. Juan will come for you in the morning after he gives the men their duties."

"Thank you. Later I would like to visit with you about the history of the ranch, if that's agreeable."

"It will be a pleasure. Now, I must go. If you wish for anything, ask Maria. Oh, by the way, Senorita Bennett, have you any published works that I can read?"

"No, this is my first attempt at a big story. I hope to follow it with articles on Spanish and Australian cowboys."

"I see. If I may ask, who is financing you?'

"I am, with money my grandmother left me."

"Good day, Senorita. Don't hesitate to call me if you need assistance."

Juan sent a young boy for Rae the next morning. Rae followed the lad to the barn where Juan was saddling a stocky gray horse for her. She wasn't familiar with the breed, but she would try riding him.

Riding wasn't a problem. Her mount was well behaved and had a smooth gait. She fell in beside Juan, and they rode to watch as gauchos began the fall roundup. Rae soon joined the guys, herding cows and picking up strays. Cowboys were just cowboys, it seemed. They all liked to show their roping and riding talents.

Rae spent four days with Juan and then took a day off to write. She was surprised at how easy it was to document the facts she gathered. Writing might become her second occupation.

She was beginning to think Jackson Cooper was no longer on the ranch. No one had mentioned him or the clinic. Rae was tempted to ask about medical treatment, but didn't think it wise. If she didn't hear something soon, she would ask Juan to take her on a tour of the ranch.

Rae had been on the ranch five days and feared she would soon wear out her welcome. Thinking about her dilemma, she walked from the barn to the guesthouse. On her way, she passed two boys chopping weeds in the garden. She had stepped up onto the porch when she heard a scream. She ran to see what happened. One of the boys was lying on the ground, thrashing about. He had slashed his leg with a machete and was bleeding profusely. Rae elevated the leg and applied direct pressure on the wound.

Maria came running to help. Rae asked, "Is there a doctor anywhere near here?"

"Si, Senorita. I'll get one of the hands to drive you to him."

A jeep soon arrived and loaded Rae and the injured boy into the back. Rae kept pressure on the leg, but couldn't stop the bleeding completely. He wouldn't make it if they had to travel very far.

The ten-minute drive seemed like three hours, and the boy was going into shock. Rae continued to apply pressure to the wound as the child was carried into the clinic and placed on the operating table.

"Let go, so I can have a look," said a man in a wheelchair.

Rae released the leg and turned to go.

"Where are you going?" the man asked.

"I thought you'd take over from here," Rae replied.

"I'm by myself. I could use some help." Pointing toward a cabinet, he said, "Grab some clamps and gauze pads."

Rae got the items he requested.

"Now soak up this blood so I can clamp off the big bleeders."

"My hands are dirty."

"Doesn't matter. If we don't stop the bleeding, infection won't be a problem."

Rae's back was killing her by the time the severed vessels were clamped and the bleeding stopped. She was turning to leave when the doctor said, "Well, aren't you going to help suture this up?"

"I will if you need me."

"Good. Grab that stool over there and we'll get this lad fixed up."

Thirty minutes later, they finished closing. Doctor Cooper gave Ramon a tetanus shot and started an IV. Rae washed her hands.

The doctor rolled across to join her and asked, "Who are you?"

"Joan Bennett, and you are?"

"Doctor Jackson Cooper. Thanks for your help. I don't believe I've seen you before."

"No, I'm here to do a story on gauchos. I've been on the ranch about a week."

"Nice to meet you, Ms. Bennett. You seem to know your way around an operating room. Have you had medical experience?"

"I was a dental assistant for several years."

"I need a drink. Would you like something?"

"A Screwdriver would be wonderful."

"Manuel, bring my usual and Ms. Bennett a Screwdriver."

Rae couldn't believe that she was sitting across the table from Jackson Cooper. She took a sip of her drink and asked, "Have you worked here long, Doctor?"

"Almost six years."

She was going to ask about the clinic when a servant came to the door and said, "Senor Doctor, it is time for you to dress for your dinner engagement."

"Oh, hell. I forgot all about that. You'll have to excuse me, Ms. Bennett."

"Certainly, Doctor. Thanks for the drink."

"Maybe we can visit when you come back to check on your patient tomorrow."

With that, he was gone from the room.

Rae finished her drink and left to go back to the ranch. She wondered how Jackson became paralyzed. Well, if all went according to plan, he'd soon be out of his misery.

Juan came for her the next morning, and they rode to the corrals where the men were working calves. The calves were branded, vaccinated, and held in a special pen away from their mothers. Some of the heifers would be kept for breeding; the others, and all of the bull calves, would be sold.

Rae told Juan she needed to check Ramon so he asked a young man to drive her to the clinic. Ramon was asleep, so she went in search of Dr. Cooper.

She heard him before she saw him. He was shouting orders. When Rae walked into the room he greeted her with, "Scrub up. We have a hot appendix that has to come out before it blows."

Rae went to the sink and began scrubbing her arms and hands. A woman, whom she assumed was a nurse, brought her a gown, mask, and gloves. She donned her new apparel and joined Dr. Cooper at the operating table. He barked commands and she followed them. Many times she thought if it weren't for the patient, she would kill him right now. Once the surgery was finished, however, Dr. Cooper became civil.

"Come, Ms. Bennett, and join me for a drink."

"I'm not sure I want to. You're a dangerous man."

He howled with laughter. "I only sound dangerous. I'm really quite harmless."

"Have you ever injured an assistant?"

"Not one time."

"Okay, I'll have a drink with you."

"Let's sit in the garden." Dr. Cooper said as he wheeled out of the room.

He shouted orders as he rolled across the patio. Rae caught up with him and joined him at a table near the fountain. In a minute she had a drink in her hand.

"Tell me about yourself, Ms. Bennett."

"Please, call me Joan."

"Then tell me about Joan. Where are you from?"

"All over. My father was in the military. I attended Oklahoma University but never graduated, worked as a dental assistant, legal aid, and now I'm into journalism."

"Where are your parents now?"

"Deceased. Killed in a car wreck ten years ago."

"I'm sorry. I shouldn't ask so many questions."

"That's okay. I'm pretty much over it. What about you? Where are you from?"

"I'm from a little town in Texas."

"How did you get from Texas to Argentina?"

"I fell in love with a friend's cousin. Carmela Isabel Francesca, the most beautiful woman I've ever known. After I graduated from medical school, I came to Argentina to ask for her hand in marriage."

"I take it she accepted."

"Yes, we were married four years."

"Were?"

"There was an accident. My wife and infant son were killed. I, unfortunately, survived."

"When did the accident happen?'

"One year, two months, and thirteen days ago. She didn't want to fly that day, the weather was bad, but I insisted it would be okay."

"I'm sorry."

"We'd best go check on our patients."

"Good idea. Then I'll head back to the ranch before you put me to work again."

"I'm sure glad you showed up. My regular nurse is visiting her family. No telling when she'll be back."

"Send a runner if you need me. I'll be glad to help if you'll quit hollering at me."

"Old habits are hard to break, but I'll try not to holler. I'd appreciate your help."

Cooper didn't call for her the next day so she went for a ride with Juan and finished writing her article. She wasn't sure that it met all of the writing requirements but it sounded good and looked good on paper. Now, what was she going to do about Cooper?

Maybe she could visit another area of the ranch and come back here to write. She would approach Carlos with that idea when she gave him the article to read. Somehow she must find a way to stay on the ranch until she eliminated Jackson Cooper.

She sent Maria to Carlos, requesting a visit. Maria came rushing back with news from Dr. Cooper. He needed her immediately. A young boy was stepped on after being thrown under his horse. A car was waiting for her.

"Did you tell Carlos?"

"Si, Senorita. He said that he will visit with you when you return."

By the time Rae arrived at the clinic, Dr. Cooper had the patient prepped for surgery. As soon as she was gowned and gloved, he put the little guy completely under and made the incision. "I'm guessing a ruptured spleen. I just hope we got to him in time. He's lost a lot of blood."

"Can you give him transfusions?"

"If he makes it through surgery."

True to his word, Dr. Cooper didn't holler at her. He started to a couple of times, but caught himself. Rae suctioned and sponged, while Cooper removed the spleen. Once the bleeding was controlled, Dr. Cooper looked for other injuries before closing.

"He was lucky. Must have been a glancing blow because the intestines and kidneys are okay. I think he'll pull through."

"You do impressive work, Doctor."

"Thank you, you're not too shabby yourself."

"Will he need someone to sit with him?" Rae asked.

Cooper replied, "Yes, I'll stay while you go clean up."

When she returned, Dr. Cooper and one of his assistants were putting the little boy into a bed. All they could do now was wait and keep a close watch.

Rae said, "If you'd like to clean up, I'll keep an eye on him."

"Okay. I won't be gone long. Would it bother you if his parents came in?

"Not at all. They need to be with him."

The boy's parents sat with him through the night. Rae stayed in Cooper's guesthouse in case there were complications and they had to operate again.

She joined Jackson in the garden for breakfast.

"How's our patient?" Rae asked.

"He's holding his own, but not out of the woods yet. His blood pressure still isn't up enough."

"Do you need me to stay and help you today?"

"What about your article?"

"It's finished."

"Does that mean you'll be leaving?"

"Probably, unless you agree to let me write an article about your clinic."

"I'll think about it, but only if you stay here and work."

"You read my mind."

"We'll discuss this later. Right now I have to check on my patients. Want to come along?"

"Lead the way."

Rae sent a man for her clothes and to tell Carlos what was going on. She stayed at the clinic and took care of Jose. He hovered on the verge of death for three days, before he began to improve. Five days after surgery, he asked for something to eat, so they knew he was on the road to recovery.

During the time she'd been there, Rae had given shots, pulled teeth and helped deliver two babies. She loved the work, the people, and even liked Cooper a little.

She was packing to leave when Jackson knocked on the door.

"Hi, Doc. Come in."

"What are you doing?"

"Packing."

"You mean leaving, don't you?"

"Well, don't you think it's time?"

"I thought you wanted to write an article."

"You never said that I could, only that you'd think about it."

"Well, you can, so unpack."

"I have to talk with Carlos."

"I'll let you have that much time off, but don't push it."

"Don't start hollering again. I'll be back if Carlos says it's okay."

Carlos was impressed with Rae's article and gave his consent for her to stay and work with Dr. Cooper.

"Jackson needs someone from his own country to talk to. He has suffered a great loss and I fear he will never recover," Carlos said.

"I know he's very sad. Perhaps time will help him heal," Rae replied.

"Perhaps."

Days at the clinic were filled with every kind of illness and injury imaginable. People came from great distances for treatment and none were turned away. The clinic certainly wasn't bringing in much money.

Rae asked Cooper, "Do you ever get paid?"

"Sometimes. It doesn't matter. I'll treat them as long as I can."

When Rae found free time, she went horseback riding. Jackson had a stable and some beautiful horses. She chose a black gelding named Ebony. He was a little more spirited than Maggie or the gray she rode at the ranch, but Rae could control him. Occasionally, thoughts of Maggie and Link drifted into her mind, but she brushed them aside.

She was riding one afternoon when she noticed a change in the weather. Ebony was nervous and hard to control so she knew something was about to happen. Sure enough, by the time they got to the barn, a storm was brewing.

Rae handed Ebony over to a stable hand and went to the clinic. The patients were settled for the evening and Cooper wasn't around. Great, maybe she'd get some sleep tonight.

About eleven Jorge knocked on her door. A woman at the clinic needed help. Rae walked through the rain to see what was going on. The woman was in labor.

"Where's Dr. Cooper?" Rae asked. Jorge shrugged.

Cooper still hadn't shown up and the woman's contractions were five minutes apart. Rae went to get him. Luis met her at the door and told her the doctor wasn't feeling well. She brushed past him and went to find Cooper. He was drunk and refused to budge. On her way out, she told Luis to get him sobered up because they had a lady in trouble.

Cooper never came to the clinic. Rae delivered the baby boy by herself. She was not happy and returned to the house to tell Cooper how she felt. Luis was reluctant to let her in, but she ignored him and went straight to the den. Cooper was slumped in his chair with a bottle in one hand and a picture of Carmela in the other.

"I just delivered a baby without knowing what I was doing. They both could have died. What's the matter with you?" Rae asked.

"I'm tired of living, but Carmela believed that suicide was a mortal sin. If I kill myself, I'll never see her or Jack again. Why don't you help me out and kill me? That's why you're here, isn't it?

Rae was stunned into silence for a moment, before finally asking, "What are you talking about?"

"I'm talking about a woman who has killed four, no...five, men from my hometown. I'm the last on her list."

"I think you've pickled your brain, but just for curiosity's sake, why did she kill them?"

"It isn't a pretty story and it haunted me until I married Carmela. When I told her what I'd done, she told me I could redeem myself by helping others. I opened the clinic here, instead of an office in Cordoba, and it has helped. I was happy for the first time in my life. Then because of my own obstinacy, I lost the two people I loved most in the world.

"I wake up every day and face emptiness. I feel that my heart is going to burst. Sometimes the loneliness causes me to be physically ill. You can't possibly know what I'm talking about."

"Oh, I think I know quite well what you're talking about, but I still don't know why you think I came here to kill you."

"I received a phone call a few weeks ago from a man named Stone. He's been investigating a series of deaths that happened recently. The men who died were involved in a crime that happened about thirteen years ago. There seems to be a woman linked to all of the men. He warned me that she might be headed my way, and then you show up."

Rae's heart was flopping around in her chest. How did Stone get involved in this? Mother. She was probably still convinced that Jane was alive. Stone might be on his way here now.

"I came here as a guest of Carlos, not you. I didn't know you existed until Ramon got hurt."

"A perfect cover. You're no dummy."

"You're not making sense. Why am I going to kill you? Just for the simple pleasure, or is it because your name starts with J?"

"It happened when I was a senior in high school. A friend of mine was crazy about this girl, but she wouldn't have anything to do with him. He kept bugging her but she refused to go out with him.

"One evening, just before dark, we were riding around drinking and smoking pot. Tom spots this girl walking through the park, so he tells Dale to follow her. Before I knew what was happening, we were getting out of the car. Tom caught her and dragged her into the woods at the edge of the park. He said for me to hold her so he could teach her a lesson. After he raped her, Dale took a turn, then Stephen, and because I was so afraid of Tom, I took a turn, too.

"Jim Garrett begged Tom not to do it, but he wouldn't listen. Garrett didn't touch her, but Tom told him if he said anything he'd say it was all his idea. We all backed Tom so Garrett didn't have any choice. He had to keep quiet. Tom jerked the necklace from around her neck and pitched it to Garrett, said it would remind him to keep his mouth shut.

"I didn't know until the next day that she fell into the drainage ditch and fractured her skull. She was never mentally right again. I'm so sorry for what I did. She was a beautiful, talented girl, and we ruined her life."

Rae sat in stunned silence. The words "Garrett wouldn't have anything to do with it" kept running through her mind. Link was innocent.

She finally found her voice and asked, "Was there a trial?"

"No, we weren't even questioned. Tom's dad bought off the sheriff."

"I'm not surprised that someone wants to kill you, but it isn't me. Now why don't you have Luis fix you some breakfast and about a gallon of coffee. I'll see you at the clinic later."

Rae fought to keep her composure and get out of the house. She stumbled through the rain to the guesthouse.

Link was innocent and she'd killed him. He was kind and good, and she shot him like he was nothing. Together they had ridden across the countryside, delivered babies, and shared a joy she had never known before. He was the only man she trusted enough to give herself to completely. Why didn't she talk to him and try to find out his past?

Why did he keep the necklace? That question would never be answered. She couldn't go back. Stone was on to her. Never again would she live in her wonderful house or ride Maggie. What was she to do? Killing Cooper didn't matter anymore, especially since he wanted to die. At this point, she didn't care. Maybe she should put him and herself out of their misery.

Rae paced the floor until the first rays of light began to show, then she rushed to the barn. She needed to ride and get her mind under control. How could she possibly live with the fact that she'd killed Link? The others deserved to die, but not Link. She rode from the barn across the wet pasture. Her body ached as though she had the flu. She cried but the only moisture on her face was from the falling rain. On she rode into unfamiliar territory, not caring that she might get lost.

When Ebony shied away from something, she almost fell off. Looking down she saw a baby calf. The mother wasn't in sight so she stepped from the saddle to check the little one. Leading Ebony, she approached the baby. Its right leg was caught in some wire. She held the reins in one hand, caught the calf with the other, and stepped onto the wire. The calf pulled away from her and the wire, but bawled in distress.

Rae turned just as the cow came to the aid of her baby. Not wasting any time she stepped into the stirrup, grabbed for the horn, and was swinging her right leg across the saddle, when the cow charged. Ebony jumped to avoid the charge. Rae's hand was wet so she lost her grip on the horn and was thrown from the saddle.

In her haste she'd failed to change into her boots. The smooth soled sneakers allowed her foot to slip through the stirrup. The scared horse bolted away, dragging Rae with him.

She called to him, but that only scared him more. Getting hold of the back cinch was her only chance. Twice she almost had it. When she tried the third time, Ebony's hoof struck her in the head.

When she didn't return by lunchtime, the stable boy went to Dr. Cooper. Jackson sent five men to look for her. The wet ground made it easy for them to follow the horse's tracks. In a short time they spotted Ebony walking toward them, dragging Rae.

The men approached the horse cautiously. He was jumpy and shied when Jorge reached for him, but the man managed to catch hold of the bridle reins. They freed Rae's foot from the stirrup but knew it wouldn't be wise to transport the unconscious woman on a horse. One of the hands raced back to the clinic to get Cooper and a jeep.

Jackson didn't think she would make it to the clinic. After a quick evaluation, he started an IV and oxygen. Her left ankle and right arm were broken, her torso was bruised and bleeding, but the greatest danger was the head injury. Jackson knew he couldn't perform brain surgery and without it, she would surely die. He would have to fly her to Cordoba.

He called Carlos and told him the situation. Carlos would have the plane ready by the time they got Rae to the airstrip and would call the hospital. Jackson asked Luis to bring the Lincoln and plenty of blankets. He switched her to a portable oxygen tank and took extra IV bags with him. He hadn't been on a plane since the accident, but he knew he must go with her.

A brain surgeon met them at the emergency room. He removed part of Rae's skull to relieve pressure on her swollen brain. Other life threatening injuries were treated, but she was too near death to worry about broken bones.

Jackson stayed with her around the clock for the first twenty-four hours. When she made it forty-eight, he returned home to close the clinic then flew back to the hospital. Rae was holding her own, but still in a coma. A week later he flew home to open the clinic.

Six weeks after the accident, Jackson flew to Cordoba to get Rae. He was taking her to the clinic so he could care for her. She would have a private room and nurse, plus his medical care. Perhaps in time she would awake, and he could tell her that he knew who she was. He knew the minute he lifted her eyelid and looked into a bright green eye. The shock was almost too much for him, especially when he pictured her with blonde hair. The only thing he didn't know was which twin she was.

Two months passed and Rae remained in a coma. Jackson thought he noticed eye movement a couple of times, but wasn't sure. The dye was gone from her hair. There was no doubt that she was one of the Hayes twins.

Jackson had about given up hope when he wheeled into her room and saw that her eyes were open. He called to her, but she didn't respond. Wheeling closer, he spoke to her and she looked at him. He recoiled from the empty look in her beautiful eyes. "Joan, it's Jackson. Do you remember what happened to you?" She didn't answer.

Jackson worked with her for days but couldn't get her to respond verbally. Several times a day nurses got her up and walking. The day finally came when she could walk unassisted. Sometimes she wandered in the garden, but most of the time she sat in the shade of the patio clutching a pair of worn leather riding gloves.

Captain Stone called and asked, “Have you had a female visitor from America?”

“No, I’ve been expecting her, but she hasn’t shown up.”

“I’m surprised. I just knew she would be there by now.”

“Maybe she changed her mind or you’re mistaken.”

“Maybe, but stay alert. Will you give me a call if a strange woman does show up?”

“Sure, let me get a pencil so I can write down your number... Got it. Thanks for calling.”

He wheeled himself toward the patio. “Captain Stone called,” he said as he picked up her hand. Leaning close to her ear, he whispered, “I explained to Carlos that you have no family and I feel responsible for you. He’s agreed to help me protect you. You’re safe here. I promise I’ll never let anyone hurt you again.”

25431755R00129

Made in the USA
San Bernardino, CA
29 October 2015